POUR CHOICES

A MIXOLOGY LOUNGE MYSTERY

ADRIAN ANDOVER

Chestnut Avenue Press

PRAISE FOR ADRIAN ANDOVER'S MIXOLOGY LOUNGE MYSTERY SERIES

Awards for *Whiskey Business*, the first installment in the Mixology Lounge Mystery series:
2026 Agatha Award winner for Best First Novel
2026 Lefty Award winner for Best Debut Mystery

What others are saying:

"A fresh pour on the cozy with so much heart, a touch of humor, and a deeper look at what it means to step into who you're meant to be."

ELLIE ALEXANDER, AUTHOR OF THE BAKESHOP MYSTERIES

"The perfect blend of mystery, mischief, and mixology. With clever twists, a setting you'll want to crawl right into, and just the right dash of danger, this cozy mystery is the perfect pour from start to finish."

ANNIE MCEWEN, AUTHOR OF THE NORTHWOODS MYSTERIES

"You'll want to craft your own literary cocktail while you *pour* over the details to help Reece shake up the suspects to find the killer."

PAULA CHARLES, AUTHOR OF THE HOMETOWN HARDWARE MYSTERIES

ALSO BY ADRIAN ANDOVER

MIXOLOGY LOUNGE MYSTERIES

Whiskey Business

*For my kindergarten through fifth grade teachers at
Oklahoma Elementary School, who nurtured my love of books
and made me believe I could do anything I put my mind to.*

Teachers are heroes.

ONE

I wiped a bead of sweat from my brow with the back of one wrist as I lugged a sandwich board sign under my other arm. The air was thick with humidity as a heat wave scorched my quaint, artsy hometown of Hope Mills, Pennsylvania, which was nestled along the banks of the Delaware River.

There. I positioned the sign, which read WELCOME TO COMEDY AND COCKTAILS NIGHT! on the sidewalk in front of our building, careful not to block the flow of foot traffic. The event that was about to start was a first for Subplot, my literary-themed cocktail and mocktail lounge, and the pressure was on to deliver a flawless event for our guests.

As customers arrived tonight, they'd be greeted by our bubbly maître d', Lainey, in the vestibule we shared with our upstairs neighbor, D'Amico's Italian restaurant. She'd open our secret bookcase entrance and lead them down a set of stairs into our cozy basement lounge.

Eager to escape the humidity, I spun on my heels to return inside through our rear entrance, which led directly to Subplot.

Just as I was about to turn onto the footpath which connected the front sidewalk with the alley behind the building, a stocky man in his mid-forties with slicked-back brown hair paced along it, blocking me. Despite the sweltering heat, he wore a button-up shirt and a suit jacket with dark blue jeans.

He held his phone to one ear and had a finger jammed in the other. "If this doesn't work out the way it's supposed to, I can kiss my career goodbye," he hissed.

"Excuse me," I whispered loudly with an awkward smile. "Gonna squeeze past ya."

He stepped aside, allowing me to pass through the narrow walkway between the brick building and shrubbery. "I hope you're right."

"Thank you," I whispered. Though it was none of my business, I couldn't help but wonder what he was so stressed about. Hopefully everything would turn out all right for him.

"Fine. Whatever," the man scoffed.

When I reached the alley which led to the basement door, I peeked over my shoulder. The man was gone.

That was bizarre. I shrugged it off and headed inside.

Stepping into Subplot, I was delighted by the cool, dehumidified air. The faint scent of pineapple lingered, thanks to the fresh fruit my fellow mixologist Ava had just chopped to garnish our beverages.

"Reece! There you are," Lainey called from the staircase on the far side of the lounge. She wore a long golden necklace over a black tank top tucked into faded black jeans. "There's a line forming upstairs, and the vestibule is filling up. Heidi is going to get antsy if we don't start letting guests in soon."

I let out a sigh. Heidi was D'Amico's owner, and there was nothing I could do right in her eyes—except maybe close Subplot so she could be the sole tenant of our building once again.

I clapped my hands together. "It's huddle time!" I called out to my team as I waved Lainey to join me at the center of the lounge.

Each evening before we opened for service, Ava, Lainey, our server Dante, and I convened in a ceremonial circle near the bar. I couldn't speak for the rest of the team, but our huddles never failed to get my head in the game, regardless of how my day was going. It was a non-negotiable part of our opening routine —even if it meant risking a complaint from Heidi.

I swallowed the lump forming in my throat. "Here goes nothing."

Ava brushed a strand of her long, straight black hair away from her face with one hand. "We've got this. We've done everything we can to make tonight perfect."

Dante, who towered over us all, reached a fist across the circle to give me a light, friendly jab in shoulder. "And I'm sure it will be." Though he had the strong, bulky frame of a line-backer, he was a gentle artist at heart, specializing in painting and pottery in his time away from Subplot.

I grinned sheepishly. "It's just...Meghan Spencer is a big deal."

Meghan would be our headliner for the evening. Thanks to some viral videos, she'd amassed a huge following on social media. Chances were good that she'd attract new customers to Subplot.

Ava's chin fell to her chest and stared at me, deadpan. "That's exactly why tonight has the potential to be a huge win for us."

Or a massive flop. I didn't dare say it out loud. I sometimes tended to jump to worst-case scenarios, but some things were better left unspoken, especially when leading a team.

With Meghan's growing popularity, I wanted Subplot to shine when our audience shared their videos and experiences from the evening online. If anything went wrong, I feared it might scare future customers—or even other performers—away. My lounge hadn't even been open for six months yet, so every move felt make-or-break.

Lainey grinned and gave two thumbs up, her bright personality outshining the all-black clothing we wore as a staff. "I'm so excited I'll get to hang down here with you guys for a change and see the show."

Because the event was ticketed, customers wouldn't trickle in throughout the night as they normally would. Rather than being posted at her host station upstairs, Lainey would be downstairs in the lounge assisting Dante with service after all our guests were checked in, freeing Ava and me up to focus solely on crafting drinks, ensuring speedy service. If anyone arrived late, they could press a button on the host stand upstairs, which would sound a chime in our staff's earpieces, signaling Lainey to escort them downstairs.

Our space had previously been a basement my landlord used for storage, but earlier this year, he had it rezoned for commercial use. With the help of my best friend Nate, a local handyman and jack of all trades, I'd transformed the dark, drab space into a literary wonderland with built-in bookshelves along the side walls, eclectic and colorful furniture, subdued neon lighting, and the emerald glow of library lamps with glass lampshades.

Nate lingered just outside our huddle. He typically wore work clothes, including paint-streaked T-shirts, carpenter pants, and work boots. For Comedy and Cocktails, though, he'd traded his workwear for a dapper golf polo tucked into gray chinos with dressy white sneakers.

Who's this guy? I almost didn't recognize you all dressed up, I'd teased him earlier that afternoon. He'd shown up a few hours before we were set to open to help me rearrange furniture, set up my new small P.A. system, and offer his support.

"You've already outdone yourselves, and you haven't even opened yet," Nate said now. He gestured at the lounge, which we'd rearranged to accommodate the evening's entertainment.

Rather than our usual seating pods, which could accommodate anywhere from two to ten guests each, consisting of plush couches, leather reading chairs, and coffee tables, we'd rearranged all our seating to face the staircase.

Near its base, Nate had built a small platform stage where we hosted an ambient music DJ on Saturday nights. It would also work perfectly for any other type of entertainment we'd host in the future, including musicians, comedians, and readings by authors and poets.

A microphone on a stand was positioned in the middle of the stage with a stool behind it and P.A. speakers aimed at the audience on both sides.

I'd opened Subplot in the spring, a couple of months after breaking off an engagement with my ex-fiancée, Chloe. After coming to terms with my sexuality and accepting I was gay, I knew I needed to break up with her, as difficult as it would be for both of us. Though I would've been content to stay together and live a perfectly happy life with her, it wouldn't have been fair to either of us if I wasn't living in my truth. I dealt with the guilt and regret I felt after the breakup the only way I knew how —by jumping headfirst into hard work as a distraction.

Besides the time and effort it took to lease a space, secure a liquor license and a small business loan, and build the lounge from an empty brick and concrete room alongside Nate, opening Subplot was a costly endeavor. It also came with a lot of risk—like most small businesses. Many didn't survive past one year.

Subplot was open on Thursday through Sunday evenings. While the first three nights were typically busy, often requiring us to rely on a waitlist given our first-come, first-serve business model, our Sunday patronage had slowly dwindled as the summer wore on.

Although we crafted cocktails and mocktails unlike any others in our charming, Colonial-inspired small town of Hope Mills, Pennsylvania and the surrounding area, serving innovative and unique drinks wasn't enough.

Customers always craved something new. Every three months, we launched a full seasonal menu to keep things fresh, along with themed decor. At the start of summer, we saw a huge spike in demand as customers returned multiple times to taste their way around our refreshed menu. Our drink menus were bound in hardcover books and broken into two sections—*Fiction* cocktails and *Non-Fiction* alcohol-free mocktails. For summer, we covered them all in dust jackets of popular beach reads, like Taylor Jenkins Reid's *Malibu Rising* and Elin Hilderbrand's Nantucket series. Guests often took photos and posted them to social media, which further bolstered business.

But in the humid heat of early August as we were hard at work developing our fall menu, which would launch the weekend after Labor Day, customers needed another draw.

Just before the July Fourth holiday, Ava and her boyfriend Logan, the owner of Delaware Crossing Distilling Co.—or DCDC, as Hope Mills locals referred to it—had attended a stand-up show at a basement comedy club in Philadelphia, the nearest major city.

When she came into work the following evening, she practically buzzed when she presented the idea to me. "Let's give our customers an experience. We can hire an up-and-coming comedian to perform a set in Subplot. It'll give us something new to promote. We can sell tickets to make it feel like a real event." She went on to explain her vision, and it sounded like a great way to drive more business for Subplot.

The following several weeks had been a mad dash to organize and promote the show, sell tickets, and make sure the lounge was set up just right. If all went well, I could envision Comedy and Cocktails becoming a monthly event.

While in Philly, Ava had collected a few business cards from comedians and their managers. I'd also leveraged my small business network in town to connect me with a booking agent who presented multiple options for acts we could hire.

After doing tons of research and spending hours online watching videos of stand-up routines from comedians in our region, our team unanimously agreed to hire Meghan Spencer to headline our inaugural comedy night.

We were drawn to the way she interacted with her crowds, often involving them in her routine. Also, given Subplot's intimate atmosphere, we figured it was best to bring in a comedian who'd make the lounge feel like a living room. Someone who engaged the audience rather than performed *at* them. Plus, it didn't hurt that she'd recently broken out in bookish corners of social media for posting hilarious skits of well-known characters from classic novels in modern situations, like Elizabeth Bennet and Mr. Darcy meeting on a dating app.

Her fee was within our budget, although at the higher end, and we knew she could draw a crowd. Though she wasn't a household name, she was well on her way, which made me feel confident we could sell out—and we did.

In addition to Meghan, we'd also hired Nick Platt, a local actor from our community theater, Washington Playhouse, to open the show. He moonlighted as a stand-up comedian, so having him kick off the evening was a way to help him grow his following and promote talent from within our local community.

I checked the watch on the wrist of my sleeve-tattooed arm. From *The Giving Tree* to Marcellus the octopus from *Remarkably Bright Creatures*—my most recent tattoo—I was inked with a colorful arrangement of motifs from my favorite books. Five fifty-eight. "All right, let's open the doors and give these people a show."

"I'll flip off the overhead lights," Ava said. She referred to the fluorescent rod lights which illuminated the lounge when we were closed. Though not the warmest of lighting, it helped us ensure safety and cleanliness when we prepped the lounge for guests.

"And I'll start checking our guests in," Lainey added.

"Ready to start taking orders." Dante hunched forward to put his hand in the center of our huddle, and the rest of us followed suit.

I caught Nate's eye over my shoulder and gestured toward our hands with a sharp turn of my head. "You, too. You're part of the team tonight."

He placed his hand over ours.

"Subplot!" we all chanted as we all raised our hands. Cheesy? Yes, but it always set the tone for a fantastic evening.

After Ava turned off the overhead lights, my eyes adjusted to the dim watermelon-pink glow of the neon lighting strips that lined the top perimeter of the lounge.

Within the next few minutes, a steady stream of customers wandered down our staircase and took their seats, which were unassigned, as the hum of conversation swelled through the room.

Ava and I floated throughout the lounge to distribute water from carafes while Dante took the first round of drink orders.

"Boy, does it feel good down here," one customer commented, referring to the air conditioning on full-blast.

The lounge was a bit of an icebox when we opened, but considering the humid, mid-eighties weather outside in the evening hours and knowing it'd be a packed house, we'd soon be glad we stayed ahead of the heat.

The first couple I waited on at the bar requested two cocktails titled The Sun Also Rises, named after Ernest Hemingway's debut novel. A twist on a classic tequila sunrise cocktail, it incorporated fresh-squeezed orange juice, our house-made grenadine syrup, and Mezcal tequila to give the drink a hint of smokiness. We served the drink in fishbowl-shaped mason jars with flat sides so the completed cocktail resembled a setting sun.

About twenty minutes after opening, the lounge was almost three-quarters full.

Ava did a happy dance behind the bar as she loaded ice, gin, our house-made rhubarb syrup, and fresh-squeezed lime juice into a cocktail shaker behind the bar. "Can't you feel the anticipation in the air?"

I loved seeing her enthusiasm. "You had such a great idea, and I'm thrilled to see how it's all come together. Amazing work, A."

I placed six cocktails at the end of the bar, ready for Dante to deliver. Since we had our drink orders under control and we'd be ready to kick off the entertainment soon, I ventured into the crowd and surveyed the lounge for customers who were still waiting to place an order, as Lainey was still posted outside of the secret bookcase upstairs.

I sidestepped toward a group of guys who'd taken their seats on a vintage velvet green couch. "Welcome to Subplot. Have you all been here before? First time?"

I blinked hard. Julian—the guy I'd been crushing on for months and the owner of a local bookstore called Ampersand—was one of them. An excited chill raced down my spine as I admired his medium-length wavy brunette hair, which flowed beautifully behind his ears.

"Hey, Reece. I'm a frequent flyer," Julian said. His voice had a subtle rasp that was smoky like Mezcal.

"Oh, Julian. Hey!" I tried to play it cool. "I realized it was you as soon as I asked."

Even after combing through the evening's registration list multiple times, I hadn't noticed he bought a ticket for Comedy and Cocktails, and it was probably for the best. Maybe a friend bought one for him. The pressure to deliver a perfect evening had just bumped up a notch.

A few months before, Julian had left his phone number on his check when I'd waited on him at the lounge. At the time, I hadn't yet come out to my family and my breakup was still fresh. I'd eventually texted him, and we'd become friendly acquaintances, but nothing more. Too afraid to make a move, I was shy any time we bumped into one another, and Julian hadn't made a move, either. As two men in our early thirties who'd recently opened our own businesses in Hope Mills, we had plenty to discuss without delving into our personal lives. And until I was more comfortable with the idea of dating again—and dating a guy for the first time —I was fine not exploring the possibility. And besides, even if he'd been interested before, he could've moved on.

"What can I get for you all?" I asked, extra cautious to make sure I evenly distributed eye contact to all three guys in the group and not just my crush.

After taking their order, along with a group seated beside them, I retreated behind the bar to shake up more drinks. I hoped Ava and Nate hadn't seen me talking to Julian. While I appreciated my friends for pushing me out of my comfort zone, I wasn't ready to take the plunge into dating. Not yet.

"It's going to be just fine," a woman's voice hissed to my left as I tugged fresh mint leaves off a plant under an indoor grow light for a mojito. As my eyes panned in her direction, I confirmed it was Meghan. She was accompanied by Tiffany, her manager, at the end of the bar.

Up until then, they'd been getting ready in my office, which I'd offered as a makeshift green room. It was down a short hallway near the bar that also led to our restrooms, small kitchen, and supply closet.

Tiffany and Meghan couldn't have looked more different. Tiffany's tall, athletic build was a stark contrast to Meghan's short, petite frame. Meghan had blue eyes and straight, long blonde hair with curtain bangs, while Tiffany had brown eyes and mid-length black hair with thick curls.

I split my attention between their conversation and the mint leaves, lime juice, and sugar I muddled at the bottom of a tall Collins glass. I worked slowly, not wanting to shred the mint too much, which would release a bitter flavor into the cocktail.

"This is a huge deal," Tiffany urged with both palms turned out at her sides. "Scott Simmons is going to be in the crowd tonight."

Meghan didn't respond. She only gave her manager a deadpan stare.

"From CineStream? He's the talent executive who's casting for *In Stitches.*"

Meghan scoffed. "*Duh.* I know who he is. I wasn't born yesterday."

"Then you know that this could be a huge step for your career, especially after their recent acquisition of Fledgling Studios. I extended the invite weeks ago. I didn't think he'd actually show." She scanned the lounge as she chomped on a cuticle. "It doesn't look like he's here yet, though."

Meghan rolled her eyes. "I have my ways..."

I hadn't heard about the acquisition—or even Fledgling Studios—myself, but I also wasn't part of the entertainment world, so I wasn't surprised I was out of the loop. Plus, while I kept up with the news, I didn't spend much time on my phone, so I often missed stories that weren't major headlines.

I added a shot of white rum and a scoop of crushed ice to the glass.

"If he likes what he sees tonight, you could have a shot. Just please act professional." Tiffany's voice was kind, yet direct.

Though I knew Meghan ran the show and Tiffany worked for her, what was the point in hiring a manager if you didn't take them seriously?

Meghan groaned. "You don't think I know how this works? You're acting like I'll sleep with the guy. Of course I'll act professional. I *always* act professional."

Sure seems like it. I was surprised by her tone. She didn't seem very easy to work with, and I wondered if her professionalism was an ongoing concern for Tiffany.

Tiffany pressed her lips together and gave Meghan a side-eye. When she looked back toward the audience, her face brightened. She gave Meghan a nudge on the shoulder. "There he is!" She gestured toward the staircase with her big brown eyes.

"Play it cool, Tiff."

Following her gaze, I spotted the man I'd seen on the phone outside taking a seat on the far left side of the lounge. His business-casual attire despite the heat gave me a strong feeling he had to be Scott.

Meghan approached Ava and me at the bar with hands on her hips. "Can I get a shot of tequila?"

Tiffany cradled her head in both hands then dragged them down her face. She marched toward us, towering over Meghan as she stood over her shoulder. "Absolutely not. There's too much at stake for you to go on stage with even a drop of alcohol in your system."

Meghan scoffed again. "I'm not a child. You're talking like I can't handle myself."

"It's not that." Tiffany rested a hand on Meghan's shoulder.

Meghan pulled away immediately. "Don't touch me."

"I truly believe in you, and we've worked so hard for this. I'm only trying to avoid risk. We'll do plenty of celebrating if this goes well. Trust me."

As fascinated as I was by Meghan and Tiffany's dynamic, I wished they'd kept their drama in my office.

They clearly had different approaches, and I hoped Meghan wouldn't take the conflict on stage with her. The last thing I needed was for her negative energy to cast a shadow upon Subplot. I needed our inaugural Comedy and Cocktails night to be a smashing success.

TWO

Later in the evening, after a smooth start to our event, the crowd erupted with laughter and cheered as our warmup act, Nick Platt, finished his final joke.

"Thank you so much." He pressed both palms together and half-bowed toward the audience. "Who's excited to see Meghan Spencer tonight?"

The audience's cheers grew louder and more boisterous.

I met him at the side of the stage, shook his hand as he jogged off, and hustled up to the mic. "Wasn't Nick great?" I rallied the crowd as their applause continued. "Meghan will be taking the stage in about fifteen minutes. If you'd like to order another drink, Lainey and Dante will be making another lap around the lounge before her set. Thank you all again for supporting our first-ever Comedy and Cocktails night!"

The audience didn't cheer nearly as hard for me—understandably—but they were clearly relaxed and having a great time.

Ava and I refilled water glasses while Lainey and Dante took orders. Although I felt a faint envy, I was mostly relieved that Dante waited on Julian and his friends. I didn't want to embarrass myself in front of my crush—or a packed room. That wasn't the comedy our guests were looking for tonight.

At the very back of the lounge, where Lainey took orders with a beaming smile, we'd turned our barstools around to face away from the bar and toward the stage.

"Can I get you another drink?" I'd overheard Lainey ask a woman I vaguely recognized as I passed them on my way back behind the bar.

Sitting on one of the barstools, she wore high-waisted denim shorts and a white crop top. I estimated she was about my age, in her early to mid-thirties. Her hair was light brown with loose waves cascading midway down her back. In recent months, I'd seen her around town quite often. She was always solo, just as she was tonight. I couldn't place who she was or how I knew her. Was she a neighbor? A friend's ex-girlfriend? Did she work at the grocery store or a restaurant in town? Someone I went to high school with? I figured I'd put the pieces together eventually, even if she was just a community member I had no personal connection to.

The woman glanced down at the menu card in her hand. "Sure. I'll have a...Giant Peach, please."

The beverage, named after Roald Dahl's beloved children's novel, was a peach and rosemary mocktail with a subtle kick of jalapeño heat.

Back behind the bar, Ava muddled a lime at the bottom of a cocktail shaker. Dante dropped off a stack of orders from his pad as Ava loaded a tray with a round of drinks she'd prepared for him to distribute around the lounge.

As much as I enjoyed focusing all my energy on mixology, I didn't think I could ever give up waiting on guests, even if only those at the bar. The connection with my community was one of the main reasons I made a career in the restaurant and bar industry.

"Man, I could get used to this. I'm in the zone." Ava pressed a lid onto her shaker. "But if I only made drinks, I'd miss interacting with our customers. It's one of my favorite parts of the job."

"I was thinking the same thing. On regular nights, I think we should both continue to wait on customers at the bar and at least a table or two each."

After Ava and I finished crafting everyone's drinks and Lainey and Dante delivered them, it was time for Meghan to take the stage.

She and Tiffany had returned to my office, so I headed back to give them a two-minute warning. After knocking, I slowly pushed the door open. They hadn't been talking to one another. Instead, Meghan sat on my gray futon, staring straight ahead with arms crossed and an angry wrinkle etched in her forehead. Tiffany, seated in my desk chair, had her back to Meghan and was scrolling on her phone.

"All right, let's do this!" Tiffany perked up. She rubbed her hands together nervously, yet still spoke with zeal. "You're gonna crush it." She raised a hand for a high five. Based on the tension I sensed between them when I poked my head into the room, I was surprised Meghan accepted it.

"*In Stitches*, here I come." She rose from her chair and left the office.

Tiffany trailed Meghan out into the hallway, and I locked my office door to keep their belongings safe inside. They both waited beside the bar when I made my way back to the main lounge.

I strode through the audience and up to the mic again as "Lovefool" by the Cardigans played over the speakers—part of our evening's music mix from my personal "Favorite Women of the Nineties" playlist. Ava, always in tune with me, turned the music down from behind the bar.

"All right, everybody, it's the moment you've all been waiting for. It's my absolute honor and pleasure to bring an incredible comedian to the stage tonight. She's here from Philadelphia, and you may recognize her from one of her many viral videos on social media. I'd like to welcome the one and only"—I paused and deepened my voice to chant her name into the mic as the audience erupted—"Meghan Spencer!"

As I stepped off the short stage, she jogged down the aisle with a playful smirk on her face. Her energy was relaxed, yet confident—a complete shift from her earlier tense interactions with Tiffany.

Grasping the mic with one small hand, she shouted into it, "We're going to make some racket in the library tonight. How about it, Hope Mills?"

Somehow the crowd's cheers grew even louder.

In particular, I watched Julian raise his hands to the sides of his mouth to amplify his hoot of excitement. My heart swelled. If he had a good time, I'd be able to call the evening a success.

"This place strangely reminds me of college, believe it or not." She paused for a beat as the room quieted. "I used to drink and read at the library all the time. Except the lighting was much more harsh. And there were no beautiful cocktails. Just cheap, blanco tequila I smuggled in a water bottle. Needless to say, I wasn't college material, which explains why I'm now a jester."

During the first portion of her performance, she leaned even further into her recent success with humorous book reviews and literary sketch comedy on social media.

"Who here has been personally victimized by a book before?" she asked early on, eliciting a few hesitant raised hands in the audience. "That's all? I've been both emotionally and physically hurt by books."

"Physically?" a woman in the front row called out.

Meghan stared at her with a poker face. "Oh, don't act like you've never dropped a book on your face before. Those suckers hurt. And they always catch you when you're in your most vulnerable state—just about to fall asleep." She raised a stiff arm with her index finger pointed upward. "Not today, book. You're not going to deck me in the face again. Not today."

Meghan's efforts to tie Subplot's bookish theme into her set made every cent of her expensive fee worth it. The way she seemed to understand the audience and tailor her performance in real time was a dazzling testament of her talent and skill.

"And don't get me started on people who say audiobooks don't count as reading. They're the same people who say mocktails don't count as a fun time." Rather than laughter, that comment coaxed the audience into cheers and applause of support. "Party poopers," she added, sparking some chuckles.

I gazed at Julian's side profile from my position behind the bar, admiring his active participation in the performance with claps, joyful hollers, and a smile that could illuminate the room all on its own.

About twenty-five minutes into her set, she concluded the bookish segment of her show to present other material.

"So, I don't know how to swim," she said, deadpan.

"What?" an audience member called out in shock.

She took an exaggerated deep breath, rolled her eyes histrionically, and shook her head. "I said, 'I don't know how to swim!'"

A few people in the crowd chuckled.

Tiffany, who'd been recording videos from multiple angles on a digital camera throughout the evening, approached the stage from the far left wall. Given Meghan's huge online following, I figured she was always capturing as much raw footage as possible. Would her next viral video be filmed in Subplot? I could only hope. It'd be a great way to keep building buzz for the lounge.

"I don't. Never learned. Probably never will. You see, it's not just that I *can't* swim. I *don't* swim. Ya feel me? Kind of like I *don't* smoke or *don't* have a relationship with my mother or totally *don't* wish my ex-boyfriend would die in a house fire." She grimaced and sucked a loud breath in through her clenched teeth. "Too far? Okay, maybe I was lying about that last one. But don't worry—he sucked. He has it coming for him. I'll tell you more about him later."

The audience was, well, in stitches. One man in the front row had an infectious laugh which seemed to influence the rest of the room to roar in an instant.

"But no joke, though... When I tell people I never learned how to swim, they act so shocked. And do you know what they always say?"

She paused for a beat as the crowd hung on every word. "They always say, 'Oh, I'll teach you,' as if no one has ever said that to me before. As if it's never occurred to me that I should try to learn. As if I've never even attempted to swim or been near a pool in my life. They say, 'Meet me at the YMCA. Give me two hours, and I'll teach you.'"

She sidestepped and did the YMCA hand motions from the song, then waved her arms in an S.O.S. gesture and mouthed, *Help me*, which elicited some hoots from the lounge.

"To which I say, 'Wanna bet?' And for some reason, these people always seem to list out their qualifications. They'll say, 'Oh, I was on the swim team in high school,' or 'I was a life-guard all throughout college,' or 'I was in the Navy,' or 'I taught my boyfriend's cousin's second husband how to swim.'" She raised an index finger. "To which I reply, 'I don't remember asking for your resume, first of all...'"

The man in the front row cackled, which sent the rest of the audience into another round of hysteric laughter and even made Meghan let out a suppressed chuckle of her own.

"'This is not a job interview, thanks. And second of all, I will absolutely waste your time.' I'm a lost cause. Me and water? We don't mix. And of course, they'll always respond with something like, 'It's a very valuable skill. You never know when you might need to know how to swim. But I'm like, 'No. I don't think I'll ever need that skill.' And they'll say, 'But what if your plane goes down over the water?' To which I say, 'Can't swim. Can't fly. I'm a land animal.'"

She got down on all fours and crawled around the stage. She pretended to graze for grass, and right in front of the man with the contagious laugh, she let out an enthusiastic, *Mooo!*

The audience erupted with laughter and cheered at the end of the bit.

Meghan sprung up to stand on two feet with victory written on her face. "Speaking of things I can't do, I can't believe—"

"You can't be funny?" a woman's voice interrupted Meghan from the audience.

Uh-oh.

She shielded her eyes from the spotlight hanging from the ceiling and squinted to search for the heckler in the crowd. "Excuse me? Did you just say what I *think* you said?"

From my position behind the bar, I also surveyed the lounge to figure out where the comment had come from.

"Can't swim, can't fly, can't tell a joke to save your life," the heckler called out again.

The audience was silent.

Toward the center of the room, I spotted a woman with long, straight brunette hair who'd interrupted with the rude remark.

A few rows in front of her, I clocked Julian wincing at the awkwardness.

Ava poked an elbow into my ribcage from my left. "Yikes!" she whispered.

"Do you think she's sloshed? Should we throw her out?" I asked.

"That reminds me of another thing I can't do." Meghan's sullen voice rang out over the P.A. speakers. A frown drooped on her face. Her shoulders slouched and arms hung at her side, dejected.

The audience was silent, hanging onto the moment in suspense for what she might say next.

Dante hunched toward us. "This is bad," he mumbled from the other side of Ava. "Do you want me to throw her out?"

I shrugged, unsure of what to do.

Looking over to Tiffany, she appeared unbothered as she filmed the interaction from her position toward the back of the aisle which parted our guests. She would've flagged me down if she thought I needed to intervene, right? The heckler had already created a scene, and I didn't want to make it any worse.

"I can't wait for you to shut the hell up. This is my show."

"Yeah!" the man with the infectious laugh in the front row sprung to his feet and cheered. The audience roared and rose to give Meghan a standing ovation.

"See?" The rowdy applause nearly drowned out Meghan's voice. She stared directly at her heckler. "Some people think I'm funny."

"What was that all about?" I asked my team in a low voice amidst the cheers. "I can't believe what just happened."

"Doesn't it seem a bit too convenient?" Ava ran her fingers through her straight black hair. "I think that might've been part of the act."

Lainey nodded in agreement. "The audience is clearly on Meghan's side."

Until they'd mentioned it, I hadn't even considered the

possibility it was planned. To me, the heckler's comment seemed too off the cuff to be orchestrated.

"I usually save my crowd work for the end of the show, but since we've already had some audience participation, maybe we should do that part a bit early. What do you think?" Meghan asked the crowd with open arms.

The audience applauded to persuade her to continue.

"The crowd has spoken." She shielded her eyes from the spotlight and pointed to a man with dark brown hair in the second row, seated directly next to Nate. "What's your name?" she asked in a playful, almost childlike voice.

Tiffany strolled down the aisle. As she did, I imagined the footage slowly panning closer toward Meghan and the man she called out.

"Garrett," the man responded. His voice was deep and raspy.

"So, are you really short, or is he super tall?" She pointed at Nate, who was seated beside him. "Now *that's* what I call a man."

A few chuckles echoed through the lounge.

At six-foot-one, Nate was on the tall side, but I didn't consider him to be super tall, even at my average five-nine-and-a-half.

From my angle, the man did appear quite a bit smaller than Nate, despite his bulky muscles which appeared to be strangled by the sleeves of his tight olive green T-shirt.

Nate slunk lower in his seat until he appeared to be the same height as Garrett.

Garrett didn't answer her question. He only shook and bowed his head, making his modern mullet haircut visible to me.

"How tall are you, Garrett?" Her sing-songy voice was condescending.

"I don't see why that's important," he answered in an even deeper tone than before, perhaps compensating.

"There's nothing to be ashamed of. Ladies *love* a short king," Meghan taunted.

"I'm not answering that question." His flat, quiet tone was barely audible from my position in the very back of the lounge.

Half of the audience chuckled, though it sounded forced. The rest were silent, glancing around at one another as if to seek validation for how to respond.

"I mean, look at this hunk beside you." Meghan gestured her open palm at Nate, practically undressing him with her eyes. "He's not exactly ripped, but he's a *big* dude." Her eye contact switched back to Garrett. "And I'll give it to you—you're *shredded*. I mean, look at those pecs on you! Yet you still look *so small* in comparison. Pocket-sized!"

A few laughs rung out, but they were accompanied by some groans and nervous whispers from the crowd.

Garrett stood up in front of the black leather reading chair he'd been seated in. Looking down at Nate, he grunted, then addressed Meghan. "I'm five-six. Are you happy?" He squeezed past a few other audience members and stormed past the stage and up the stairs toward the secret bookcase.

"Call me," she said with a quick giggle. It was unclear to me who her comment was intended to address.

I focused on Nate, who sat next to Garrett's now-empty chair in the second row. He rubbed the back of his bald head. I caught a glimpse of his profile, which revealed a grimace painted on his face. He slid even further down in his chair—a perfect reflection of the rest of the clearly uncomfortable audience.

Would Meghan recover after her crowd work segment went terribly wrong? Or was her set beyond saving?

THREE

Meghan's performance recovered, thanks to a brazen segment about her ex-boyfriend. Many attendees had tears in their eyes from laughing so hard. By the end, Garrett storming out midset and her tense interaction with the heckler seemed like a distant memory. The audience was putty in her hands, and they rewarded her with a standing ovation

Once she stepped off the stage, audience members swarmed around her to offer their compliments and appreciation. Luckily, she kept her charisma rolling and interacted with the crowd with grace, even hugging audience members who approached her.

Hopping back onstage, I thanked everyone for coming to the show and encouraged the crowd to continue hanging out in the lounge. "Tiffany from Meghan's team will be setting up some merch here on the stage, so if you'd like to purchase any, you can stop by and see her. I believe Meghan will be mingling, doing some signing, and taking photos with anyone who wants one. We'll also rearrange some of the furniture to open up space in the lounge, so we hope you'll stay and enjoy the rest of the evening with us."

Nate and I worked our way around Subplot, positioning furniture into circles so customers could chat more naturally. We'd have to arrange everything to its original configuration later. I never took his support for granted. At one point, Subplot had been nothing more than an empty basement and a dream. Thanks to his skill and hard work, we were able to bring it to life. Tonight's event made the space feel more alive than ever.

As we rested a heavy wingback chair at an angle on an area rug, I spotted a small bouquet of sunny yellow tulips abandoned on the concrete floor near where Nate had been sitting,

"Well, well, well..."

The critical female voice I recognized without a doubt seemed to come out of nowhere. I looked up to see Heidi D'Amico, the owner of the restaurant upstairs, standing in the middle of my lounge.

What now? I inwardly cringed. "Hey, Heidi. How's it going?"

With a fist planted on each hip, she tapped the toe of one of her tall wedge sandals. "Awfully convenient that your little comedy show ends just as my restaurant is about to close. It's neighborly to share business, wouldn't you say?"

Not far behind her, Julian and his friends congregated in a small circle. I hoped he wouldn't hear Heidi reading me the riot act.

I sighed. "I'm sure some of our guests tonight had dinner upstairs before they came down to the show."

She rolled her eyes and didn't respond directly, perhaps realizing I was right. She often brought petty, baseless grievances to me. More than anything, I think she just loved to complain. "You know what the one bright side is?"

Nate, who was standing just behind Heidi, covered his mouth, clearly stifling a laugh.

I forced my tongue into my cheek, fighting my own urge to smile. "Hm?"

"You think this is funny? The bright side to you *stealing* guests away from me at the end of the night is that I didn't have to deal with any unsavory behavior."

Unsavory. She loved to use that word—perhaps more than she loved to complain. Though I'd seen her soft side peek out on occasion, she was generally a tough nut to crack. She'd shown me grace after my tense confrontation with the killer during a murder investigation which shook Hope Mills several months ago. However, she'd returned to her rigid, uptight ways.

"I'm sorry, Heidi." Sometimes it was easier to let her win— or at least create the illusion that she'd won—than to try and argue with her. "Next month, I'll be more mindful when building the schedule." Knowing she'd inevitably be upset about something else in a month, it wasn't worth following through.

"Next month?"

"Yeah, we want to make Comedy and Cocktails a regular event here."

"I don't think there will be a next month. Not if I have a say in the matter."

You don't have a say in the matter, I wanted to respond. "Have a nice evening, Heidi."

She scoffed and retreated toward the staircase which led up to her restaurant.

After Nate and I finished rearranging the furniture, Lainey returned to her maître d' stand upstairs to accept walk-in guests since the performance had finished. Dante took orders around the lounge, and Ava and I resumed our roles as mixologists. Though some audience members left shortly after the show, I was ecstatic that the majority stuck around.

While Tiffany sold merch at a table we'd set up on the stage, Meghan hung out near the bar as various audience members continued to approach her to talk, take selfies, or sign a T-shirt, poster, or baseball cap. Everyone was kind and respectful, giving her space and not crowding, hovering around her, or monopolizing her time.

Despite the chatter which filled the lounge, Meghan anchored herself close enough to me that I could overhear snippets of a conversation she had with an audience member—a man with dirty blond hair peeking out of his coral baseball cap. He was tall and fit, wearing a short-sleeved button-up shirt with khaki shorts and white sneakers.

"I can't believe what you said about me." He shook his head.

"David, not here. Not now," Meghan pleaded through clenched teeth. She kept a smile on her face despite her aggravated tone.

"Die in a house fire? That's low."

Her eyes darted in every direction, as if she was nervous someone might overhear.

I kept my eyes focused on the orange peel I twisted into an Old Fashioned. Luckily, I had no shortage of work behind the bar to keep me busy, so I hoped they wouldn't suspect me of eavesdropping. Because of my proximity, and the fact that everyone else was engaged in conversation, I figured I was the only person in the lounge who could listen in.

She scoffed. "It's called comedy. Ever heard of it?"

I snuck another peek at the man—David—who spoke with animated gestures. "Come on, Meg. Give me a break. I know it's comedy, but nothing you said about me in the second half of your set was true. You made me sound like the worst person in the world."

"Would you drop it?" She continued to speak through gritted teeth. "I'm working right now. Can't we talk about this later? You're not supposed to be here, so scram."

He smacked the back of one hand down on his open palm. "You told everyone I locked you out of the house and made you sleep on the front porch in the middle of winter. You know that's not true. *You* did that to *me*."

"Not everything in my set is autobiographical. You should know that more than anybody. I can use creative license, you know."

David tsked. "Whatever, Meg. We can talk about it later, but I'm out of here. Your set was funny, but what's even funnier is how you only show empathy when you have an opportunity to act like a victim. I was the victim in our relationship, and we both know it. Have fun using me as material."

She gave him a coy smile. "I'll keep an eye out for the cease and desist."

He grunted before walking away and retreating upstairs.

Dante was busy taking orders, so I loaded cocktails on a tray to distribute around the lounge.

As I did, I kept an eye on Meghan, who remained upbeat and friendly as other audience members approached her after her ex-boyfriend left.

While delivering drinks throughout Subplot, I noticed the heckler from earlier in the set speaking to Scott, the CineStream talent executive, in a corner. Though I didn't overhear any of their discussion, their interaction appeared friendly, even with an occasional chuckle exchanged between the two of them. He appeared much calmer than when I'd seen him on the phone outside before the show. But then again, if he was working, he likely had no choice but to remain poised and professional.

It seemed odd that a heckler felt comfortable approaching someone in Scott's role. She must not have been aware he was in the lounge to evaluate Meghan for a role on *In Stitches*. Though I hadn't talked to him, I was surprised he even entertained having a conversation with someone who showed such blatant disrespect. Perhaps the heckler had cornered him.

Considering Lainey and Ava's theory that the heckler had

been planted by Meghan and Tiffany, maybe Scott approached her to figure out why she'd heckled Meghan and whether it was part of the bit.

At about a quarter till eleven, shortly after we announced our last call, we distributed the final round of drinks. Our team closed out customers' tabs and guests gradually trickled out of the lounge. I always felt relieved seeing customers use rideshare apps or hearing them mention designated drivers.

When I realized Julian and his friends had already gone, I was equally relieved I didn't have to face my nerves in front of my staff and disappointed that we didn't have a chance to chat.

Earlier, Ava had let Meghan and Tiffany into the office to collect their belongings, and they each packed up and left the lounge without saying goodbye. Luckily, I had their contact information so we could connect on final details for payment, since the remaining installment of Meghan's fee was due after her performance.

Lainey and Dante got a head start cleaning up the lounge while Ava tidied up behind the bar.

As Nate and I reset furniture to its original layout, he patted down his front and back pants pockets.

I wrinkled my forehead. "Looking for something?"

"My pocketknife." He always carried a multi-tool Swiss Army knife around with him. It was set in walnut wood and engraved with his initials. Given his occupation, it often came in handy for small jobs on the go.

"Did you leave it in your work pants?"

"Maybe." He didn't sound convinced by the possibility. "It doesn't matter what I'm wearing. Along with my keys, it's the first thing I take out of my pockets when I get home and the first thing I grab before I head out the door to leave. I'll bet it fell out of these loose pockets."

"Blame it on getting all dressed up." I shrugged. "Maybe it'll turn up once we get all the furniture back in place."

"I hope so," he said as we each picked up an end of a yellow art deco-style couch.

"How about that crowd work segment?" I teased.

"Dude. That was so uncomfortable for me."

"Sure looked like it."

We lowered the couch, resting its front feet on a floral area rug and back feet on the lounge's smooth cement floor.

"It's like she was implying I was more of a"—he made air quotes with his fingers—"*real man* than Garrett, just because I'm a bigger, taller guy."

"The joke seemed mean-spirited, but I'm still surprised he stormed out the way he did. It was a comedy show, after all. I'm not making excuses for Meghan, but comedians push the limits. And she's known for her crowd work."

Nate slid his hands into his back pockets and rocked on his heels. "About that…I overheard Garrett talking to his friends after the opening act left the stage and before Meghan started. He said he wanted to try asking her out after the show."

"I guess that explains the bouquet of flowers I noticed near your seat?"

He grimaced. "Yeah."

I coughed to stifle a chuckle. "Seeing how he left, I'd say he probably didn't follow through."

"By the sounds of it, he'd been eyeing her up on social media for a while and had even slid into her DMs. Maybe when she teased him for his height, he took it personally because he was hoping to spark some romance. Some people can't handle rejection."

"Aww. Poor guy."

Nate crossed his arms and stared straight ahead contemplatively. "Honestly, I almost feel like I should apologize to him."

I lifted the back end of a reading chair to angle it just right around a bean-shaped coffee table. "You didn't insult him, though."

Nate placed a hand on one hip. "True, but Garrett is one of my clients. I'd rather apologize, even if I don't need to. I should make sure we're cool so he doesn't choose another handyman."

I respected Nate's perspective. It was the right thing to do. He cared deeply not only for his clients, but the community as a whole. Nate came from a military family that had moved around a lot up until he was a teenager. Once his family had settled for good in Hope Mills, he'd vowed it would be his hometown forever.

I cocked my head to one side. "Really? You've worked with him before?"

"Yeah, he's a barber here in Hope Mills—at TAME. I helped them install some new mirrors earlier this year."

"No kidding."

"In fact, I think he owns the place, but I'm not sure." Nate scratched his thick red beard, which had sprouted its first gray hairs in recent months. "Regardless, he basically runs the place. He's the one who schedules maintenance when it needs to be done and signs all the checks."

I rocked on my heels. "You've got me thinking. How he was treated probably isn't a good look on Subplot, either. Maybe I should swing by there tomorrow and offer my own apology. I can invite him back for a free round of drinks. He came to our comedy show for a fun night out and left feeling antagonized. I hope he realizes that's not what we're about."

Nate nodded. "I don't think that's a bad plan. Like you told me, I don't think an apology is necessary, but since we both know where to find him, I don't think it hurts to extend some goodwill. We small business owners need to look out for each other. Plus, the world could use a bit more empathy and compassion, don't you think?"

I couldn't ask for a more thoughtful, friendly, and caring best friend than Nate. I appreciated his sensitivity and genuine concern for others. Even if Garrett hadn't been his client, I knew he'd want to make things right out of the goodness of his heart.

I was grateful that Nate inspired me to do the same.

Unfortunately, the situation took a turn for the worse before we'd had a chance to smooth things over.

FOUR

The next morning, I awoke to a series of buzzes as my phone vibrated repeatedly on my bedside table, a recent addition to my room as I slowly furnished my bachelor pad.

I squinted at my alarm clock in my disoriented, half-awake state. Six forty-seven.

Something's happened to one of my parents. Besides being sleepy and tending to hop to worst case scenarios, I never received calls so early, so I had a feeling something was wrong.

My cat, Jameson, stretched and yawned at the foot of my bed, where he slept most nights—if he wasn't attempting to smother me in my sleep by lying on my face.

A few months prior, I'd found Jameson as a tiny kitten in the alley behind Subplot. Although I'd originally agreed to foster the friendly orange tabby until his original owner was found or the local shelter had placed him in a new home, I was a classic foster fail. After a few days with him, I couldn't imagine my life without his playful personality, and I certainly couldn't bear the thought of him living with anyone else. He'd grown like a weed in the months since, and he was shaping up to be a long boy.

The vibrations continued to rumble on my nightstand. Who possibly needed to get ahold of me at such an early hour?

Monday mornings were usually calm. I typically didn't set an alarm and gave myself permission to stay in bed as long as possible since Mondays were the start of my weekends.

I reached for my phone as it continued to buzz in my hands.

My home screen was plastered with notifications of multiple missed calls and a string of cryptic text messages from Nate.

> Bro. Call me right now.

> Are you awake?

> Come on, answer!

> It's urgent.

> I need you, man. Please call me as soon as you see this

Without thought, I tapped the call button in the upper-right corner of our text conversation.

Nate was my best friend. My ride or die. He'd do anything for me, and I'd do the same in return. We'd sworn we'd always have one another's back.

The phone rang once in my ear.

He'd answered almost immediately. "Oh my God, Reece. You'll never believe it." No greeting, no pleasantries. He sounded out of breath.

"What happened? Is everything okay?"

"I swear it wasn't me. I didn't do it."

"Didn't do what?"

"I only found it." In all of our years of friendship, I didn't think I'd ever heard Nate sound so flustered and out of sorts. He was typically the level-headed one. The one who remained calm in the face of chaos. The one who pushed me out of my comfort zone. The one who talked me off the ledge when my over-thinking spiraled out of control.

"Would you please calm down and tell me what you found?" I knew I needed to be direct to get through to him. "It'll all be okay. Whatever's going on, I'll help you through it." Without knowing, though, I hated feeling uncertain about whether it was actually within my power to help him at all.

"This is bad, Reece. Really bad. I was out for my jog earlier this morning—around five-thirty. I wanted to see the sunrise over the river, so I jogged down to the Promenade." The River Promenade was a wide cement walkway along the Delaware River. In addition to being a popular walking, jogging, and bench-sitting spot, it also provided access to businesses located along the waterfront. "But something caught my eye in the water, just over the edge of the walkway. At first, I thought it was trash clumped together on the riverbank. But my curiosity got the best of me." His voice sounded rough.

"What was it?"

"A body. Caught up in the brush on the bank."

My jaw hung open. "You're kidding, right? This isn't funny."

When Nate didn't respond, only panted shallow breaths on the other end of the line, I knew without a doubt he was serious.

I ran my fingers through my hair, which had grown quite a bit longer than my typical buzz cut, as if it might soothe my growing unease. "You called the police, right?"

"Of course, I did. Right away."

"Did you figure out who it was?"

He sounded breathless. "Meghan Spencer."

Heat rose on the back of my neck. It was a good thing I was

still in bed, because my vision grew dark as my heart pounded. If I'd been standing up, I think I would've passed out.

Immediately, I considered whether the contentious moments from the night before could've contributed to her unexpected demise. "This *is* bad. Really, really bad."

A few months prior, I'd discovered a dead body in the alleyway behind Subplot after a disastrous whiskey tasting in the lounge. I still suffered from terrible flashbacks of my discovery. I often saw the victim's limp, outstretched arm covered in red-and-black checkered flannel in my mind.

Acknowledging my own trauma, I realized I'd better make sure Nate was okay and knew he had my support. He'd been a pillar for me when I'd needed it, and it made all the difference.

I swallowed my own fear, knowing Nate needed me to be strong. "I've got your back no matter what. Whatever you need. I know all too well how you must be feeling right now, and I wouldn't wish it on my worst enemy, let alone my best friend. Where can I meet you?"

Nate let out a heavy, wet sigh, which made me wonder if he'd been crying. Considering his discovery and his general sensitivity, I wouldn't have been surprised if he was. "I'm near Riverside Roastery now."

"I'll be there in fifteen minutes—or even faster, if I can. Don't go anywhere."

Jameson leapt off the bed, as if he sensed my unease, knowing I was about to get up as well. Or perhaps he knew it was nearly time for his automatic feeder to release his next portion of dry food at seven.

I left my bed unmade—which I never did—and threw on a pair of blue athletic shorts and a white T-shirt. Knowing I didn't have time to tame my sandy-brown hair, which appeared disheveled thanks to my loose curls starting to grow out, I pulled a rugged tan DCDC baseball cap over my head. In the kitchen, I refilled Jameson's water dish and topped off his feeder.

"No parties while I'm gone today, Jame." I had no doubts Jameson was in tune with my emotions, whether by reading my body language or smelling my stress hormones, and I didn't want him to worry about me.

Jameson let out a long, annoyed meow, as if to play along.

"I don't want to hear any ifs, ands, or buts."

"Meow," he chirped as if to say, *Whatever.*

"I love you, Jame," I called before hurrying out the door.

"Meeeooow." It was feline for, *I love you, too.*

FIVE

I practically jogged to Riverside Roastery. Although it was shortly after seven, the air already felt hot—likely in the mid-seventies and exacerbated by the high humidity.

In light of my rapid heart rate and internal panic, I wished my feelings reflected the peaceful scenery of Hope Mills in the morning. The ivy-covered buildings and brick sidewalks which lined Main Street were washed in a tranquil golden light. With the exception of birds chirping their morning songs, I only heard the faint whisper of tree leaves swaying on the gentle breeze. I reminded myself to take deep breaths as I rushed to meet up with Nate.

The coffee shop's back entrance led directly to the Promenade, and caution tape, police officers, an ambulance, and a forensics team came into view as I approached Riverside Roastery.

When I turned the corner onto the Promenade, Nate was sitting alone at a table outside in his running clothes—a rare sight. He wore a tattered baseball cap over his bald head, a paint-splotched green T-shirt, and shorts. He sat on the front edge of his seat and leaned forward with elbows resting on each knee and one leg bouncing ferociously.

"Are you okay?" I called out as soon as he was within earshot. The question felt dumb as soon as the words escaped my mouth, as he clearly wasn't. "Can I get you something to drink?"

He didn't look up at me. "My heart rate is already through the roof. Caffeine wouldn't be a very good idea."

"How about a pastry? I've never known you to pass up a chocolate croissant." It felt strange to stay upbeat and try to keep the situation light, but I had to stay strong for Nate.

His bouncing leg stopped. One corner of his mouth stretched to form a forced, painful smirk. "Okay, you've got me there."

I headed inside to order my favorite summer coffee beverage—an iced blueberry pie latte, which tasted exactly like taking a sip of iced coffee after eating a bite of delectable blueberry pie. The blueberry flavor and sweetness weren't overwhelming, balanced by the coffee's bold flavor and a touch of vanilla.

After collecting my beverage and a chocolate croissant for both of us, I took a seat at Nate's table beneath string lights of Edison bulbs which draped between the building and wooden posts along the perimeter of the outdoor seating area.

He pinched the bridge of his nose. "Like I said, I just happened to see her body floating on the riverbank. I'm surprised I saw it, actually. It was foggy when I was running."

Though a thin layer of fog still lingered over the Delaware River, most of it had lifted for the day.

"After I called 911, a couple of police officers arrived within minutes. Cam was one of them." Cam, as most people called him —short for Cameron—was my ex-fiancée's older brother.

"Detective Sharp got here not long after. She listened to my observations while the police, EMTs, and a forensics team worked around us. It seems there's little doubt it had to have been…" He got choked up as he hesitated to say the next word. "Murder."

I'd become well-acquainted with Detective Joanne Sharp during the investigation which resulted from my own horrifying discovery. She took her work very seriously while also leading with compassion and extreme care for the safety of our community.

"Did she ask you many questions? Did she seem to have any idea of what might've happened?"

He let out a loud exhale. "Not really. I need to go to the station later to give my official statement. She asked if I was able to identify the victim. I told her I thought it was the comedian Meghan Spencer. That led to me explaining how she'd performed at Subplot last night and that I was there. I hope this doesn't come back to bite you."

I gulped down a swig of my latte. "Me? I'm more concerned about you."

He swallowed a small bite of his croissant. "Well, the detective mentioned she'd like to speak with you, too, especially since you worked so closely with Meghan leading up to last night. In case you saw or heard anything unusual."

Great. I almost asked Nate if we could go inside the air-conditioned café as my body temperature rose with my increasing nerves.

While I felt duty-bound to share what I knew with the police, I hated feeling like Subplot would once again be under a microscope. A viral comedian's last show took place in my lounge, and I couldn't stomach the thought of the negative attention it might attract. But far worse was knowing my best friend stumbled upon the tragedy.

"I'm doomed," he said. "I'm sure they'll be suspicious of me."

"Why would you say that?"

"Well, for one, I found her body. How many true crime shows have you seen where the murderer calls in the discovery?"

"Even if they consider you, I think they'll find pretty quickly that you have no ties to Meghan."

"Except I do."

I tilted my head.

"She called me out during her crowd work segment last night. She put me in a really uncomfortable situation in front of all those people."

"Did you tell the detective about that?"

He stared at the table and fidgeted with the paper sleeve his pastry came in. "No. Not yet. I stuck to the basics. If it comes up in her questioning at the station, I'll answer to it then."

"But you're not the one who had a big reaction and stormed out. Plus, she only had flattering things to say about you. In fact, it kind of felt like she was flirting with you. If anything, I think they'd be suspicious of Garrett."

Nate's skin flushed. He removed his hat and rubbed his scalp. "True. But the authorities still need to investigate every possibility. And besides, it probably appears I physically could've tossed her over the railing. She pointed out my big stature herself."

"She was tiny, though. Even though she poked fun at Garrett's height, he was still bigger than her. Even she acknowledged his muscular build. She really twisted the knife by insulting his masculinity. I think it's a stretch to assume last night's events alone would've driven him to murder, but he was clearly upset."

Nate squinted with one eye—a telltale sign he was deep in

thought. "She didn't only insult him. He wanted to ask her out —remember? Rejection can drive some people off the deep end."

I swirled the iced coffee in my glass as condensation dripped onto the table. "But to drive someone to murder?" Though I initially thought it was a stretch, I paused and reconsidered. "Sadly, plenty of men have murdered women who said no to a date, so it's possible. Speaking of romance, I think Meghan's ex-boyfriend was in the crowd last night."

"No way." Nate sat up straight, appearing even more dialed in to our conversation. "I wonder if he was the ex she trashed during her set."

I nodded. "By the sounds of it, I think so." I recounted the tense conversation I'd eavesdropped on between Meghan and the tall man in the baseball cap.

"Similar to those who find the bodies, ex-partners always seem to be top suspects in these types of cases. I wonder if the police knew he was there. If so, I'd bet they're looking into him."

I took a quick sip of my latte. "And let's not forget about the woman who heckled Meghan in the middle of her set. After the events of this morning, I'm wondering if her comments cut deeper than simple teasing."

"Good point," Nate said through a mouthful of chocolate croissant.

"And!" I raised an excited index finger. "I saw the heckler speaking to the talent executive who was in the audience after the show."

"Talent executive?"

I filled Nate in on Scott Simmons from CineStream. As I described his appearance, Nate made the connection of the dressed-up man in the crowd with slicked-back hair. "I couldn't tell who approached who. Ava and Lainey thought the heckler was part of Meghan's act, but I wasn't convinced."

"They thought the incident was planned?"

I bobbed my head up and down. "You saw how Meghan handled that. It completely won the crowd over. Maybe Scott was talking to the heckler as a way to figure out if her interruption was truly off the cuff. If it was, though, I don't know why she would've stuck around after the show."

"Man, Meghan had a lot of enemies, huh?"

"Sure seems like it. Who would've thought?"

"I didn't realize all of this happened last night." Nate's energy seemed to lighten as he considered how many other people could've played a role in her demise.

"And we haven't even talked about the tension between Meghan and her manager, Tiffany. Before the show, Tiffany reminded Meghan to be professional, and it clearly annoyed her."

"She recorded a bunch of videos last night. I'm guessing they were for social media. She filmed from multiple angles and panned to capture the crowd's reactions to certain jokes. If she cared so much about Meghan's career, do you think she would've killed her?"

I stroked my stubbled jawline. "Honestly, I'm not sure. I don't think so. But then again, until I learn more, I'm suspicious of anyone who had any sort of relationship with Meghan who was present last night."

Nate drummed his fingers on the metal tabletop. "I also keep thinking about the joke Meghan told about not knowing how to swim. Doesn't it seem strange she was found dead floating in the river?"

"You think that could've played a role?"

Nate furrowed his brow. "How could it not? It seems like whoever did this used that knowledge to put her in a helpless situation. Several people could've physically done it. I just hope it doesn't end in disaster for me."

I hated the thought of Nate being mixed up in the investigation. I knew him better than anybody, and I was certain he couldn't have killed Meghan. I felt a duty to ensure the authorities believed the same. I was committed to doing whatever I could to help him prove his innocence without a doubt.

Furthermore, with Meghan's body being found mere hours after her performance for Comedy and Cocktails at Subplot, and given that another murder had taken place in the alley behind my lounge a few months prior, I also needed to prove my business wasn't responsible for the recent uptick in violent crimes in Hope Mills.

Though I'd proven my innocence once before, I was concerned a second crime connected to events at Subplot might create negative associations with my lounge, especially considering Meghan's virality. I still had quite a way to go before my business became profitable, and I feared any bad press could be detrimental.

Clearing Nate of suspicion and showing once and for all that Subplot had nothing to do with Meghan's death was a no-brainer. I planned to learn as much as I could about the tragedy and find justice.

Nate and I sat in silence for a couple of minutes. Though we'd both finished our pastries, I continued to savor my delicious latte, wishing it would never end or leave Riverside Roastery's seasonal menu.

I rested my glass on the metal table as a thought came to mind. "You know what?"

"Hm?"

"You were right yesterday about smoothing things over with Garrett." I removed my cap and ran my fingers through my hair. "Plus, I'm getting a bit shaggy. I think I'm due for a haircut, don't you think?"

Nate, mirroring me, removed his baseball cap and slicked a

hand over his bald head. "I wouldn't know anything about hair."

I chuckled. "Since I'm on my weekend, I think I'm going to drop in to TAME later today—see if they'll take a walk-in. I'm not sure if any of the other possible suspects we talked about are still in town, but we know he works here in Hope Mills. Maybe I'll learn something."

Nate's eyes widened. "Be careful, man. Please? I don't want a repeat of last time. Especially not for me."

He was referring to the last murder I'd uncovered, in which the killer had held me at gunpoint. The flashback sent a jolt down my spine that made my entire body twitch. Usually, Nate was the one to push me out of my comfort zone, but now it was my turn to rise to the occasion.

I put the ballcap back on, pulling it down tight over my messy hair. "Don't you worry about me. I'll be just fine."

SIX

Before I could swing by TAME, though, I already had plans to go for a walk with my parents at eleven, followed by lunch.

Though working on the weekends had its drawbacks, I loved being off during the week while most other people were at work. Since I'd made my career in the bar and restaurant industry, I was used to my routine and wouldn't want it any other way. On Mondays, when the rest of the world seemed to be dreading their work week, I was free as a bird, able to engage in any recreational activity or go to the grocery store when it was practically empty.

I also felt fortunate to have a close relationship with my parents, who still lived in my childhood home in a residential area not far from downtown Hope Mills.

Since they were recently retired and lived locally, I made an effort to get together with them at least a couple of times a week.

As I strolled along the red-brick sidewalk toward their house, a TV news van from one of the local Philadelphia news stations zoomed by me in the direction of the Promenade.

I took out my phone and opened one of my social media

apps, which I only used to manage Subplot's accounts. I didn't even have to scroll to see the news was actively breaking online. Though my conversation with Nate still felt surreal, seeing posts about a suspected homicide in Hope Mills made me realize the weight of what was going on. And in our tight-knit community, it wouldn't be long before it was the talk of the town.

I swiped over to my messaging app and typed a quick text to Tiffany as I approached my parents' street.

> I just heard the terrible news, and I am so sorry for your loss. If you need anything at all, I'm here for you. I'll be in and out of Subplot throughout the week.

Figuring she likely spent the night in town after last night's show, and considering she'd likely want to stick around while the police investigated her client's death, I thought she might feel isolated here without her support system nearby. I also needed to pay the last installment for Meghan's performance, but considering the circumstances, it wasn't the best time to chat business.

I slipped my phone back into my pocket as I turned onto the front cement path leading up to my parents' front steps.

After three quick raps on their canary-yellow front door, I inserted my key with a matching yellow cover into its lock.

My mom was headed toward the door when I stepped inside, and I pulled her in for a tight hug.

Ah, I'm home.

She sat on a wooden bench by the front door. "Frank, are you ready?" she called out to my dad as she put her sneakers on.

"I'll be there in a minute," his muffled holler bellowed from the garage.

She let out an exaggerated exhale while tying her laces. "He's always tinkering with something."

When my dad entered the house through the door from the garage and down the front hallway, he opened his arms for a hug.

"Are you two ready to walk?" I asked.

My mom hoisted herself up to her feet. "Ready to walk? Yes. Ready to brave the heat? No."

"It's not the heat that's an issue. The humidity is what really makes it feel oppressive out there," my dad said with a grin.

My mom and I both groaned at his comment.

My dad's smile grew larger.

He knows what he's doing every time he says that.

We started our walk on the Delaware Canal Towpath trail, which was easily accessible from my parents' backyard. The red dirt path paralleled the Delaware Canal and stretched nearly sixty miles in its entirety.

"Have you heard the latest scoop on what's happened in town?" I asked amidst the steady drone of insects humming around us in every direction.

My dad fought a grin, trying to appear serious. "Scoop? Is there a new ice cream shop opening?"

"Oh, Frank," my mom groaned. I clenched my eyes shut and pinched the bridge of my nose. That was my father, king of dad jokes.

"I haven't read any news yet today," he said.

"Me either," my mom added. "It's been glorious. What's happening?"

I tucked both hands into my pockets, hesitating a few times before I could bring myself to utter my next words. "There's been another murder in town."

My parents both gasped and froze in their tracks.

"*Alleged* murder, I should say." I kicked a stone in front of me. My parents picked up speed to catch up as I continued forward. "Based on what I've heard, though, it doesn't sound like it could've been an accident."

"I sure hope you didn't stumble upon the body this time, too," my mom said.

"I didn't." I took a deep breath. "But Nate did."

"Oh my word!" She placed a hand over the chest of her flowy white shirt. "He's such a nice guy. What a shame he had to come across that." She froze again, prompting my father and me to pause as well. "Do you know who was killed?"

I swallowed hard. "Her name was Meghan Spencer. She was the comedian I hired to perform at Subplot last night for our first Comedy and Cocktails event."

She shook her head in disbelief. "This can't happen here. Hope Mills is such a sweet, safe town. Violent crime doesn't just happen out of nowhere, let alone twice in the same year."

I kept my gaze focused on the fine red stone at my feet. "Which is exactly why I'm nervous people are going to connect the dots back to Subplot."

"Oh, no. You're not saying you think your comedy night had anything to do with the murder, are you?" Both of her hands were now firmly planted on the sides of her head, her fingers laced through her now-disheveled hair. "You can't take responsibility for that."

"Did anything suspicious happen last night? Anything that might be tied to her death?" my dad chimed in, always the one to want to get down to the facts.

I summarized all the strange tension and uncomfortable interactions between Meghan and members of the audience, her manager, and ex-boyfriend.

"Where did Nate find her?" my dad asked as two bicyclists passed us on the trail.

I waited for them to be far ahead of us before answering. "In the river. Along the Promenade. He was out for a jog at sunrise. He said it was foggy, but he noticed something floating out of the corner of his eye. Sure enough, after he got a closer look, he confirmed it was a body."

My parents looked at one another as if in disbelief and both shook their heads.

"I hate that this happened at all, but since it did, I'm glad it happened on a Monday morning. I feel relieved I don't have to open the lounge tonight. I can spend the next few days decompressing."

"And who knows"—my dad chimed in—"maybe this'll be figured out by the time you open again on Thursday."

I focused my gaze on the thick green moss which covered the canal. "I sure hope so, but I'm not counting on it. If someone did indeed kill Meghan, there must be a deep, dark motive. I don't feel like someone would've killed her over a joke alone. Who knows how long it'll take for the police to piece the truth together."

We continued our light hike along the path for another thirty minutes or so, mostly sharing and discussing our theories about the crime in town, before we exited the trail near downtown Hope Mills.

Our next stop was the Dublin Ale House for a bite to eat. Our waiter seated us at a table beside a window which looked out into the restaurant's back garden and patio. Not wanting to sit in the heat, we opted for the air-conditioned dining room with its cream walls, adorned with framed local sports memorabilia, and laurel-green wainscoting. Though the restaurant was Irish-themed, it offered a broad menu with pages of options—a challenge for someone as indecisive as me.

I finally decided on a grilled chicken salad served with French fries and a sun-dried tomato balsamic vinaigrette. My parents' choices adhered to the restaurant's Irish theme, with my dad ordering classic fish and chips while my mom ordered a full Irish breakfast platter.

"Have you heard from Chloe at all?" my mom asked after the server retreated.

If she'd asked a few months ago, the question would've irked me. Before I came out, my mom had been devastated by my broken engagement, using any opportunity she could find to pry for details, reluctant as I was to share. Now that the truth was out in the open, it felt like we'd all found some peace.

"Funny you should ask. We actually have plans to get coffee at Riverside Roastery tomorrow morning. She just returned from a trip to Florida, and she's going to tell me all about it."

My dad wiped a glistening sheen of sweat from his brow with the back of his wrist. "Florida in the hottest stretch of the summer? I would've waited until at least November. I'm dying in the heat and humidity of Pennsylvania."

"She's actually exploring job opportunities down there."

I was fortunate to have maintained a friendship with Chloe. Though she and I had both grown up in Hope Mills and lived here all our lives, she was exploring options for her next step— from nearby Philadelphia all the way to Florida. Given the demand for workers in the restaurant industry, her opportunities were endless, especially since she was an extremely qualified and accomplished manager that any restaurant would be lucky to hire. Though it was a small town, Hope Mills was a well-known day trip destination for its arts, theater, and fine dining scenes, which could go a long way as she pursued potential employers.

My mom set down her water glass after taking a sip. "Please tell her your father and I say hello. I'm so grateful she was so supportive and understanding through this all."

I fidgeted with my straw wrapper. "She's one of a kind. Even though we weren't meant to spend our lives together, I'm so grateful for the time we shared. If I meet a guy one day who's even a fraction of who she is, I'd be the happiest man alive. And the fact she's still part of my life is icing on the cake."

Her face brightened from across the table. "So, does that mean you're dating again?"

It felt like all the air had been sucked out of the room. I had no doubts her question was well-intentioned, but I hadn't been prepared for it. I should've been, though. It was in her nature to want to know all the details.

Dating wasn't in the cards for me. Or at least not for a while. I was still too fresh on the heels of coming out and dealing with the residual guilt of breaking off my engagement to Chloe. Plus, I'd never been with another guy before. It was something I knew I wanted, but I was too afraid to take the next step.

I started, "Oh, no...I—"

"Come on, Stace," my dad admonished my mom.

"What? I can't ask a simple question?"

"He'll tell us when he's ready."

"I sure hope he will. I still want grandkids one day."

Grandkids. I didn't think she'd ever let that topic go. Though it was still completely possible for me to have children, I was undecided about my future as a potential parent. Her ceaseless pleas for grandchildren didn't help with my indecision. Ultimately, it was up to me.

I cleared my throat loudly. "I'm still sitting right here, you two."

My parents exchanged an embarrassed glance before turning back to face me.

Luckily, our waiter arrived to drop off our food before the conversation grew more tense and awkward than it'd already become.

As we ate, we discussed lighthearted topics—my parents'

foray into pickleball, the autumn cocktails Ava and I were developing, and I showed them the latest cute photos of Jameson which took up the majority of my phone's camera roll.

Once we finished our meals, I asked my parents what they had in store for the rest of their day.

My mom poked her thumb into my dad's arm. "I don't know about him, but I'm going to curl up in my hammock with a good thriller novel. I need to pick a new one off the shelf."

He mirrored her pointing with his thumb. "And I'm building a Little Free Library for the front yard so we have a place to put all of this one's books when she finishes reading them. I swear she finishes a new one every two or three days."

My mom let out a serene sigh. "Ah, retirement is grand."

"And how about the rest of your day off?" my dad asked.

I removed my hat and once again ran my fingers through my hair. "My curls are starting to feel a bit unruly, so I'm going to head to the barber shop."

I was careful not to mention my haircut would hopefully double as a suspect interview as I searched for the truth about the murder of Meghan Spencer.

<h1 style="text-align: center;">SEVEN</h1>

"Good afternoon—do you have an appointment?" I recognized the barber who greeted me from the comedy show the night before. He'd attended with Garrett, who was deeply focused on aligning his current customer's sideburns when I arrived at TAME.

"I don't. Sorry. Do you guys take walk-ins?"

He gestured to a row of chairs lined up behind the barber stations. "Absolutely. You can grab a seat along the wall. Garrett should be able to take you soon, since he's wrapping up."

"Awesome, thank you."

The barber who greeted me returned to cutting his client's hair.

I swallowed hard, hit with the reality of facing Garrett directly. But that was exactly what I'd come here for. To my relief, he didn't acknowledge or seem to recognize me when I took a seat on a pastel-blue metal chair. I didn't want to cause a scene, especially knowing how worked up Garrett had been the night before and considering there were other customers in the shop. My approach would have to be delicate.

Techno music pulsed through surround speakers placed

around the barber shop's bright walls. TAME had an artsy, modern-industrial vibe with neon-colored, graffiti-inspired murals painted on the walls. Books of abstract art rested on end tables throughout the waiting area.

Four barber stations were side-by-side in front of my chair, but only two were being used, likely because Mondays were slow in the daytime while most of the town worked their nine-to-fives.

Each barber's name was displayed on a sign above their station, which confirmed the guy who'd greeted me was Eric.

At first, I thought I'd lucked out by coming in while Garrett was working. Although, if he owned TAME, as Nate had theorized, I wouldn't have been surprised if he was always there.

"Have you heard any chatter about the situation down by the river?" the client asked as Eric scissor-cut the man's medium-length gray hair.

Eric stopped cutting and held his scissors at his side. "What situation?"

"You haven't heard? Aren't barber shops supposed to be a breeding ground for town gossip?" the customer quipped.

"Nah, buddy. Try heading to a *salon*"—Garrett groaned the word as if it was beneath him —"if you want gossip."

Luckily, no one saw me roll my eyes. It was exactly what I'd expect a guy with fragile masculinity to say. *This is a barber shop! For men! We talk about sports and cars and grilling steaks!*

Eric combed a tuft of the man's hair and pinched it between his index and middle fingers, ready to resume cutting. "Well, spit it out."

"I'm surprised you haven't heard about it. It's all over the news and social media. Someone was found dead in the river. They think it might be murder."

"Murder?" Eric's heightened pitch made him sound

surprised. He pivoted his head in Garrett's direction. "Did you hear about a murder in town?"

Garrett stayed focused on his client's haircut, and with his back toward me, I only saw the loose brunette waves of his modern mullet from behind. "No, I didn't. I think I would've mentioned it if I had." He spoke nonchalantly, and his reaction seemed awfully subdued if it was the first he'd heard about a murder in our typically peaceful borough.

"So, what's the deal, then?" Eric asked his customer.

Garrett looked up for the first time since I'd been in the shop. He rolled his head in a circle. Was it a gesture of irritation? Or was he loosening his neck muscles after being so laser-focused on making sure his customer's fade was perfectly even and seamless? Perhaps I was reading too far into every move and assuming the worst.

"I'm surprised you guys haven't heard. It's the buzz around town. The woman who died was a comedian."

Garrett and Eric exchanged what looked like nervous glances as the customer continued.

"I never heard of her before, but apparently she was a big deal on social media. I watched a few of her clips, and they were hilarious. I can't imagine why someone would do such a thing."

Eric covered his mouth with his free hand and stepped back from his client. "We were just at her show last night."

Garrett continued working on the final details with his customer. "She had it coming," he mumbled in his raspy voice. He puffed out his arms as he said it. He oozed bravado, but I couldn't tell if it was authentic or overcompensation.

Eric's customer tsked. "No one deserves to be thrown into the river."

Garrett grunted. "Whatever."

Thankfully, the upbeat music thumping through the barber

shop kept the room from falling into an awkward silence as the conversation tapered off.

Garrett didn't show any signs of concern about Meghan's death, and he didn't even seem to be surprised by the news.

After he finished with his client, the two men headed to the front of the shop to complete their transaction. He returned to his station shortly thereafter to sweep up the hair from the gray faux-wood floor and sanitize his tools.

Despite his short stature, he had a hulking frame. His biceps and triceps were so big that his beige T-shirt sleeves stretched tightly over them, never getting any relief, regardless of how he moved his arm.

He swiveled the front of his barber chair toward me. "Whenever you're ready, boss." We made eye contact, but it didn't seem like I set off any alarms. Maybe he didn't remember me or realize my connection to Subplot.

We briefly discussed my haircut. While I told him I sought a basic trim, keeping it a little longer on top with a tight fade on the sides, I complimented his hair. He made a recommendation for how he could shape the back and sides of my hair to replicate his hairstyle without going into full mullet territory.

I gave him a thumbs up and realized too late he couldn't see my hands under the barber's cape. "You're the expert here."

Though I had no solid evidence to believe Garrett played a role in Meghan's death, besides their interaction during the show, this haircut was my opportunity to glean whatever information I could.

However, it was difficult for me to broach the topic in front of his fellow barber—potentially his employee—and a customer in the shop.

Luckily, a minute or two into my cut, Eric wrapped up with his client, leaving me alone in the shop with the two barbers.

"You guys were at the comedy show last night, weren't you?" I asked.

Garrett switched off his electric razor. He froze in the mirror and glanced over at Eric, who swept up his station while he waited for another customer to enter the shop.

He eyed me skeptically. "Yes ..." Garrett let his answer linger, not providing any additional explanation.

"Look, I'm the owner of Subplot, and I'm not happy about what went down last night. I want to make things right." I hoped coming from a place of empathy might coax Garrett to open up more.

"What she said about me last night has nothing to do with this, okay?" Garrett's tone had grown defensive on the subject, unlike his bold claim earlier that Meghan had it coming for her. Was he backpedaling now that he knew who I was?

"I never said I thought the two things were related. I just... Regardless of what ended up happening to her, I don't like what she said. I'd like to invite you both to come back to my lounge sometime for drinks—on the house."

Garrett rocked on his heels. "Thank you, but it's not your fault. There was no way you could've known she was going to fire off like a loose cannon." His tone was lighter and friendlier, as was his entire demeanor. Why the sudden shift from how cold and emotionless he'd been when I arrived?

"I'm serious, though. From one small business owner in town to another, we've gotta have each other's backs. I want to apologize whether you think I need to or not, and the offer for drinks stands."

Garrett crossed his arms over his bulky chest and grasped each of his elbows tight. "I swear I couldn't have killed her. *Shoot!* I bet the police will come looking for me. I'm sure it looks bad, but I wouldn't harm anyone, especially a woman. She was just making a joke." If the police hadn't paid him a visit yet, I wondered if he was on their radar, or if they were still figuring out next steps for their investigation.

"But even so, what she said must've gotten under your skin." It was probably an unwise thing to say to someone with potential anger issues who also held a pair of scissors behind me.

"You think I would've killed her over a joke?"

"What? No." I shook my head adamantly, though theories brewed in my mind. "I don't think you killed her. But I can see how what she said would've bothered you."

Garret rested his scissors on the wooden desk below his mirror and pinched the bridge of his nose.

"I found a bouquet of flowers near where you were sitting last night. Were you going to ask her—"

"Flowers? I don't know anything about flowers," he interrupted. "I wasn't going to ask her anything."

Eric, who sat in his barber chair, swiveled himself from side to side with one foot controlling his movement on the shop's faux-wood floors. The forced neutral expression on his face said, *If you say so ...*

Garrett's immediate dismissal of my question told me everything I needed to know. It seemed he didn't handle rejection well and resorted to denial when questioned. "I was frustrated, that's all. I didn't kill her."

"No one said you killed her, man," Eric chimed in.

Garrett's head swung in his colleague's direction so fast he could've gotten whiplash. "Oh, you know what I mean." He practically spat the words. "The police can't hear about what went down last night. If they knew what happened, of course they'd be suspicious of me."

"If you didn't do it, you don't have anything to worry about." Eric's choice to use an *if* statement made me question whether he knew more than he let on. "Just be confident and tell the police the truth if they question you. You'll be fine."

Garrett stared blankly at the ground. "I don't even know when she was killed or where her body was found. I'm literally learning about this right now." I couldn't tell whether he was bluffing.

I debated letting him in on what I knew. Providing details gave him a chance to fabricate an alibi, which could make him look less suspicious and complicate the facts of the case. But if he was innocent, my information could bring him peace. Knowing I likely needed to share something to learn more from Garrett, and trusting Detective Sharp's ability to sniff out a lie, I decided to mention a few general details.

"Her body was found on the riverbank near the Promenade. From what I've heard, the time of death is uncertain, but it had to have happened very late last night or early this morning."

"I was home by ten-thirty last night." He pointed his index finger toward the barber shop's high ceiling with exposed beams and ductwork. "My apartment's upstairs."

The night before, we'd kicked off our entertainment at seven. Our opening act took the stage for about half an hour, followed by a twenty-minute intermission, so I estimated Meghan's hour-long set began at seven-fifty, give or take ten minutes. Garrett had stormed out about halfway through her set, so he would've left by about eight-thirty.

Meghan had stayed for a while after her set to mingle with the audience while her manager sold merch, but I had no clue of her whereabouts after she left Subplot. I also wasn't one hundred percent sure what time Meghan departed the lounge, but it must've been before ten-thirty.

"Did you go anywhere besides home after you left Subplot?" I figured he had, considering there were approximately two hours between the time he left Subplot and claimed to get back home.

"I walked to Bridge Street Bar." He rested his electric razor on its charging stand in front of me, my hair only half-cut. Since we'd begun discussing Meghan, he hadn't trimmed a single strand of hair. "I was there for a couple of hours. Come to think of it, I saw Meghan again when I left the bar."

If he'd continued to drink after leaving Subplot, was it possible he'd gotten excessively intoxicated? If so, I wondered how reliable his post-bar recollections were. Additionally, I wondered how he typically acted when drunk. Did he get angry or aggressive? Silly? Numb? Depending on how alcohol impacted his behavior—especially knowing it impaired cognition and decision-making—I wondered if he'd made a decision he'd regret after leaving the bar.

I reached a hand out from under the barber's cape to brush an itchy loose hair from my temple. "You saw her on your way home?"

"Did you say anything to her?" Eric added.

Garrett let out a single chuckle as if Eric's question was ridiculous. "No. I'll admit I was angry after she said what she said about me. But after I got a few beers in me, I cooled down."

Ah, so maybe he gets more chill when he drinks. From my experience, though, that usually wasn't the case. Plus, statistics showed that alcohol played a role in nearly half of all murders and a significant number of violent crimes.

If I'd been in Garrett's shoes, I wouldn't have admitted to consuming more alcohol so openly. I didn't trust that the extra drinks gave him any restraint if he was already outraged. However, it seemed like my questions put him on the spot.

"Plus, she was with someone. I wasn't going to interrupt them," he said.

Oooh. Now that's juicy. If he was telling the truth. Was Garrett making up a story to distance himself from suspicion?

I made eye contact with Garrett through the mirror. "Do you know who the other person was? Were they at the show, by chance?"

He directed his gaze up at the ceiling as he thought. "Now that you mention it, I think he was. The guy was tall. He had a beat-up, pinkish baseball cap on. He wore a nice shirt and shorts. They were arguing."

Garrett likely spotted Meghan with her ex-boyfriend David. His description was spot-on when recalling the man I'd seen her speaking with at the lounge.

I grasped the swishy nylon fabric of the barber cape draped over me, eager to learn more. "Did you catch any of their argument? Any idea what it might've been about? This could be important information to share with the police."

"He was pleading for her to give him another chance."

Based on what I'd witnessed last night, it didn't make sense to me. David had seemed pretty ready to be done with her.

Garrett smoothed down the stubble on his cheeks with one hand, clearly stifling a grin. He seemed pleased, as if he'd made a sudden connection. "I just remembered something. You'll never guess how Meghan responded to his begging."

"How?"

"She yelled, 'I'd rather die than spend another day with you.'"

In my reflection in the mirror, I watched my eyes widen. "She really said that?"

"Mm-hmm." Garrett picked up his razor from the charging station and returned to his position behind my chair. His overall demeanor relaxed. Was he satisfied by remembering what he'd witnessed—or proud of a lie he'd just invented?

He went on to say, "That's when I turned left to head

toward my apartment here. The two of them walked off in the opposite direction—toward the Promenade."

I wasn't sure if I bought his story about Meghan and David. Based on his accurate description of her ex-boyfriend, it was possible he might've spotted them together. If there'd been discussion about giving someone another chance, it also made sense that Meghan was talking to an ex. However, I knew what I'd overheard between Meghan and David earlier in the evening, and it didn't add up. Based on that conversation, I highly doubted he would've begged to have her back. Plus, a comment that she'd rather be dead than get back together with him seemed awfully convenient, given what happened to her hours later.

On the other hand, if he told the truth about them walking toward the Promenade, could their argument have escalated and ended with Meghan drowning in the river?

Garrett admitted to consuming several drinks throughout the night. Could I really believe a word he said?

I also remembered Nate's recollection that Garrett had planned to ask Meghan out after the show. Could he have killed her in a crime of passion, and everything he'd shared with me in the barber shop was a ruse?

Giving Garrett's story the benefit of the doubt, though, was it possible David actually did want to rekindle his relationship with Meghan, even despite his clear frustration with what she'd said about him during her set? If David was angry about Meghan telling false stories about their relationship, could he have killed her out of revenge?

Or had Garrett misheard their argument on the street near Bridge Street Bar? Did he see them arguing at all? I still had my doubts about Garrett, but his revelations increased my suspicions about David.

There was one major problem, though. If David wasn't local, how would I ever find him?

"You need to tell the police about what you saw last night," I urged Garrett.

"What? No."

Eric, still waiting on another customer to arrive, sat in his barber chair, swiveling himself back and forth with his foot. "Bro, that's your key out of this." I was glad he supported my stance.

Garrett shook his head. "Out of this? I'm not even part of this. If I tell the police what I saw, they might flip the script back on me. 'Anything you say can and will be used against you,' remember? I don't want that. I'm innocent."

Eric let out an exhausted sigh. "If you're so innocent, why are you so concerned?" I couldn't tell if he was playing the devil's advocate to make his co-worker feel better or if he was skeptical of him.

"Plus, we don't know if the guy she was arguing with is local." I split my eye contact between the two of them. "If he was responsible, he could be long gone by now. The faster you share this info with the police, the faster they can track him down, question him, and potentially learn other details that can clear your name."

Eric stood up and approached my chair. He poked his thumb into my shoulder. "This guy is spitting straight-up facts."

"Fine. I'll call the non-emergency line and fill the police in on what I saw. Happy?"

Eric and I both looked at Garrett in the mirror in front of me, nodding our heads in approval.

But would he follow through?

EIGHT

Despite the sticky, hot, and humid August weather, I felt marginally cooler as a gentle breeze swept over me on my walk home. I carried my cap in one hand.

Maybe I should've gotten my entire head buzzed.

Though the heat was borderline rage-inducing, remembering the sting of bitter, cold winter winds kept me from complaining.

As I ambled down the red-brick sidewalks of Main Street from its north end, under baskets of vibrant pink and yellow flowers hanging from the lampposts, I fished the phone from my pocket and put my hat back on. I'd received a response from Tiffany while I'd been at TAME.

Hi, Reece. Thank you for your support. I'm devastated. I can't believe what's happened. It doesn't feel real.

I started to type a response multiple times, but nothing I wrote could possibly fill the hole she must've been feeling. Despite the strain I'd sensed between her and her client, I was sure she was grieving. Given the tragic circumstances, though, I knew I couldn't immediately rule Tiffany out as a suspect. I wanted an opportunity to speak with her again, though I knew I'd have to remain cautious.

> Are you still in Hope Mills?

Three dots appeared at the bottom of my screen as she typed a response.

> Yes, I'm not leaving until we figure out once and for all what happened to Meg.

Perhaps I could use the remaining payment for Meghan's performance as my chance to speak with Tiffany.

> If you're feeling up to it, maybe you can swing by Subplot and get away from it all for a little while. Plus I have a check for the last installment I owe you for last night, but I'm sure it's the last thing on your mind

I hoped mentioning a physical check and offering an escape would entice her to visit and give me a chance to gather more information. Though I felt guilty for indirectly persuading her to talk to me, I tried to come from a place of compassion.

> I think I'll def need to get away. Maybe I'll pop in tomorrow if you're around. I don't have the heart to do anything today…

I replied right away.

> Yes, I'll be there tomorrow. Let me know when you're thinking of stopping by, and I'll make sure I'm around. If you need anything while you're in town, please reach out

Although Subplot wouldn't be open for business the following day, I typically spent a few hours there on Tuesdays and Wednesdays to craft new cocktails, accept deliveries from our suppliers, take care of administrative work in the office, and do other chores.

As I strolled south down Main Street in the direction of Subplot and eventually home, I approached Ampersand, the bookstore which my new friend—and secret crush—Julian opened around the time I'd launched Subplot. From the moment I first met him, I had been captivated by his deep brown eyes, wavy brunette hair, and breathtaking smile.

I had an inkling he might be gay, but I had no way to know for sure, and I hated to make assumptions. Perhaps my inclination was a projection of my own desires. One night when visiting Subplot with his friends, he'd left his number for me on his check. Based on similar scenarios I'd seen in my fifteen-plus years working in the restaurant biz, I thought he was flirting with me. It'd taken me a few days to muster up the guts to text him, and when I did, there was nothing flirty about the conversation which followed. Had I missed my chance? Or had I completely misread his gesture? Perhaps he wanted to connect as friends—just two young small business owners in Hope Mills. Or did I approach him with energy that seemed closed off to romance? Honestly, considering all I'd been through in breaking off my engagement with Chloe, I wouldn't have been surprised if that was the case.

I admired the corner bookstore's summer romance display in its front picture window as I strolled by. While I enjoyed reading the classics—with a dash of contemporary thriller, horror, or occasional science fiction—I'd recently felt an urge to get lost in the pages of a romance novel. While I didn't feel like I was quite ready to date anyone, it felt safe to experience romance in a book where I knew I'd find a happily ever after. I had a lot of figuring out to do.

I debated going inside to ask Julian if he knew of any highly recommended gay romcoms.

Was it presumptuous to think he'd have a suggestion? *He's a bookseller!* It was his job to make book recommendations across all genres and interests.

I sighed and spun on my heels to continue walking along Main Street.

Out of the corner of my eye, though, I saw faint movement inside the bookstore. I squinted and shielded my eyes from the bright sun with both hands to get a better view inside.

Julian waved his arms, inviting me in.

My chest tightened, and without giving it much thought, I headed inside.

"You look like you could use a respite from the heat." He smirked as the bell above the door tinkled. "Welcome to the A/C." Unlike me, who dressed purely for function rather than for style, he dressed fashionably any time I saw him. Today, he wore a forest-green T-shirt with sleeves that fit snugly around his muscular arms and light wash blue jeans that were rolled above the tops of his white sneakers.

I took my sunglasses off and folded them over the collar of my T-shirt.

The bookstore's soft olive walls and sleek white crown molding made the space feel inviting, yet sophisticated. Books filled the built-in shelves lining each wall, with literary quotes accompanying the signs above each section. I stepped further into the shop, over its light, rustic wood flooring and past tables which displayed the latest hardcover releases, books from local authors, and the top staff picks. There were no customers inside —only Julian and me.

"I was just checking out your awesome new window display."

"Anything catch your eye?"

My heart raced. The store may have been air conditioned, but I radiated heat. "I'm not usually much of a romance reader, but I've been thinking about trying a new genre."

"Any particular type of romance you're looking for? Any tropes you like or dislike? I swear there's a romance involving characters with almost any interest or profession."

Was he feeling me out? Was this how I'd come out to him?

I wiped my damp palms on the sides of my shorts, grateful I could blame my profuse sweating on the heat outside rather than on nerves.

Here goes nothing.

"I've never read a male-male romance before. Are there any that have been popular this summer?" It wasn't quite coming out, but perhaps he'd connect the dots.

Julian clapped his hands once and pointed at me. "I have a bunch I can recommend. We have a few that are selling like hotcakes this summer. I love to occasionally read some male-male romance myself."

Did that confirm he was gay after all? Or did he like to read romances across all orientations and representations? Or perhaps he was simply a bookseller, happy to be making a sale on a slow Monday afternoon.

Regardless, the butterflies in my stomach fluttered out of control as I began to fall even harder. Hopefully my irises hadn't taken the shape of hearts. *Play it cool, Reece.*

He waved for me to follow him toward the romance section near a reading nook in the shop's back corner. The scent of teakwood grew stronger, emanating from a pool of melted wax in a candle warmer behind the checkout counter. After he presented me with a few of his personal recommendations, I decided to purchase a gay soccer romance.

At the checkout counter, Julian tapped my credit card on his point of sale tablet. "I also wanted to ask you a question."

The bell above his front door rang as a group of customers trickled into the store.

His gaze drifted to them and then back to me. "On second thought, would you want to stop by later this week?"

Whatever his question was, it didn't seem like he wanted to ask it in front of customers. Or maybe he wanted to appear more available for them.

I grasped the paperback book he'd sold me and tucked my receipt into the front cover. "Yeah, of course."

"Awesome. I'll text you."

I couldn't decipher whether he was interested in me romantically or if he saw me as a friend or local business contact.

What stopped me from making a move? I could think of a thousand reasons.

As I headed out the shop's glass front door, the woman I'd recognized sitting at the bar during the Comedy and Cocktails event browsed the two-dollar used book cart outside. She wore a blue and yellow sundress, and her wavy, sandy-brown hair flowed over one shoulder.

How do I know you? I'd been seeing her around Hope Mills more and more in recent weeks. Was she just another woman around my age?

Making the connection that she'd attended the comedy event, I wondered if she might've seen or heard something which could help me learn more about Meghan's death.

"Hey," I said just above a whisper.

She gasped as soon as she made eye contact with me. Confusion was written across her wrinkled forehead, but she didn't say a word.

I unfolded my sunglasses and put them on. "Do you have a moment to chat?" I hoped I didn't appear unhinged.

She snapped the paperback she'd been leafing through shut. "Sorry, I got to run." She slid the book back onto the cart and fled in the opposite direction of where I was about to go.

My breath caught in my chest as I resisted a small urge to call out for her to stay. Had I said or done something wrong?

I turned right and strolled down Main Street toward my apartment, which was located in one side of a duplex house on the other side of town, as I reflected on the woman's frantic response to my simple question.

I couldn't place how I knew her, but my suspicions about her involvement grew. Given how often I'd seen her in recent weeks—it almost seemed as if she was seeking me out—I had no doubt we'd cross paths again. When we did, I hoped I could gather some new intel.

I exhaled a defeated sigh and shifted my focus to the present moment. I stepped along the red brick sidewalk, admiring the quaint ivy-wrapped facades of homes and businesses in my charming, historic hometown. Flowers draped over the window baskets in front of many of the businesses' front windows.

Because Hope Mills played an important role in the American Revolution and its roots dated back to Colonial times, I often envisioned how the narrow streets might have looked in the late 1700s as I ambled through town. With my love of classic literature, I imagined someone reading my favorite books or plays throughout town over the years.

Just over the crest of Main Street, a jogger came into view on the opposite side of the street. I first noticed his rugged, coral baseball cap before seeing the rest of his body.

Was he Meghan's ex-boyfriend David? *I'm bumping into everyone this afternoon.*

If it was him, I wondered why he'd stick around town. Considering his ex-girlfriend had just been found dead in the river, I figured he was likely a top suspect in the eyes of the police. Was he staying in town to strategically plant or remove evidence? Maybe he stayed in town to pull strings, so everything played out in his favor. Would he try to silence or harm anyone who might uncover clues that pointed to him? Or maybe the police requested his cooperation with their investigation, perhaps advising that it'd reflect poorly if he were to leave town.

Despite the grueling heat wave, I shivered at the thought. Though I wanted to speak to him to see what I could learn, keeping the potential risk in mind gave me pause.

However, he hadn't been arrested, so the police must not have had enough solid evidence in that regard. It didn't seem like he was trying to disguise himself, either. His pink baseball cap seemed to be his most recognizable feature. Even Garrett had mentioned it in his recollection from the previous evening.

I picked up my pace as he continued in my direction, raising an arm to try and flag him down.

He was focused on every stride, and as he jogged closer, I noticed the ear pods plugged into each ear. He was probably preoccupied with music or a podcast.

Just when I hoped he might glance in my direction and spot me trying to catch his attention, he made a sharp turn to his left, continuing his jog up the front steps of the Colonial Inn.

For a moment, I hoped I might be able to gather some intel from the inn's staff about his whereabouts the night before. Then I remembered the inn was self-serve with no front desk staff to witness what time he'd returned.

Though I didn't have a chance to chat with David then, I made a mental note about where he was staying.

A small pocket park, adorned with more hanging flower

baskets, sculptures, a couple of benches, and a classic red British phone booth was nestled between two brick buildings across the street. I planned to return with my laptop during the week to get some online work done for Subplot while I staked out.

Whether David was responsible for Meghan's death or not, he likely knew her better than anyone, so I was hopeful I could learn something—anything—from him which might clear Nate of suspicion and avoid possible damage to Subplot's reputation.

Bzz-bzz. Bzz-bzz. My phone vibrated against my thigh in the pocket of my shorts. I fished it out to check who was calling. It was someone with a local 267 number, and my phone provider identified it as coming from Hope Mills, PA.

I veered to the far right of the sidewalk to make room for other pedestrians to pass me.

"Hello, this is Reece."

A familiar woman's voice spoke on the other end of the line. "Reece, hi. Good afternoon. It's Detective Sharp."

I gulped. "Oh, hi, Detective. Is everything all right?" Though I trusted her good nature, I couldn't help but feel intimidated during my interactions with the police, especially with an active investigation taking place in town.

"When you have a moment today, can you please stop by the police station? We need to document your statement in relation to the murder of Ms. Meghan Spencer."

NINE

Hope Mills Borough Hall was located in a former church perched atop a hill a couple of blocks over from Main Street. The municipal building housed most aspects of our town's local government—from council meetings under the high, vaulted ceilings to our small police force in its basement.

After receiving Detective Sharp's call, I trekked to Borough Hall right away, despite the dread which burrowed deep within my stomach.

I was committed to doing anything I could to keep the police's suspicion away from Nate, so I needed to share whatever I knew with the police. *I might as well get this over with.*

I walked through the glass front doors of the deconsecrated church, and the receptionist inside greeted me as she chomped on the back end of a pen. I gave her my name and let her know I was there to meet with the detective.

She pointed toward a row of five wooden chairs with simple blue upholstered cushions behind me. "You can take a seat over there, and Detective Sharp will come meet you shortly."

My leg bounced as I tried my hardest to sit still and stay calm in my seat. Although I'd built some rapport with the detective after my run-in with the killer from the last murder that took place in town, I had a feeling she wouldn't be happy to see me again—especially in conjunction with another homicide.

I could already hear her stern voice in my head, lecturing me not to interfere with her investigation and recounting the danger I'd faced the last time I'd sleuthed around for answers. I also feared she might allege Subplot was the common denominator between the only two murders in Hope Mills' recent history.

I let the sinking feeling in my chest be a reminder of why I needed to continue my quest for justice.

The glass door I'd entered through swung open, and I immediately recognized Cam, thanks to his clean-cut blond hair, as he sauntered inside in uniform, a half-eaten red apple in one hand.

As he headed toward the counter, presumably to head back to his desk, he froze in his tracks when he caught a glimpse of me. "Reece?"

I pressed my lips together and gave him a quick wave. "Hey, Cam."

During my seven years with Chloe, he and I had become very close—almost like brothers. On occasion, we'd even hung out together without her, going to concerts or for hikes when Chloe's work schedule didn't allow her to join. She'd always encouraged us to develop a friendship. However, when I'd ended our engagement, things had understandably become awkward between Cam and me.

Luckily, though, after coming out to him and making it clear I only wanted the best for his sister, our interactions had become a bit more relaxed whenever I encountered him around town.

"Are you here for ...?" The way his unfinished question

lingered made me feel like he already knew I was here to answer questions about the recent murder. He took a bite from his apple, likely a fuji or gala, as he listened for my response.

I sighed. "Yeah, I am. Detective Sharp called me in to answer some questions about yesterday."

"Mr. Parker," a woman's voice called from across the room. The detective's voice was firm but not commanding.

I'd been so focused on my casual conversation with Cam and the flood of memories from my past relationship which always accompanied when I saw him that I hadn't noticed her enter the waiting area through a large archway behind the receptionist.

Cam swallowed the bite of his apple. "I'm headed back this way, too."

I rose and followed him to the counter, where Detective Sharp had opened a waist-high wooden gate. We proceeded to walk down a short hallway and down some stairs into the basement of the former church. Because the building was situated on a steep hill, one side contained windows which allowed natural light to spill in.

At the bottom of the steps, we split off from Cam, who walked in the opposite direction, and we exchanged see-you-laters. I remembered my plan to meet up with Chloe tomorrow morning. I was eager to learn whether she planned to leave Hope Mills, although I secretly wished for her to stay.

Detective Sharp gestured for me to go inside.

The walls were painted baby blue, and the room contained one window to the outside, its glass frosted so no one could see in or out. Cameras pointed at the small table in the center of the room from all four corners. A one-way mirror was centered on one wall, and I couldn't help but wonder if I'd be observed in real time or only by the cameras.

The detective closed the door behind her and took a seat on the opposite side of the faux-wood table. "So, we meet again."

"I wish it was under better circumstances. I've heard the tragic news."

"I understand you had quite a bit of contact recently with Ms. Spencer—not just in the hours leading up to her death yesterday, but also over the past few weeks."

I nodded. "Yes, that's right. We hired her to perform in my lounge for a new comedy series we launched."

"Did Ms. Spencer do or say anything that seemed paranoid? Like she thought she might be in danger or concerned for her safety?"

I bit at my lower lip as I tried to recall every interaction I'd had with her. "No. She always seemed bold—very confident and in-control. We really only talked about the business side of things, though." It was the truth.

"And how about other people who interacted with her last night? Did anyone act strangely around her?"

Where would I begin? There'd been so much tense energy between Meghan and almost everyone she interacted with.

While I didn't want to throw any innocent people under the bus, it was in my best interest to tell the detective everything I knew. The quicker she could gather facts, the faster she could make moves and find Meghan's killer to restore peace in our charming town. I just hoped it wouldn't make her more suspicious of Nate in the process.

"There seemed to be some tension between Meghan and Tiffany, her manager. Tiffany urged Meghan to take the evening seriously and act extra professionally. They had a small quarrel...but it seemed to work itself out. I guess some casting director or talent executive from CineStream was in the audience. I think they said his name was Scott Simmons, and he was there to vet Meghan as a potential competitor on a reality TV comedy competition called *In Stitches*."

Detective Sharp scribbled notes in a small notebook. She glanced up at me to signal she was ready to hear more.

"A heckler also gave Meghan a hard time during the show. I don't know her name, but she was Asian, probably in her mid to upper thirties, with straight, very long brown hair. But Meghan responded back and had the whole crowd in a standing ovation by the end of their interaction. After the show, the heckler was speaking to Scott the talent scout, but I'm not sure if Meghan realized it."

The detective furrowed her forehead and twisted her lips to the side. "A lot of this seems quite...interconnected. Continue."

I debated sharing more about what I'd learned from Garrett, but I feared doing so might make it appear like I was meddling with her investigation. Gathering my own details created a blurry line when it came to deciding what was worth sharing. That was a lesson I learned the hard way the last time someone had been murdered in town. Plus, I had no way to know if Garrett was a reliable source of information. I decided to limit my testimony to what I'd observed directly. Surely she'd find a way to speak to him if I mentioned his name, right? He was a local business owner; he wouldn't be difficult to track down.

"About halfway through the show, Meghan did an unscripted crowd work segment. She teased a guy in the audience for being short. He was White, muscular, and he said he was five-six. From my perspective, she insulted his masculinity, basically saying he had a Napoleon complex. He stormed out because of it."

"Do you have any idea who he was?"

I pressed my lips together and allowed my eyes to wander, hoping she'd think I was racking my brain.

"When you're unsure of someone's name, you usually give me a disclaimer up front. But this time you didn't."

Dang, she's good.

"I believe his name's Garrett. I'm not sure of his last name. I recognized him from TAME barbershop here in town."

Detective Sharp squinted and craned her neck, as if her line of vision was a helicopter inspecting me. "It looks like you got a nice, fresh cut recently. Very stylish."

I should've suspected she'd have me all figured out.

"In my defense, I was overdue for a haircut. I feel shaggy when my curls start to grow out. Plus, as a fellow business owner in town, I felt like I had a duty to smooth things over with Garrett after Meghan insulted him last night. He clearly took offense to her jokes, and I didn't want it to reflect poorly on my business."

The detective crossed her arms. "Don't you remember what happened the last time you got involved in my investigation? You got a nice look down the barrel of a gun."

The words made my entire body quiver.

"Please leave this to me. If not, there will be consequences. Capeesh?"

I took a deep breath. "Understood." I continued to explain the flowers Garrett had brought for Meghan and his possible intentions to ask her out.

"Now, do you remember any other strange behavior from anyone in the crowd last night?"

"There was a tall guy, White, probably around thirty—I think Meghan called him David. It sounded like he was an ex-boyfriend. She said some pretty cruel things about an ex during her set—like she wished he'd die in a fire. She also told stories about what a terrible partner he'd been, but after the show, I overheard them talking. He argued with her about how nothing she'd said was true."

I shared additional details about their tense interaction and answered clarifying questions about the suspects I'd mentioned.

"You're sure there's no one else who might have played a role?" she asked.

"No, ma'am."

"Not even your friend who discovered her body this morning?"

I scooched forward to the edge of my seat. "Nate? No. He'd never do such a thing."

"Well, for the safety of our entire community, I need you to answer these next few questions honestly. I need to do my due diligence here."

I shook my head and let out a defeated sigh. "Sure thing."

"Did Nate have any interaction with Meghan last night?"

I told her about how Meghan had compared Nate to Garrett during her crowd work segment as briefly as possible.

"How did he react?"

"He looked uncomfortable—sliding down in his chair. After the show, he told me it had been awkward, but we didn't discuss it in any more detail. He seemed to move on from it pretty quickly."

"And do you know what Nate got up to after the comedy show?"

"He hung around Subplot with me, and at the end of the night, he helped me clean up and rearrange our furniture back to its original positions."

"And after you all left?"

"He would've gone home. He's an early to bed, early to rise kind of guy. And he was up before sunrise to jog this morning."

"But you don't know for sure?"

I shook my head, upset with myself for not having more

concrete evidence of his whereabouts. "I know Nate well enough to feel certain he would've gone straight home."

She bit her bottom lip, appearing hesitant to share more. "The problem is...we found a pocketknife engraved with his initials near the body."

My stomach dropped. "He realized it'd gone missing last night. Someone in the lounge must've picked it up and planted it there. Who would do such a thing?" For it to end up at the crime scene, someone must've been trying to misdirect suspicion or frame Nate. There was no way the culprit could've known Nate would discover Meghan's body, but I could see how the coincidence appeared shady to the detective.

"We're going to run it for fingerprints, but if you know anything else, I need to know, regardless of how it makes your friend look. The safety of Hope Mills is at stake."

"Well, if you're concerned about Nate's whereabouts, can you share the estimated time of murder?"

"We still need to wait for the full autopsy to be completed, but based on the condition of the body, it seems like she was likely in the river by one or two a.m."

"Well, in that case, I feel certain Nate couldn't have done it. He was up past his bedtime as it was just by helping me close the lounge. But her body being found in the river makes me curious about another theory."

Detective Sharp clicked her pen open and closed repeatedly. "Mr. Parker, I'm looking for facts here, not theories."

"Please—stick with me," I pleaded.

She spun her hand in a circular motion, gesturing for me to keep talking, reluctant as she seemed.

"During her set, Meghan made a joke about not knowing how to swim. Knowing that, doesn't it strike you as odd that she'd end up dead in the river?"

The detective's eyebrows lifted. Did she think I was on to something?

Since she didn't respond right away, I continued talking. "Maybe she was intoxicated and somehow ended up in the river on her own. It's been oppressively hot outside, and maybe she decided to go for a swim in a drunken or drug-induced stupor."

I didn't think Detective Sharp's posture could be any straighter, but when she shifted her weight, she somehow sat taller and even more confidently. "Everything we've observed so far points toward her being murdered. Forensics is performing an autopsy, which will include bloodwork to determine if she had anything in her system. They'll do a thorough scan of her body to confirm or rule out various methods by which she could have died. But like I said, we need to proceed as if foul play was involved. From what we can tell, it looks like someone tried to stage the scene to appear like an accident."

Had someone used their knowledge of her inability to swim to put an end to her?

"Did you have a chance to review any camera footage from the nearby businesses, like Riverside Roastery?" I asked.

Her eyes rolled quickly at my nosy question. I imagined her response: *Are you doubting our team of professionals?*

"It was super foggy last night," she said. "None of the cameras in the vicinity picked anything up."

Remembering the dense fog from the humid morning, it made sense.

I leaned forward and grasped both hands around my knees. "Well, if there's anything I can do to aid your investigation, please let me know. I'm happy to help."

"Thank you." She snapped her notebook shut and placed it, along with her pen, inside her cobalt-blue blazer. "The best thing you can do to help is to leave the investigating up to me. Do I make myself clear?"

"I completely understand." I stood up and extended my arm across the table for a handshake.

While I planned to leave the investigating to Detective Sharp and her team, I couldn't promise I wouldn't stumble upon more information.

Hope Mills was a small town. People talked.

TEN

The following morning started almost exactly like the day before—foggy and with an early-morning walk to Riverside Roastery—but thankfully without the discovery of a dead body. I was heading there to meet up with Chloe for coffee.

As I strolled along a silent Main Street, a man hurried down the sidewalk across the road, headed away from me. I wouldn't have thought much of it if it weren't for his dark, slicked-back hair and a light-blue sports coat.

The casting director. Scott.

Though I had no concrete reason to wonder if he might know something about Meghan's death, I felt wary of anyone who had a connection to her. While he could've just been having a bad day when I'd briefly overheard his phone call before Meghan's show, he'd sounded concerned about his career. If he was worried he had so much to lose, could he have been involved somehow?

What was he still doing in town? Wouldn't someone working for a major streaming service have other, more important places to be?

Where was he headed? *There's only one way to find out.*

I checked the time on my phone: ten till eight. With a few minutes to spare until my plans with Chloe, I looked both ways before I crossed the street and tiptoed as quickly and quietly as I could behind him, passing my destination as I did.

Though he was about my height, he speedwalked with an impressive stride that made it difficult for me to keep up with him. If I moved any faster, he would hear me. I couldn't let that happen.

He reached the corner of Main and Bridge Street and turned into Provisions, an upscale version of a convenience store. The faint tinkle of a bell floated on the breeze as he pushed the door open.

If he'd extended his stay in Hope Mills, maybe he needed to pick up some essentials at the store. I couldn't fight my curiosity. As badly as I wanted to follow him inside and try to strike up a conversation, I wasn't prepared. Instead, after making sure no one else was out and about to see me, I stationed myself on the sidewalk outside the shop's faded pink brick exterior and peered into the tall storefront windows. With my phone in hand, I was ready to appear busy texting if he looked in my direction. Observing him would have to do for now.

His back faced me as he observed the store's small newspaper rack in front of the checkout counter. Its selection had greatly dwindled in recent years, and I was surprised they still sold any newspapers at all. He picked out a couple and reached into his back pocket for his wallet.

I glanced down at my screen immediately and pretended to text, although the only thing on my screen was my wallpaper of a sleeping baby raccoon snuggled up in a fluffy white blanket. Even Scott's small reach-around for his wallet had been enough to make me paranoid he'd seen me. I took a deep breath to refocus.

As the bell above the door tinkled again, I realized I hadn't planned for what I'd do when he walked out of the building. What if he turned toward me?

I hustled down the street in the direction from which I came, back toward Riverside Roastery, and I tucked myself into a small walkway around the corner of a building a few doors down.

Do I take the chance of sneaking a look? I didn't feel like I had much of a choice. My desire to know where he was headed next was too strong.

I poked my head around the corner and stared down the sidewalk. Fortunately, Scott walked in the opposite direction, clutching his newspapers.

Back to following him. Once again, I tiptoed as fast and as silently as I could.

His pace had slowed. Though both hands were at his sides, I faintly heard him talking. Maybe he was on the phone with someone through his earbuds. If so, that was good news for me; he'd be less likely to hear me trailing behind.

Just don't turn around.

I tried to catch up to him to get a better sense of what he was saying, while taking note of spaces between the buildings which lined Main Street where I could leap behind if it seemed like he'd turn around.

"I can't have that in my search history." Those were the only words I could make out, since he shrouded his deep voice with a whispery tone.

Whoa.

Though I wasn't sure what he was looking for in the newspaper, it was clear he was trying to fly under the radar. Was he avoiding searching for details related to the investigation of Meghan's murder? Being wary enough to not leave behind any record of his search history wasn't only paranoid—it was super sketchy.

I pulled out my phone and checked the time. Seven fifty-seven. I tapped over to my messaging app to text Chloe.

> Running a few minutes behind. See you at the roastery in ten

My breath constricted in my throat as I fell forward. I'd been so fixated on Scott that I tripped.

Instinctively, I stomped my other foot on the ground to stabilize myself, which unfortunately made noise as I tried desperately to stay quiet. I looked back to observe a brick which protruded from the sidewalk. Though the gorgeous brick sidewalks added charm to our downtown, their occasional unevenness didn't aid my stealthiness.

Shoot! I hoped he hadn't heard me.

When I caught my bearings, I faced straight ahead to see Scott frozen in his tracks, looking at me over his shoulder.

My stomach dropped.

"I'll call you back later," he mumbled as he reached into his pocket for his phone. "I gotta go." He tapped the screen to end the call. "You all right?"

"Me?" I glanced around. Of course, there was no one and nothing around me to blame for the sound of my stumbling. "I hoped no one saw that."

He pulled the earbuds from his ears and placed them in their charging case. "You following me?" I couldn't tell if he was being playful, or if he legitimately believed I might be onto him.

A chill rushed down my spine. *Think, Reece.* "Nah, I'm out for my morning loop through downtown. These brick sidewalks will trip you up."

He furrowed his brow and bit his lower lip. "Hmm ..."

I pointed toward the intersection ahead of us. "I usually walk all the way to the end of the business district, then I cross the street and walk back the other way." North of downtown, with its ivy-laced brick buildings, stood ornate Victorian houses. They'd been converted in recent decades to business spaces for realtors, lawyers, psychologists, and financial advisors. Less than a block from where we were standing, the commercial zoning ended, and the houses further north were all residential.

He pressed his lips together and gave me a curt nod. "Ah. Well, have a nice walk."

"You, too." It killed me to not ask any more questions, but I couldn't afford to get on Scott's bad side. His presence in Hope Mills two days after Meghan's show—and the day after she was found dead—might mean he was a witness or even a person of interest.

He continued straight ahead, strolling through the residential neighborhood. Where was he headed? Maybe he was staying at an independent bed and breakfast outside of downtown.

When I reached the intersection, I crossed the street, staying true to the story I'd told him about my morning walk.

Once I reached the Bridge Street intersection, the warm light glowing from the front window of Provisions caught my eye as the fog began to clear. I crossed diagonally and went inside.

The woman at the register was about my parents' age, and she was in the middle of a coughing fit as I approached the newspaper stand.

"Popular day for newspapers," she said. She raised her arm to her mouth and continued coughing into the inside of her elbow.

I let out a single chuckle. "Is it?"

"It's not every day there's a murder in Hope Mills."

I nodded. "You're right about that."

I read the headline of the *Hope Mills Local*—INVESTIGATION

Begins as Authorities Search for Culprit in Comedian Meghan Spencer Murder. An accompanying photo showed flowers and stuffed animals arranged near the crime scene along the River Promenade.

On the rack below, the Philadelphia newspaper displayed an unrelated main headline about the upcoming gubernatorial election for governor of Pennsylvania in November. Just above the fold, though, another headline about Meghan caught my eye. I picked up the paper and unfolded it to skim the narrow column. Fans Mourn the Loss of Viral Comedy Sensation Meghan Spencer.

As I scanned the text, the word *CineStream* caught my eye on the lower half of the front page. Two Plead Not Guilty Amid Insider Trading Charges During Recent CineStream Acquisition.

I let out a gasp which must not have been subtle, because the cashier asked, "Are you okay over there, sweetie?"

I waved off her concern. "Oh, yeah. I just can't believe this news."

"Me neither, honey. Me neither."

Though Scott's name wasn't listed anywhere in the article, two of his Fledgling Studios colleagues were. Had he been associated with—or even facilitated—their wrongdoing? Was he concerned his name might come up during the forthcoming trial?

If this doesn't work out the way it's supposed to, I can kiss my career goodbye. Those were the words he'd said before Meghan's show on Sunday.

Though I didn't have any plausible reason to connect the two headlines, I couldn't help but wonder whether the trouble brewing at Scott's company could somehow be related to Meghan's demise.

ELEVEN

"I'm so sorry I'm late." I opened my arms to hug Chloe after stepping into the café, which smelled strongly of freshly roasted coffee.

With a smile, she took a step closer and wrapped both arms around me. Though I'd broken off our engagement about nine months before, her embrace still felt familiar. I was grateful she was still part of my life, even though I knew we weren't meant to get married.

We found a table in the back right corner of the air-conditioned coffee shop, and I slung my backpack over the back of my chair. After our meetup, I needed to get some online work done for Subplot, including answering emails, doing payroll and bookkeeping, and researching vendors who offered some new ingredients at the best price. Even when the lounge wasn't open, the work never stopped.

Massive floor-to-ceiling windows formed the entire back wall of Riverside Roastery, giving us a clear view of the Promenade and Delaware River.

The heat wave over Hope Mills persisted, and even at eight

a.m., the air was uncomfortably hot and humid, though the fog lingering over the Delaware had mostly lifted. Seeing the crime scene for myself—the yellow police tape and the impromptu memorial that was on the front page of the paper—was a grim reminder of the darkness haunting our town.

I'd ordered another iced blueberry pie latte with almond milk, and Chloe ordered an iced Masala chai tea latte.

"How was your trip?" I asked as Chloe took a long sip from her chai.

"A dream." A gentle smile grew on her face. She wasn't one to get overly excited. "But if you think it's hot here, you haven't felt St. Pete in August. The days aren't too bad, but it doesn't cool down at night quite like it does here. This heat wave seems a bit unusual, though."

I swirled my latte in my glass, sure to incorporate all of the flavors since the espresso floated at the top. "Did you make any moves?" The purpose of her trip had been to do some business networking and see if there were any golden opportunities to manage a bar or restaurant in the tourist and snow bird hotspot.

"Nothing too concrete. I met with some restaurant owners and toured some kitchens. A few of the restaurants were in fancy resorts, and I had some discussions about open management roles."

"Anything of interest?"

She pinched her straw and bounced it up and down in her drink. "Maybe." She didn't look back up at me.

"You don't sound too thrilled."

She released the straw, allowing it to float freely in her glass. "No, I am. I really am. It's just...these restaurants are next level. We have an awesome culinary scene here, and we draw a lot of visitors, but the opportunities I explored down there were especially exquisite. When you're working at a restaurant on a resort property, the clientele can be"—she scanned the restaurant, as if searching for the perfect word—"demanding. Leveling up my career would be exciting, but I'm not sure I'm ready to make that big of a leap."

Based on everything I'd learned about her during our nearly seven-year history, I never imagined Chloe would want to leave Hope Mills. But when I broke off our engagement, I'd set off to find myself. If Chloe felt the same urge, I couldn't blame her for it. Thinking of her potentially moving away was painful, but I was happy she was exploring her options and taking steps to figure out what she wanted to do next.

"If there's anyone who can do it, it's you." Though I hated the thought of her leaving, she deserved the love and support she always offered me, even after I'd pulled the rug out from under her earlier in the year. "Plus, you already have such great experience. I'm sure you'd thrive anywhere."

Though we were a small town, critics highly regarded Hope Mills as a foodie destination. Even if potential employers in St. Pete hadn't heard of it, a quick online search would reveal the many accolades our town and its restaurants had received. I figured Chloe wouldn't have a problem aligning her experience with the strong reputation of our local culinary scene.

"Thanks." She took a slow, contemplative sip from her iced chai. "Now the question is if I even want to do it."

I knew it wasn't my place to judge or worry about Chloe.

As a matter of fact, she'd taken a huge chance by saying yes when I'd gotten down on one knee in front of the Washington Playhouse about two years before. Our engagement had ended up in heartbreak, so what did I know about what was best for her?

I should be happy for her. She's always supported me, no

questions asked. "I'm sure no matter what you do or where you go, you'll make the best decision for yourself."

Though I still dealt with the residual pain from our breakup, I was grateful we could still get together and have honest conversations without hard feelings or bitterness.

I wanted the best for Chloe, and I genuinely believed she wished the same for me. She'd made that clear after I came out to her, devastated as she'd been in the moment.

She turned her head toward the tall windows lining the back of the roastery. "The fog's finally lifted."

The sky was completely blue with not a single cloud, except for wispy white streaks from planes.

She shook her head. "I can't believe there was another murder in town." I presumed her attention had fixated on the yellow caution tape near the crime scene.

"I suppose Cam's filled you in?"

"He's told me a little bit. The victim was a comedian, right? She performed at Subplot? And Nate discovered her body in the river?"

I nodded. "Wow. He's really given you a briefing, huh?"

She didn't confirm or deny it. Her brother tended to let some details slip when it came to the goings-on around town. "Bad luck seems to follow you around when it comes to this stuff."

I sighed. "Oh, I know. I can't seem to escape it. I bumped into Cam at Borough Hall yesterday. The detective called me in to give a statement."

"He mentioned he saw you."

"Detective Sharp warned me to not interfere with her investigation—and I don't plan to—but I feel like I need to prove I'm not inviting murder and mayhem into Hope Mills."

She reached forward to touch my forearm with her soft fingertips. "It's not your fault. You can't control other people."

"But this is the second murder in a row with ties to Subplot. I'm worried people will start to think it's a pattern. And with Nate tied up in this, I feel a duty to make sure he's cleared, too. His pocketknife ended up at the crime scene somehow."

Chloe craned her neck and scanned the interior of Riverside Roastery in every direction, perhaps to make sure no one could overhear our conversation. "I'll let you know if I learn anything from Cam. And if you need me to weasel any info out of him, you know how to find me. As long as you don't let anything I share trace back to me."

"You have my word." I knew I didn't need to give Chloe some grandiose gesture or say anything over the top for her to trust me. I could say those words and know it was enough for her to believe me in return. "That being said, have you learned anything?"

"It's a small piece of intel I overheard him mention over the phone, but it feels significant." She spoke softly, and her eyes constantly darted around.

I leaned in. "Continue."

She took a deep breath. "He said even though the body was found in the water, the preliminary autopsy results didn't find any water in Meghan's lungs."

"So she couldn't have drowned ..." My mind began to race with possibilities for how she'd ended up along the riverbank and what actually caused her death. "But she didn't know how to swim."

"How would you know that?"

"She did a whole bit in her show about how she never learned to swim. I thought maybe someone used that knowl-edge to kill her, but if she didn't drown, she had to have been killed another way."

Chloe sucked in a shallow breath through her teeth. "Well,

it sounds like there might have been signs of trauma to her head ..."

I gasped. "This just got a whole lot more complicated. Does that mean a concussion? Brain bleed? Was she bludgeoned somehow? Maybe she took a hard fall?"

Chloe shrugged. "He didn't go into specifics about her head injuries. I think it's the question on everyone's mind after the preliminary autopsy."

I covered my mouth with both hands before folding them in my lap. "Whoever killed her must've had some sort of rage."

As our conversation on the topic came to its natural end, I flipped over my phone, which had been screen side down on the table. I couldn't keep my eyes from bulging slightly as I read the notification which had come through.

Chloe covered her mouth. "Is everything okay? What is it?"

I cleared my throat. "It's a text from the comedian's manager, Tiffany. She said she might swing by the lounge early this afternoon."

"Are you sure that's a good idea?"

As I prepared to justify my reasons, I scratched at my cheek. "I was hoping she'd stop by. She's been through a lot, and she's staying in town until she gets answers. I'm sure she must feel isolated, and I'm somewhat of a familiar face to her. Plus, she might share something which might help me get closer to an answer."

She massaged a temple with one hand. "Be careful, Reece. Remember, the detective told you to steer clear of this."

Based on the details I'd uncovered so far, it seemed like whoever killed Meghan acted fast. Perhaps they had a fit of rage and killed her, only to be horrified by what they'd done. On the other hand, though, dropping Nate's pocketknife at the crime scene made the act seem pre-meditated. Her killer must've done what they could to cover their tracks before fleeing. I figured the culprit was likely highly reactive and would go to great lengths to avoid being found.

Though I was relieved to consider her death might not have been meticulously orchestrated, I felt uneasy knowing a loose cannon could potentially still be somewhere on the streets of Hope Mills. Would they kill again if it meant keeping their dirty deed a secret?

TWELVE

I didn't waste any time after my morning coffee meetup with Chloe. Hopeful I might have a chance to speak to David, I made my way down Main Street toward the pocket park across the street from the Colonial Inn, iced latte in hand. Obsessed as I was with the roastery's blueberry pie latte, I'd ordered a decaf version to go before heading to the park, fully committed to my sleuthing.

With any luck, David was still staying there and would need to come outside eventually. I was eager to get some admin work done for Subplot and could still make progress on my laptop while I staked out.

Though Garrett was local and I'd already bumped into Scott this morning, I had no confirmation David or the heckler from the other night were still around. Since I'd seen David the prior afternoon, I hoped he hadn't checked out of the inn yet, considering it was still before ten a.m. Even if he wanted to leave, I had a feeling he'd realize he had a huge target on his back. The ex-boyfriend of a murder victim didn't get off the hook that easy, so being available to cooperate with the authorities was in his best interest.

David had reason to be frustrated with Meghan based on some of the things she'd said about him during her routine, especially if she'd made false claims. Plus, if Garrett had truly spotted them walking together toward the Promenade after he left Bridge Street Bar, he was the top suspect in my mind. And if the crime scene had been sloppy—her body thrown into the river after being bludgeoned over the head—David might have killed her in a fit of rage.

The temperature continued to rise, which made me question whether I actually wanted to set up shop in the pocket park. Before committing to my stakeout, I stood at the base of the Colonial Inn's smooth concrete stairs with ornate wrought iron railings on each side.

Do I try to peek inside?

I carefully climbed the steps and peered into a thin window to the left of the door which spanned the full height of the inn's common area. A red brick fireplace with a mirror over the mantel was the centerpiece of the room. A pine-green wingback couch, centered on a vibrant area rug, faced it.

Though there was a small desk nestled in the corner, it wasn't attended. The Colonial Inn leveraged a self-service model with keyless check-in. I glanced at the numbered keypad to the right of the door and considered which of the thousands of possible codes might unlock it.

When I glanced inside again, a woman with curly red hair strode toward me through the front room.

Shoot.

I spun around and rushed down the steps, hoping she wouldn't think anything of my lurking.

As I reached the crosswalk near the front of the inn, I heard the hotel's door unlatch.

I snuck a quick glance over my shoulder. The woman shielded her eyes from the sun as she stared in my direction.

"Trying to get inside?" She traipsed down the stairs and along the brick sidewalk toward me.

I had to think of a story. And fast. "I'm waiting to meet up with a friend who's staying here. He's not answering his phone."

"What does he look like? I feel like I've bumped into most of the other guests." It made sense, as there were only eight rooms at the inn.

Do I give her an actual description of David? Mindful that the red-haired woman might've seen him interacting with the cops—and considering she already seemed wary of me—I was hesitant. However, it was my chance to get a sense of whether I might get to talk to him myself. "He's a tall guy. Dirty blond hair. Fit." I fumbled through my description.

Her breath hitched, almost as if she was afraid. "Oh, I think I know who you mean." Was she aware David was a person of interest? Certainly, I figured, she'd be aware of the murder investigation, with all of the chatter around town and online. "I held the door for him earlier. He must've been coming back from a coffee run. Hopefully he'll be out soon to meet you." She didn't give me a chance to get inside—and rightfully so.

I raised my beverage toward her as if to say, *Cheers.* "Thanks. Have a great day."

The woman rushed away toward the shops on Main Street as I crossed the road. Knowing she'd likely seen David earlier, I felt marginally better about sitting in the humid heat in an attempt to connect with him.

When I took off my gray vegan leather backpack in the pocket park facing the hotel, my thin shirt clung to my back. I sunk into a yellow Adirondack chair in the shade next to the red British phone booth which decorated the park. Despite the heat, I found serenity in my surroundings. A hydrangea bush with indigo flowers was planted beside me, and bright pink, yellow, and orange zinnias were scattered throughout the small park as birds chirped from the trees which towered overhead.

I placed my condensation-covered plastic cup on one arm of the chair and pulled out my laptop. My first order of business was researching vendors who carried specialty ingredients, such as the rare Green Chartreuse, a liqueur made by French Carthusian monks and produced exclusively in their distillery, which was becoming increasingly difficult to procure.

Over the next half-hour, I'd been so locked in on my work that I almost missed the Colonial Inn's front door slamming shut.

David hustled down the front steps in sunglasses and athletic clothing, looking like he was ready to go for another jog. He turned to the right at the base of the stairs, moving away from me.

I needed to make a move...and fast. Otherwise, he'd be too far down the street for me to catch him. I snapped my laptop shut, zipped it into my backpack, picked up my almost-full iced latte, and made a run toward him through the thick, humid air.

Crossing the street toward the Colonial Inn, I reached into my pocket for my wallet. Inside was my customer rewards punch card for Riverside Roastery—buy ten coffees, get the eleventh free.

Here goes nothing.

"Hey!" I called out to him as he picked up his warm-up walking pace. "Hold up! I think you might have dropped this."

THIRTEEN

David froze and glanced cautiously over his shoulder. Even with sunglasses on, he placed a flat palm above his eyes to form a visor and appeared to squint as I approached.

I held out the business card-sized rectangle of cream card-stock with seven star-shaped holes punched over coffee bean clipart. "This was lying at the bottom of the stairs. I thought it might have fallen out of your pocket. It's a rewards card for Riverside Roastery."

David patted the front pockets of his shorts, then pointed toward their closed zippers. "All of my stuff is locked away."

I shook my head and pressed a thumb and index to my brow, putting on an act of embarrassment. "Sorry to bother you. I guess I wasn't paying very close attention. I saw this card on the ground and thought you might've dropped it." I swirled the iced latte in my other hand.

He chuckled. "It must be your lucky day, then. Finders keepers."

"Nah, why don't you take it? Only three more to go for a free coffee."

He swiped his hands in front of him. "No. You keep it."

I wagged a knowing finger at him. "Wait. You look familiar."

"Really?" He removed his sunglasses. "You know what, I think I recognize you, too. You own the cocktail lounge, right?"

My improvised plan was playing out better than I thought it would.

"Yep, that's me."

He observed the backpack slung over my shoulder with striking hazel eyes which bordered on green. "Are you a student, too?"

"No, I like to get work done around town when the lounge is closed." With my thumb, I pointed at the pocket park across the street behind me. "I was working at the park, but the heat was getting to be too much."

He put his sunglasses back on. "I was at the comedy event you hosted the other night. Your team really knows how to entertain."

"Ah, that's probably why you looked familiar. Thanks so much for the support. Are you here on vacation? I saw you leave the Colonial Inn."

He sidestepped toward the wrought-iron fence which lined the red brick sidewalk, giving a group of pedestrians space to walk past us. "I live in Philly. Even though Hope Mills is close enough to be a day trip, I love coming here for longer. I work remotely, doing finance for a tech company, so I stay up here a few times a year. I work out of the inn and at the Roastery since work gives me that flexibility. It's always a much-needed change of scenery." He made his extended stay here seem completely voluntary and pre-planned.

"That's awesome. We're happy to have you. So, you enjoyed the show?" I was careful not to mention Meghan or my awareness of his past with her.

"I did, but I'm horrified by what happened to Meg."

"Were you a big fan of hers?"

He tucked his chin down to his chest and let out a deep sigh. "Oh, sorry. I...Uh...I'll be honest with you. She...she was my girl-friend...at one point. Even though we're not together anymore, I still wanted to support her."

I sucked air in through clenched teeth. "I'm so sorry for your loss." I glanced down at the zinnias planted on the other side of the fence. "I can't imagine what you must be feeling right now."

"I can't believe she's gone. I was supposed to check out yesterday, but I decided I can't leave until I find justice." His voice grew increasingly shaky, and his face reddened as he spoke. "I need to find whoever did this to her. She might've been my ex, but she didn't deserve to die." He shook his head. "What am I doing? Opening up to a stranger on the street like this. I'm sorry."

"No, please don't worry about it." I tucked the punch card in my pocket before extending my free hand for a shake. "I'm Reece."

He grasped my hand. "David."

"You're going through a lot right now, and if there's anything I can do to support—"

"She didn't deserve to die this way. It's so unfair, man. And then to make it worse, the police must assume I had something to do with this, being her ex and all."

Why was he being so open and honest with me? Perhaps it was his grief response to unload, even to a stranger.

"Please don't take this the wrong way, but she said some pretty terrible things about an ex during her routine."

David shrugged and waved off my concern. "That'd be me. But hey, comedy is comedy. Anything for a laugh, right? A lot of what she said isn't true. The audience seemed to think it was funny. She and I got along great."

That hadn't been his perspective during their argument

after her show. Was he aware I'd overheard them? If he'd recognized me so easily, I thought it was a good possibility he was. And if so, it seemed like he was trying to ease any suspicions I might have.

On the other hand, I wondered if I'd read their conversation wrong when he pleaded with Meghan. *You made me sound like the worst person in the world*, he'd said. It didn't seem like a statement which could be misinterpreted, though.

And although I questioned Garrett's credibility, he also claimed he'd seen the former couple arguing, so I doubted David was so cool with Meghan's vicious jokes about him.

"Have you learned anything more while you've been in town?" I asked.

"I'm suspicious of a few people. I've talked to some, and there are a couple of others I'm waiting to have words with. I hope I can keep my cool. Whoever did this to Meg deserves to pay dearly for what they've done, and I hope it's as painful as possible for them."

I felt my pulse accelerate in my chest. Knowing he was chatting with other suspects reminded me to be careful as I sought to do the same. If he planned to try his hand at uncovering Meghan's killer, I hoped I could learn something new from him. However, as the victim's ex-boyfriend, I had no doubt the authorities were keeping a close eye on him, so I had to be careful.

I cocked my head to the side. "Oh, really? Are you making good headway?"

"Two people are really sticking out to me right now. You know the short king she joked about during her crowd work session?"

Garrett. I smoothed down my stubble, acting like I was racking my brain.

David continued. "She clearly got under his skin. He was mad. And you saw Meg's manager Tiffany recording video clips for social media last night, right?"

I nodded. I remembered her filming videos from almost every angle in the lounge, but what did that have to do with Garrett?

"I think he went to great lengths to keep the videos from hitting the Internet."

"But then why wouldn't he have targeted her manager? Don't you think he would've stolen her phone, or at least tried to get her to delete the footage, rather than killing Meghan?"

"Because she didn't offend him. If he went after Meg, there'd be no reason to post any new videos to social media—especially one featuring a joke that likely led to her death. By killing Meg, he could get payback and prevent his humiliating video from surfacing—a two birds, one stone kind of thing."

While I could follow David's logic, it seemed like a massive stretch to me. Wouldn't that have been too obvious on Garrett's part? If that theory was true, it seemed like an easy case to prove.

If Garrett had killed her, it was likely the video clip would have eventually surfaced as evidence in a court case and potentially circulate online. But under that same scenario, Garrett would also be sentenced to prison for the rest of his life, so what would it matter? On the other hand, if Garrett managed to cover his tracks and avoid being charged with her murder, it was likely the video would never see the light of day. Either way, though, the video on its own didn't seem like it created the strongest motive for Garrett.

"Did you get a chance to chat with Meghan after the comedy event the other night?" I asked, leaving my question up to interpretation.

"Very briefly." He thankfully didn't mention I was within earshot. If he had, I would've blamed my lack of attention on being in the zone behind the bar.

"Did she seem concerned she might be in danger or afraid someone might be after her?"

His body wilted. "No. And after leaving your lounge, I never saw her again. I can't believe it was the last time I ever saw her."

There was a key discrepancy. Garrett claimed he saw Meghan and David fighting after he left Bridge Street Bar, but David claimed he never saw her again after leaving Subplot. One of them had to be lying. And lies meant someone was trying to hide something. Who was telling the truth?

He removed his baseball cap, revealing his thick, moppy hair, and wiped the sweat from his brow with his wrist. "But you know who I did see later that night?"

"Who?"

He put the cap back on his head, pulling his bangs back to keep them off his forehead. "The short muscle man." He had to have been referring to Garrett. His teasing, especially considering the circumstance, rubbed me the wrong way.

"The guy who stormed out of the show? Did you talk to him when you saw him?"

He bit his lower lip. "No, but I wish I would've. He stumbled out of a bar near the main drag." He pointed down Main Street in the direction of Bridge Street Bar. "He looked like hell—with messy hair and glassy eyes. And in his stupor, he staggered down toward the waterfront. It kills me to think he could've been headed to the Promenade. That's where her body was discovered, in the end. What if he saw Meg there and ..." His shoulders deflated even more than they already had. "You know."

If David was telling the truth, I had serious questions about the story Garrett told at TAME. If he was as drunk as David claimed, I couldn't believe a word he'd said—not just because it meant he was lying, but also because he was seeing the world through intoxicated lenses.

"Have you told the police about this?"

"Yeah, yeah. They're going to question the guy. Yada, yada, yada." He swatted at the air. "I don't trust law enforcement, though. I want justice for Meg, which is why I'm taking matters into my own hands. And he's not the only one I find suspicious. Any guesses who else is at the top of my list?"

I pressed my lips together. "No. Who?"

"Remember the woman who heckled Meg in the middle of the set, right before she started doing crowd work with that short beefcake? She has long, straight brown hair."

"Mm-hmm. How could I forget her?"

"Her name is Kari."

"Whoa, how'd you learn her name?"

He crossed his arms over his chest. "Oh, I've known it. She's part of the comedy community. She's a stand-up comedian herself. I spent years in comedy clubs going to Meg's showcases and open mic nights. It was my role as the supportive boyfriend. I've seen a lot of different comedians, and Kari was one I saw regularly. I recognized her immediately in the audience the other night, even before she started heckling Meg. You better believe I was keeping a close eye on her."

Ava and Lainey's speculation that Meghan and the heckler knew each other had been correct, if David was telling the truth. But had they coordinated their intense interaction as part of Meghan's set?

"Here's where things get dicey, though. Remember the joke Meg told about not knowing how to swim?"

"Yeah..." I bit my lip. Where was he going with this?

"She was an excellent swimmer."

A heavy feeling sunk in my stomach. "So she lied?"

I made a mental note. If Meghan was actually a good swimmer, then I figured whoever killed her must not have been well-acquainted with her. Perhaps her killer had staged her death to align with the joke, not realizing she could actually swim. It aligned with the information I'd learned from Chloe, too, considering there was no water found in Meghan's lungs.

"Well..." His voice fried and dragged like the air squealing slowly out of an untied balloon. "I wouldn't call it lying. I'd call it creative license. Storytelling, if you will. The only problem is... that joke was stolen from Kari's routine."

I couldn't suppress a gasp. "Really?"

"Oh yeah. I heard Kari do that bit years ago, back when Meg was still in her open mic days. Meg's career grew, and Kari's career tapered off. While Meg's comedy went viral and she started to headline events like the other night, Kari is still struggling in the open mic circuit."

I crossed my arms as I pondered his revelation. "I'm not saying it's worthy of killing someone over—nothing is—but surely Kari would've been outraged to see Meghan's popularity grow so much and doing it with stolen material."

David nodded, but he didn't respond.

I drummed my fingers along my bicep. "But Meghan was clearly talented. Her career was taking off. Why would she feel the need to copy someone's old material?"

He shrugged with both arms slackened at his sides. "I don't know what Meg was thinking. As much as I loved her, I'm not surprised she stole the joke. After the show, I overheard the CineStream talent scout in the crowd compliment Meghan on that bit. He loved it." He was referring to Scott. "But guess who I saw nearby, definitely within earshot, when he gave her such high praise?"

"Kari?"

"Bingo." How convenient. "And Kari attended the show with someone I assume was a friend of hers. You know what she told them shortly after the talent executive praised Meg for that joke? 'Karma is going to get her for this. I'll make sure of it.'"

FOURTEEN

David jogged away from the Colonial Inn after our insightful conversation, leaving me with no reason to keep working in the August heat.

I swung by my apartment to freshen up, relax, and give Jameson some belly scratches before heading to Subplot. He was the only cat I'd ever met that would stretch out with his stomach exposed, almost as if begging for a rub. And when I did, he actually enjoyed it.

On my way to the lounge, I sent Tiffany a quick text message to let her know I'd be arriving to the lounge shortly and planned to be there for the next few hours, once again offering her an escape. Her previous messages had been noncommittal, and if she didn't visit Subplot, I'd need to think of another way to chat with her in-person.

When I reached the front of D'Amico's Italian restaurant, I turned down the cement path which led to the alley behind Subplot. I preferred to enter Subplot through the nondescript alley entrance because it reduced the likelihood I'd run into Heidi.

Unfortunately, as I ambled down the cement walkway,

Heidi turned the corner from the back alley.

Here we go. Let the accusations and blame begin.

She dusted off her hands when she spotted me. I supposed she'd taken some trash to our shared dumpster in the back, though she typically used D'Amico's separate alley door, which led to a side staircase up to her restaurant.

"Just who I've been looking for. I've been meaning to talk to you." The condescension in her voice made me cringe inside.

It was too late to turn around and run away now.

"Hey, Heidi. How's your day going?"

"Why don't you take a guess?" She planted a fist on each hip. "All anyone can seem to talk about in my restaurant is the terrible tragedy that occurred down by the river. And do you know what they all say?"

I shrugged. "Enlighten me." While I always tried to be respectful, even when she didn't do the same in return for me, I found keeping a firm tone and slight edge with her was essential to keeping boundaries in place between us. Otherwise, she could easily steamroll me.

"They talk about how the victim performed in your establishment mere hours before she was found dead." She scoffed. "How many times do I have to tell you I don't appreciate all of the *unsavory* behavior you welcome into our building? You don't own the place, you know."

Neither do you, I wanted to retort. We each leased our spaces from a shared landlord.

"This is a shared building," she went on to say. "Whatever goes on down in that speakeasy of yours has a direct impact on my reputation, and I won't stand for it any longer. Comedy and Cocktails is officially canceled. No more of that nonsense."

I'd grown accustomed to her empty threats, though I sometimes wondered what would happen if she actually snapped.

"What happened to Meghan—the comedian—was a

tragedy. No doubt about it. But I swear my lounge had absolutely nothing to do with her death. I've talked to the authorities, and I'm cooperating with their investigation. This case is much more complex than anything that could've happened in a one-night comedy event at Subplot."

She crossed her arms, not seeming to believe me. "Oh yeah? Then prove it."

"I'm working on it." I proceeded to give her a very light summary of what I'd uncovered so far to give her faith that I wasn't involved whatsoever.

"Well, that does sound like a complicated situation, but I want this funny business resolved ASAP." She shook her head. "I need to get back to work." As she traipsed up the cement-paved path toward the front of her restaurant, she let out a disgusted exhale.

I turned the corner and entered Subplot through the heavy metal door in the back alley.

From the second I pushed the door open, ice clinking on metal echoed through the lounge. Ava vigorously shook up a beverage. The cool, air-conditioned lounge was inviting.

"Hey, A. What are you doing here on your day off?" I asked once she finished shaking.

She removed the lid of her cocktail shaker and replaced it with a strainer attachment. "I could ask you the same thing." She smirked. "I'm working on some fall cocktail ideas. The fall menu will be launching before we know it."

Ava's commitment and innovation were a constant reminder that I'd chosen the right person to work alongside me at Subplot.

She'd crafted a mocktail she called Frankenstein's Monster, named for its pale green color, which came from its blend of matcha, coconut milk, pear puree, and a dash of cinnamon. She poured it into a tall, skinny glass and added a curly purple straw. "Did you see the heckler on your way into the lounge, by chance?"

I pulled out a barstool and sat facing Ava at the bar. "Who? Heidi? Yeah, I saw her in the alley."

She swatted at the air dismissively. "She's not the heckler I was referring to, but I'll send you my condolences anyway."

"Wait. You saw the heckler from the comedy show? Why would I have seen her on my way into the lounge?"

Ava nodded. "I bumped into her in the alley on my way in today. It was very strange, and it made me super uncomfortable."

"That's weird. I didn't even realize she stuck around town. Maybe she's local."

"No clue. I turned the corner from the path along the side of the building, and there she was. She looked like a deer in headlights. I didn't say anything to her, but she fled immediately after we made eye contact. She acted like I'd caught her in the middle of committing a crime, although she wasn't doing anything wrong, from what I could tell."

"But standing in the alley for no reason is very strange. I wonder if she's scoping us out." I pulled at my earlobe as I considered possible reasons for her lurking. "I'll keep an eye out for her. I wonder if she's trying to get in touch with us for some reason? Maybe something connected to Comedy and Cocktails?"

Ava shrugged as she took a sip from her mocktail. "I'm not sure. She seemed pretty avoidant, but I guess it's a possibility."

I eyed the Frankenstein's Monster mocktail in her hand. "How is it?"

She smacked her lips together as if to enhance the flavor. "I think I went a little overboard on the matcha, but it's nothing a little tweaking won't fix."

Ava continued experimenting behind the bar as I took care

of a few tasks around the lounge—doing a brief inventory in our supply closet, placing some online ingredient orders on my laptop at the bar, and planning out social media posts for the upcoming week.

A hard knock slamming repeatedly on the basement door sucked me out of my intense focus.

I gasped and held my breath. *Who could it be?* The knock was uncharacteristic of anyone who'd usually come to the downstairs door.

"Maybe the heckler's back," Ava said.

"I'm not sure."

More thuds on the metal door. They grew louder and faster, as if someone was striking it with their open palm.

I stood up from my barstool and hustled toward the exit. "Coming!" I bellowed.

I unlocked the door and pushed the crash bar, hoping I wouldn't accidentally hit the person on the other side with it.

Tiffany raced inside.

"Close it," she demanded. "Quick. Hurry!"

I pulled the door shut and locked it immediately. "What's going on? What's wrong? Are you okay?"

Tiffany pressed her back against the brick wall just inside the door with both hands clasped over her chest. Her black, curly hair was especially voluminous today, though it was also somewhat disheveled. I feared she might have been on the brink of a panic attack as she tried to catch her breath.

"He's after me. I should've known he was up to no good."

"Who?" I asked, playing dumb, figuring she meant David. Though he seemed like a nice enough guy during our earlier conversation, I struggled to think of a good reason for him to come to his ex-girlfriend's show. Even if he'd tried to win Meghan back, it didn't add up—especially considering her fate.

Her eyes darted around the lounge. She contorted her lips to one side as if she was hesitant to say any more, but with an exasperated exhale, she answered.

"A talent executive from a production company. He was interested in casting Meg for a TV series. I should've known it was too good to be true when he showed up the other night. I wish he hadn't come."

"My phone's on the bar," I said. "I'm calling the police right away."

She gasped. "No! Don't. It's fine. You don't have to. I've already told the police he's up to no good."

"Why not?" I asked.

Ava pressed a fist into her hip. "Yeah. If he's chasing you, we should absolutely report it."

Tiffany removed a hand from her chest and pressed it against her forehead. "Because he wasn't chasing me."

My chest grew tight—a physical manifestation of my confusion and concern. "He wasn't? But you just said he's after you. And you're panting to catch your breath."

She let out a whimper. "Gosh, I feel so stupid. I'm overreacting, that's all. The trauma from this week is getting the best of me, I guess." Though she was a couple of inches taller than me, her sullen demeanor made her appear small. She buried her face in her hands and whimpered.

Ava opened an arm and approached Tiffany. "Can I give you a hug?"

Tiffany lowered her hands, revealing streams of tears crawling down her cheeks. "Yes."

The two of them exchanged a loose embrace.

Ava rubbed Tiffany's shoulder. "Let me get you a glass of water," she whispered warmly before going behind the bar.

"Thank you. I really needed that." Tiffany wiped the tears from her eyes.

I stepped toward one of our seating pods, although the

heaviness in the room made me feel like I was walking through wet cement. "Why don't we sit down? Can I offer you something to drink? Cocktail? Mocktail? Juice? On the house."

"Hmm..." She wandered toward a forest-green velvet armchair and sunk down into it. "I'm not much of a drinker, but since I'm here, how about a dirty martini—vodka, shaken, dry? Actually, make it filthy." *Dry* meant she wanted it made with only a little Vermouth, and *filthy* meant she preferred extra olive brine. It was a fluent martini order, coming from someone who didn't drink much.

Although she appeared rattled, Tiffany didn't show any signs of intoxication, so I figured one drink wouldn't hurt. Beyond helping her relax, I hoped she might open up a bit more in conversation.

"On it," Ava called from behind the bar.

I settled on a vintage mustard-yellow couch directly across from Tiffany. After a couple of minutes of small talk about the heat wave, Ava joined us. She handed Tiffany a glass of ice water and rested her martini on the coffee table between us. She removed a clean hand towel that had been draped over her forearm, offered it to Tiffany, and took a seat beside me.

Tiffany dabbed her sweat-glazed forehead with the towel. "Thank you so much. You two are the best."

"So, first things first. You weren't being chased? I want to make sure you're safe."

She let out a refreshed exhale after taking a sip of water. "No, I wasn't. But I saw him on my way over here." She exchanged the water glass for her martini and took a sip.

"You...saw him?" It seemed understandable her emotional responses—and potentially paranoia—were heightened in the aftermath of Meghan's death.

She let out a small chuckle and quickly rolled her eyes. "I feel dumb. I just know Scott's up to no good. I learned...things.

I've informed the police, and they're coordinating with investigators in another jurisdiction, but it's not like he's in custody yet. So, when I saw him on the street a few minutes ago, I freaked out. I was worried he might've suspected I tipped off the cops, so I booked it."

Could this have something to do with the headlines I'd seen about CineStream's acquisition of Fledgling Studios?

I tapped a finger over my lips. "You think he might've had something to do with Meghan's ..." Unable to fathom the grief she must've experienced, I couldn't muster words like *death* or *murder* in her presence.

She fidgeted with the tag on her towel by looping it around her pinky finger. "I think so."

"But what motive would he have had to ..." I couldn't find the strength to utter the word *kill*. "I mean, from my understanding, Scott was in a position of power. If he wanted to cause Meghan harm, wouldn't passing on her for *In Stitches* have been enough?"

Her breathing had finally slowed to a normal pace. "You'd think. But this...this cut deeper." She took another sip from her drink.

Ava sat up straighter to my left. "Why? Did it not go over well with him?"

She didn't make eye contact with either of us. "No. Quite the opposite—from a career standpoint, at least. He was quite interested in casting Meg on the show, especially with her recent success in online book communities. He thought her niche in literary comedy might bring an interesting dimension to the show."

"So, why do you think it was too good to be true?" Ava asked.

Her breath caught in her throat. "I think he had other reasons to come see Meg perform. He could've cast her based on the hours of footage available online. I don't think Scott's interest in her set was authentic."

"Really? Why would he sign someone he had doubts about?"

She took a swig from her martini glass in one hand and covered her eyes with the other, clearly worked up. "It's not about what he had to gain—it's about what he stood to lose. I think he was under duress."

I cradled my chin in one hand. "Duress? But how? Wasn't he the decision maker?"

Tiffany sighed deeply. "I figured out Meg had been blackmailing him."

My jaw dropped.

Between the alcohol and the relaxed atmosphere, it wasn't the first time secrets had been spilled in Subplot. The old adage that people tended to tell their bartenders everything once again proved itself to be true.

She pressed her lips together and nodded. "I think he turned on her to guarantee his secret would never get out."

FIFTEEN

"Blackmailing him? About what?" If it was true, Meghan must've had some nerve. Blackmail was risky and illegal. If she'd been found out, she could've lost her career. Had it also cost her her life?

Tiffany shook her head. "I don't even know where to begin." She put her martini down and gulped the rest of her water. "Could I please have some more?"

"Sure thing," I said.

"I got it," Ava whispered to me. She rose from the couch and took the glass from Tiffany.

I continued the conversation as Ava retreated behind the bar. "If she blackmailed him, then when Scott came here for the show, it wouldn't have been the first time they'd been in contact."

My mind echoed back to seeing Scott in the alley before the show. *If this doesn't work out the way it's supposed to, I can kiss my career goodbye.* Had he been referring to something related to his company's acquisition? Or was he referencing a plan to deal with Meghan's blackmail?

With her drink in hand again, she stared forlornly at the

pink-and-blue patterned rug at her feet. "From what I can tell, that's right. As her manager, it is—or was—my responsibility to make connections, but she was extremely well-networked in the entertainment industry in her own right. I created all her social media content, but I never had access to any of her accounts, which I guess isn't all that unusual. It just meant I had less visibility into certain opportunities, like this one with *In Stitches*."

"Was that frustrating for you?" I asked as the *whoosh* of the soda gun behind the bar filled the awkward silence which followed.

"It could be if we weren't on the same page. The real issue here wasn't that I was out of the loop about Scott. The problem was that she blackmailed him. She committed a serious crime and expected me to help clean up the mess? What was she thinking?"

Ava returned with a fresh glass of water and set it down on the coffee table.

"Did it ever make you consider dropping Meghan as a client?" I asked.

She wrinkled her forehead in a dumbfounded expression as she grasped the glass. "I don't know. We'd worked so hard to build Meg's career. And with Scott in attendance, our hard work was about to pay off. She was about to get her big break, and I was excited for her. But learning it was for the wrong reasons— it was a tough pill to swallow. It all happened so fast, and she was gone before I could even think about her future as my client."

Ava sat beside me on the plush couch in her original spot.

I raised one leg to cross an ankle over my other knee. "How did you take the news when you learned she was blackmailing him? I mean, that's a huge deal—especially with the acquisition. He works for a major, powerful corporation now."

Tiffany shifted around in her chair as if she couldn't get comfortable. "I'm kicking myself because I should've done something about it. I mean, her career wasn't the only one at stake. If the news came out that she'd blackmailed an entertainment exec, it wouldn't have been a good look for me, either. But I barely had time to react. She told me shortly before her performance on Sunday. When Scott arrived, she got all nervous. She said if anything happened to her, it'd be because of him. I didn't know what to do." That probably explained the tension I'd sensed between the two of them before Meghan took the stage.

I nodded along, though I didn't feel satisfied with the details she shared. "But if she'd blackmailed him in the first place, why was she so afraid? She took a huge risk. People get defensive with their secrets—especially when they're at risk of getting out. Didn't she know what she was getting into?"

Tiffany took a long sip from her martini. "I guess she felt like she no longer had the upper hand. She didn't go into specifics. I don't think I realized the extent of the danger she was in, but if I could go back in time, I would've intervened somehow."

"What did she blackmail him over?" Ava asked.

Tiffany huffed. "I really shouldn't say." Her anxious body language—fiddling with the towel in her lap, constantly shifting positions in her chair, her eyes darting around the room—seemed to signal she didn't want to keep the information to herself. "But...have you seen the news about CineStream's recent acquisition of Fledgling Studios?" She drank her cocktail faster, as if it might make sharing more information okay.

Aha! I knew it had to be connected somehow. "It sounds vaguely familiar," I lied. "I think I saw a headline during my morning news scroll."

She rested her water glass on the coffee table between us. "I don't know all the details or how Meg dug up this dirt, but she somehow learned Scott was privy to sensitive information related to the company's acquisition. Apparently, he'd shared it within his network before the news was public knowledge, giving some of his associates an unfair advantage."

"Wait, so Meghan had intel that Scott was insider trading? That's a very serious accusation. People go to jail for that." Based on the headline I'd seen this morning, it appeared he already had colleagues under fire. Though Scott hadn't been named in the newspaper article, was there a possibility he'd acted unethically?

She ran both hands up and down the wooden armrests of her chair over and over again. "I know it is. And Scott obviously knew it, too. When Meghan put the pieces together, she tried to use the intel to advance her career."

"So, you think Meghan accused him of insider trading and said, 'Put me on *In Stitches* or your secret gets out?'"

"Essentially. Unfortunately, I didn't get much detail from Meg. We talked about it while the opening act performed, so we didn't have much time to chat between the time her show ended and ...' I felt sure she would've referred to the end of Meghan's life if she'd been able to finish her sentence.

"Do you know why Meghan waited so long to share this with you?" I asked.

"I can think of a bunch of reasons. Because she was worried about how I'd react. Because she was committing a crime. And because she was terrified of Scott."

"But she could've avoided this situation altogether by not blackmailing him in the first place," Ava chimed in.

She chuckled numbly. "Yes, but she was impulsive. Thinking through consequences? She didn't act with that kind of foresight. She knew what she wanted, and she had her eye on the prize. I think she thought she had Scott exactly where she wanted him. I don't think she considered the great lengths he might go to keep his secret from getting out. I wish she thought things through more before she acted."

"How do you think it...ended?"

She pinched the bridge of her nose. "I'm kicking myself. I shouldn't have let her out of my sight, knowing how afraid she was. After we left the lounge to go back to our hotel, she didn't text or call to say anything strange was up. But at that point, we were already on rocky terms. I mean, how did she think she could blackmail someone so powerful and get away with it? I think she snuck out to meet Scott for a conversation, and he killed her to keep his secret from getting out. That's why I'm so afraid of him finding me. I alerted the police *and* I know his secret. I'm worried he might kill me to keep me silent, too."

"But if Meghan was so afraid of Scott that she came clean with you about blackmailing him right before her show, I have a hard time believing she'd willingly meet up with him later." There were gaps in Tiffany's story, and I couldn't figure out if she was lying or if she was as baffled as I was. Perhaps she was trying to piece together what had happened with the limited information she had.

She furrowed her brow as though she pensively considered my doubt. "The sad thing is we may never truly know what happened, although I keep playing out every scenario I can imagine. Maybe Scott's enthusiasm about her set gave her an illusion of safety. If she got what she wanted, then maybe she thought they were even. I can't imagine Scott would've been content with his secret being known, though."

She had a point. Blackmail was a slippery slope, especially when it came to secrets. Even if both parties upheld their end of the bargain, the collateral—Meghan's knowledge of his insider trading—couldn't be magically wiped from her brain.

"Did you have a chance to speak with her about it after the show?"

Her breath began to shake. "No, I didn't. I was fuming and, honestly, kind of freaking out about what she'd done. I couldn't be near her. She went to her hotel, and I went to mine."

"You weren't staying at the same place?"

She sighed. "No. I put Meg up at The Flora House." It was a luxury hotel along the riverfront—a few minutes south of Hope Mills' main business district by foot. "I booked the last open room I could find downtown, and it was the nearest available hotel I could find. I figured I'd let her have the nicer room. Even though it seemed like Scott was going to give her a spot on *In Stitches*, I was sick to my stomach thinking about how every-thing could blow up if Meg ever got caught. But then with what happened the next morning...it haunts me."

If Meghan and Scott had a confrontation which led to her demise, had she told him that she filled Tiffany in? I hoped not. If so, she could be in danger as well.

I felt minor comfort in knowing she was in contact with the police, but I couldn't bring myself to rest until the killer had been found and brought to justice.

As nervous as I felt about the situation, I hoped I could track down Scott.

But there was just one problem. If Scott knew Tiffany was aware of his white-collar crime and found out she'd shared it with me, my safety could also be on the line.

SIXTEEN

"That was bizarre," Ava commented as soon as the heavy metal door slammed shut.

I strode back toward my laptop at the bar, ready to check my inventory spreadsheet against our stock in the back room before I placed any liquor orders. "You think? It seemed like she was grieving."

She nodded. "Oh, absolutely. But her visit was pretty random. What was the point of coming here?"

"I forgot to mention that I texted her earlier. She's been through a lot, and I thought she might've wanted to get out of her hotel room and step away from reality for a while. I wasn't expecting her to open up so much, though."

"Liquor sure does have a way of pulling out the truth." Ava's eyes drifted toward the door, and she tapped her lips with her fingertips. "I hope she didn't run into the heckler out there."

I raised an index finger. "Oh, right. You saw her lurking in the alley earlier. Do you think I should check?"

Ava grimaced. "It was quite some time ago, but it couldn't hurt."

I headed to the exit and poked my head out into the humid

air, which felt like dunking my face into a bowl of soup. I scanned the alley for a few seconds before stepping back inside and allowing the door to shut on its own. "No sign of either of them."

"Maybe I'm just being paranoid." She shrugged. "All right, time for more experimenting. Back behind the bar I go."

I grabbed my laptop off the bar and danced into the stockroom as "I Want To Come Over" by Melissa Etheridge played over the speakers throughout the lounge. From Shania Twain to Fiona Apple, my mom listened to a broad span of female singer-songwriters of the nineties in the car when I was growing up. Between rides to school, running errands around town, and our day trips to Philadelphia when my dad worked weekends, her Lilith Fair music crept into my psyche and never left. I could get down to some Sarah McLachlan, and luckily, Ava could, too.

I took note of shelves where quantities were dwindling, both for our house spirits as well as specialty liquors that were much more difficult to procure, and recorded them in my spreadsheet.

My phone vibrated in my pocket as I slid bottles across the stockroom shelves. I pulled it out, and my heart skipped a beat when the screen illuminated. A text from Julian Garcia.

> Hey, man. Good to see you yesterday. Want to swing by the store tomorrow after close to chat about my idea?

Did I want to? Absolutely, I did. Was I terrified? Yes. Yes, I was.

I felt incredibly attracted to Julian, and I feared I might mess things up. I wanted him to like me in return. I worried I'd say the wrong thing and scare him away. But even if I managed to not screw things up, was I ready to even *think* about dating again? Was it too soon after coming out? Would my previous engagement be too much baggage for a potential partner to bear?

My heart pounded like a kick drum in my chest, and I trembled as my thumbs hovered over the screen to type a response. *You're getting way ahead of yourself here. Take it one step at a time.*

> Hey, good to see you too. Let's do it. I'm free tomorrow night

I darkened the screen and returned my phone to my pocket right away, too nervous to anticipate his response. Out of sight, out of mind.

When I returned to the bar, Ava finished shaking a beverage and poured the light green mixture into a tall, skinny glass.

"Another Frankenstein's Monster?" I asked.

"I need to get the recipe just right." She planted a bendy purple straw into the glass and took a sip of the mocktail. "Ah, now that's better. Much more balanced. Want a taste?" She slid the glass toward me and jotted a few notes in her mixology journal, which lay open in front of her on the bar.

I took a sip from the glass's rim. "I can taste the earthiness of the matcha, but it's subtle. The sweetness of the pear really shines, and the coconut milk ties it all together. This is fantastic! You have a golden palate, as far as I'm concerned. I couldn't ask for a better person to help design our menu."

She waved me off. "Aw, shucks. Don't make me blush."

I rested my forearms on the front edge of the bar and leaned on it. "Not to change the subject, but taking stock of our bottles got me thinking...how are things going with Logan?"

Ava's boyfriend Logan owned Delaware Crossing Distilling Company—also known as DCDC—one of our local liquor suppliers.

She blushed for real and fought the grin growing on her face. "Things are going very, very well. He's the sweetest, kindest, most caring guy I've ever been with. We're going out for sushi tonight in town. I have to remind myself we've been dating for several months because every single time I see him, I get butterflies. I never want them to go away. He has this magical way of sweeping me off my feet. Am I rambling too much? See, when I talk about him I get all giddy and can't stop going on and on." She covered her mouth.

"Sounds like someone's falling in—"

"Don't say it!'

I laughed, allowing my shoulders to bounce. It warmed my heart to see Ava get excited about Logan. Originally, she'd wanted to keep her relationship hidden. In addition to her role as a mixologist, she also had aspirations to begin distilling, and Logan had been showing her the ropes. However, she was initially fearful that their relationship might make it look like she was riding on his coattails. Unfortunately, women in mixology often didn't receive the same respect as their male counterparts. But knowing her exquisite palette, I knew she could make a name for herself in the industry regardless of their relationship. I was glad to see she'd let love win and was allowing her relationship to be known. Her happiness was paramount to what anyone else might think about it.

She crossed her arms and smirked. "I'd say we're long overdue for an update on your love life."

I should've known my light teasing would come back to haunt me. I shifted my gaze in multiple directions, as if searching for something I'd misplaced. "Love life? I don't have one of those."

I never used to talk about my personal life at work, but that started to change after I'd come out to Ava. Now that everyone in my life knew I was gay, I didn't feel like I had anything to hide in that regard. But with my hesitation about dating in general, it wasn't a topic I felt comfortable talking about—except maybe with Nate.

"You don't have your eye on anyone?"

"No, I don't," I answered, as if by instinct. As soon as the words left my mouth, my phone buzzed in my pocket, a reminder of the certain someone I *did* have my eyes on. Julian. But I wasn't ready to clue Ava in. I trusted her good intentions, but she had a way of persuading me to share more than I wanted to. "I'm really just trying to focus on the lounge right now and paying off my business loans. It's been a busy year with a lot of change, so I'm not looking. I was with Chloe for seven years, so I'm taking some time to be single." It was my convenient, rehearsed response to the question.

In many ways, opening Subplot had been my outlet after breaking up with Chloe and as I came out. While it continued to serve as a great decoy to draw attention away from my personal life, I'd become more self-aware of the reasons why the thought of dating made me so uneasy. Dating men was uncharted territory for me. I could blame timing and being busy all I wanted, but at the heart of the matter, I was afraid of exploring that part of myself. I feared that dating might reveal some hard truths I wasn't ready to face. As sure as I felt about being gay, I worried I might discover that being with another man wasn't what I actually wanted. And if that were the case, would it mean my breakup with Chloe had been in vain? Perhaps I was only making excuses for being afraid to let my guard down and try something new.

Ava sighed. "All right, I'll take your word for it, then."

I hoped she didn't have any suspicions about my crush on Julian. He'd come into the lounge several times with friends since I first met him a few months ago. Any time they were seated at the bar or at a section I was responsible for serving, my nerves always got the best of me, requiring me to focus all of my attention on not acting awkward—and often ending up with me acting awkward.

Luckily, she let the conversation fizzle out there.

As nonchalantly as I could, I reached for my phone to read the message I'd received as we talked.

> Awesome. The store closes at 7 tomorrow, if that works for you

> Perfect! See you then. Looking forward to hearing your idea

I continued working at the lounge for another couple of hours, completing the liquor and ingredient orders I needed to place on my laptop, and later hopped behind the bar alongside Ava to experiment with fall cocktails myself. I tried to block out my anxious feelings about meeting up with Julian. Was it wrong to collaborate on business projects if I was harboring feelings of attraction? What if he didn't feel the same way about me? Or even worse—if he *did* like me back, what if I accidentally made things weird and scared him away?

Luckily, being behind the bar eased my mind. It was my favorite escape—a safe place for me to go when I didn't want to face my feelings. Though I always put pressure on myself to craft the next bestselling drink on the menu, there was something freeing about experimenting with flavor. When I gave myself permission to experiment and occasionally have some flops, I gave myself the space to create something new and exciting. If I didn't take risks, I'd never stumble upon something great.

It also made me feel connected to my dad, who was a renowned, award-winning mixologist himself. He'd once traveled to Italy to compete in the Martini Grand Prix, an international cocktail competition. His dedication to the craft inspired me to follow in his footsteps, and so I began bartending and experimenting with cocktail recipes as soon as I'd turned twenty-one.

Today, I formulated a hickory-smoked maple Old Fashioned, which I planned to add to our fall menu when it launched in September.

I poured a shot of rye whiskey into a glass and placed a cocktail smoker top snugly over its rim. The attachment looked like a small, thick plate, but it contained a smoking chamber, vented at the bottom to allow smoke into the glass. I scooped hickory wood chips into it and lit them on fire with a blowtorch. A cloud of smoke plummeted into the glass, which would infuse the rye with a smoky, hickory flavor. I placed a lid over the smoker to trap the smoke inside. The lounge smelled like a delicious campfire on a chilly fall day, making me yearn for mountain pies and rosemary beef stew.

When experimenting, I was meticulous about writing down every step and measurement in a notebook as I went to ensure I'd never forget what I did. Doing so made it easy to tweak the recipe to get it just right. My biggest fear was making a great discovery I couldn't replicate.

After allowing the rye to smoke for four minutes, I added a local farm's fresh maple syrup to the glass along with housemade Angostura and orange bitters. I stirred the ingredients together, then poured the liquid over a large ice cube in a separate rocks glass, and garnished the drink with a twisted sliver of orange peel.

I was planning to title the drink Sappy Place, fusing a syrup pun with the title of Emily Henry's novel *Happy Place*. Taking a sip, the cocktail's sweet smokiness warmed me up from the inside, almost making me forget it was a hundred degrees outside. Fall couldn't come soon enough.

After jotting down the final recipe and cleaning up after

myself, I packed up my belongings, ready to head home and relax for a while.

I let Ava know I was heading out and told her not to work too hard. She told me to be safe in return and said she was planning to finish up shortly before going home to get ready for her sushi date with Logan.

As soon as the door slammed shut behind me, I tugged on the hot metal handle to confirm no one from outside could get in.

Footsteps rustled nearby.

I spun around. "Hello?" I held my breath.

No response.

I took a few steps forward, scanning the alley from left to right.

As I approached the dumpster, I peered around the corner, once again haunted by a flashback to the dead body I'd found in that area months before.

A woman crouched beside it. Although she was dressed casually in a cropped white tank top and gray shorts with her long, straight brown hair tied up into a messy bun, I recognized her.

The heckler. Kari.

My jaw tensed as I clenched my teeth together. "What are you doing here?"

She sprung up and darted away without a word.

"Hey!" I projected my voice down the alley. "Come back here. Don't run away."

She hustled toward the sidewalk which led to Main Street.

"Kari." I didn't shout, but the sound of her name was enough to make her freeze in her tracks.

She gasped. "How'd you know my name?"

"Sources." I couldn't reveal I'd learned her name from

David. And I certainly couldn't let her realize I was trying to learn all I could about Meghan's murder.

She turned her back toward me and continued to jog away.

"Please, let's talk," I called out to her.

"Why should I?"

"I know your name, and I'm in touch with the police. I'll tell the detective you're acting suspicious."

She froze again, turned around, and paced slowly toward me.

SEVENTEEN

"I swear I didn't mean any harm." She raised both hands as if to show she was unarmed. "Please, I beg you. Don't mention anything to the detective."

Clearly, my warning about informing Detective Sharp worked. I hoped it would also give me leverage to ask questions and learn more.

"Why are you hanging out back here?"

The alley's gravel crunched at her feet as she took a few more cautious steps toward me. "What day of the week does your trash company empty the dumpster?"

"Monday mornings." I furrowed my brow, both confused and annoyed she'd answered my question with an unrelated question of her own. "Should I ask why that's relevant?"

Her posture deflated. Her messy bun bounced as her gaze fell to the ground. "Dang it! It's gone!" She pressed both hands to the sides of her head. "It can't be."

"What's gone?"

"It can't be lost forever. Maybe it was stolen." Her words of denial were punctuated with quick, choppy breaths.

I took a step closer to her so I could speak in a calmer, softer voice and still be heard. I wanted to prove I was approachable and willing to help. "What are you looking for? If you tell me, I can do my best to help you find it."

"It's no use." She let out a deep, frustrated sigh. "I had a small pocket journal with me at the comedy show. There was some important, very personal, very private information written inside."

I recalled rearranging the furniture with Nate and cleaning up that night after everyone had left. "Maybe one of my teammates found it and put it in our lost and found. I can check now to see if it's there. What color was it?" Knowing Nate's pocketknife had also gone missing that night and ended up at the crime scene, I didn't have high hopes. It seemed as though someone had been swiping other people's belongings to complicate the investigation.

"Could you please?" she replied without missing a beat. "It has a black cardboard cover. There's a sticker of a pink rose on one side."

I backtracked to the door, keeping an eye on Kari and hoping she wouldn't use the opportunity to dart off without continuing our conversation.

I slipped the carabiner out of my pocket and found the silver key in a blue cover to unlock the door. I poked my head inside.

"Did you forget something?" Ava called out from behind the bar.

"No, but I'm checking on something for a customer."

"Is it the heckler? Is she back?" she whispered as loud as she could.

I gave a quick nod and formed my lips into a shushing shape, not wanting Kari to overhear us. "Did you see a little pocket-sized notebook anywhere in the lounge after the comedy show? It's black with a pink rose sticker on it."

Ava's eyes danced around the lounge. "Not that I remember. Maybe Lainey or Dante found it. Let me check the office."

While I waited for Ava, I turned back to Kari to let her know she was searching for it.

A few minutes later, Ava returned to the bar area, empty-handed with palms out. "Sorry, no luck."

I thanked her and stepped backwards into the alley, allowing the weighted door to shut on its own. I tugged on the handle to ensure it was locked before stepping closer to Kari. "I'm sorry, but my colleague just checked our lost and found, and it unfortunately wasn't there."

Her eyes blinked rapidly. "Great. Just my luck." She exhaled an audible breath.

"I won't pry about what's inside—you said it was personal —but do you think there was reason someone might have stolen it? In my experience, people are pretty honest, especially in Hope Mills."

Her face went slack. "There was literally a murder here a couple of days ago. I have my suspicions there are some people around here who aren't exactly a shining example of integrity."

Touché. She wasn't a shining example of poise herself, given her little outburst during the comedy show.

What could've been written inside the journal? If she'd been willing to dumpster dive for it, it must've been important—and potentially relevant to the case. Had she been keeping tabs on Meghan's every move? Had she plotted out a plan for murder? Did the notebook even belong to Kari, or was she trying to locate someone else's? Though I had no way of knowing what it contained, I felt determined to find it. If I did, I could catch a peek at whatever was inside and maybe get closer to solving Meghan's murder.

"I know I look super sketchy right now, especially considering what happened to Meg, but I swear me being here right now has nothing to do with her," Kari said. I found it strange that she called the comedian by her abbreviated name. I'd only heard Tiffany and David—people she'd been close to—call her that. "I want my journal back. That's it."

"You're the person who heckled her in the middle of her set, aren't you?"

Kari's breathing quickened again.

Please don't hyperventilate. The last thing I needed was to have to take care of her or call in a medical emergency when I'd been warned not to meddle in the police's investigation.

"Yes." She covered her face with her hands. "And I know that makes me look even worse. What do you want from me? I'll do anything. Just please don't say anything about this to the police."

Though I couldn't make any promises not to share details with the police, I was glad to have the upper hand when it came to speaking with her.

"What compelled you to call her out in the middle of her show?"

She sighed. "I'm not proud of it. I wish I could take it back. But in the moment, I couldn't help myself."

"Why, though? Something must've set you off."

She crossed her arms and rolled her eyes. "It's not that deep. I just wanted to get a rise out of her. That's all."

I didn't find her nonchalance to be very convincing, especially considering how Meghan's story eventually ended. Plus, knowing Meghan had stolen her bit about not knowing how to swim, I had a feeling Kari's interruption was real and personal, especially since it came right after the joke in question.

"Getting back to the journal, if you think someone could have stolen it, do you have any ideas of who might've been responsible? Maybe my team or I saw something. I can ask around."

"I have a couple of ideas. There was this bigshot from a major streaming service at the show."

If Tiffany's claim about Meghan blackmailing Scott was true, could the notebook have contained dirt on her? Maybe he used it to bargain with her. If that were the case, though, how had he gotten his hands on it? Did he somehow grab it when the two of them talked after the show?

"Oh, yeah. I thought I saw the two of you talking afterwards." I made no mention of how strange the interaction was, given Kari's interruption.

Her eyes bulged. "You did? How'd you know who he was?"

"Meghan and her manager briefed me about a talent executive attending the show, and he looked the part—all dressed up in this summer heat. Did he mention anything about Meghan? Do you know if he was planning to move forward with her?"

Her lips tightened briefly. "He's a tough nut to crack. It sounded like he planned to advance her, but he didn't seem thrilled about it."

"Really? How so?"

"Well, if you were looking for America's next top comedian, and you watched a set so incredible you wanted to make a deal to cast them for your show, don't you think you'd be excited?"

It took a lot of suspension of disbelief to put myself in Scott's shoes. "I guess so. You didn't think he was?"

"Not at all."

"I'm sure everyone would act differently. Plus, this is his job. Maybe he was having a rough day."

Kari clenched both of her hands, clearly passionate about what she was saying. "It'd be like striking gold. But instead, he seemed kind of bored. Or maybe preoccupied. It was almost like he was obligated to move her to the next round. A check of a box, shall we say?"

If she sensed obligation on his part, it aligned with Tiffany's revelation. Regardless, Scott's interest in Meghan gave Kari an even stronger motive if her jealousy related to the stolen joke had taken over.

"Why do you think he'd want to steal your journal, though?"

She flicked her wrist. "Oh, you know… Reasons."

Sensing her unwillingness to elaborate, theories about the journal raced through my mind. Was there damning information about Meghan inside? Was the missing journal a farce meant to distract me?

"No, but really. Why would a casting director have any motive to take your journal?" I pressed again, not satisfied with her non-answer.

Her dark brown eyes darted in all directions. "Because there was information inside, okay? Important information. I've already said too much." She couldn't look at me directly. Did the so-called important info in the journal incriminate Kari?

I slicked a hand over the top of my freshly cut short hair. "If not him, who else do you think might've taken it?"

"Maybe Meg's manager."

If she suspected Scott or Tiffany of taking the journal, what could've been written inside that would've been of interest to both of them?

"Her manager was here not long ago, actually."

She blinked hard. "She was?" I took her question as confirmation that they hadn't bumped into each other in the alley after Tiffany left the lounge.

I nodded but didn't provide any additional context. "I saw you chatting with her after the show, too."

"You were really keeping tabs on me, huh?"

"You interrupted the show. I had to make sure things didn't get out of hand."

Kari let out a small chuckle. "Well, funny enough, her

manager Tiffany didn't seem too happy about Meg as her client. I sensed a lot of anger on her part."

I found it interesting that the two people she suspected of stealing her notebook were people she spoke with after the show—though it offered a possible explanation for how they'd taken possession of it. Given her rude interruption, I was shocked either of them had anything to do with her. Unless her journal contained coveted information. I wondered if one of them had stolen the notebook or if Kari had given it away freely, perhaps as a form of sabotage. If that were the case, maybe she was trying to track it down, fearful it might be entered as evidence into the investigation.

I bit my lip and chose my next words carefully. "I'll admit I sensed a bit of frustration between them, but it seemed like Tiffany was genuinely invested in growing Meghan's career."

"True, but everyone has a breaking point."

"And if the casting exec had shown interest in having Meghan on the comedy competition, I'd think Tiffany would've been buzzing with excitement."

She wagged a finger at me. "That's my point exactly. The fact she wasn't made me think the vibes were way off. So, I pried a little. Turns out, Tiffany was contemplating bailing on Meg as a client. After Scott expressed interest, though, she felt like she had too much to lose in her career. Regardless of her feelings about Meg, it was her meal ticket to becoming an established talent manager."

"I'm going to go out on a limb here, but something just dawned on me."

Kari squinted. Either the bright sun was getting in her eyes, or she was eagerly anticipating what I'd say next.

"When we were planning our Comedy and Cocktails night, I swear my team watched video clips from every up-and-coming comedian in the Philadelphia metro area. I had a feeling you looked familiar. Did you ever do standup of your own, by chance?"

She took a step back. "I did…"

"Have you ever dealt with a heckler in the crowd?"

She rolled her eyes. "Yes, of course."

"And how does it feel?"

"It's the worst. You have to scramble to say something back while not allowing the interruption to throw off the pace of the entire rest of the set. It can totally kill the energy."

"So, if you know how it feels, then you knew what you were doing to Meghan. Did you come to her show to sabotage her?"

Thinking about Kari's conversation with Scott after the show, I wondered if she'd had a clue he might be there. Did she see it as her golden opportunity to throw Meghan off and disrupt her career?

"No." She started to speak a few times but stopped herself before finally saying, "It was to help her."

"*Help her?*" I blurted out. "But you just admitted a disruption like that could throw off the entire flow."

"I know, but"—she glanced around in all directions and lowered her voice—"Meg put me up to it."

Had Ava and Lainey's theory been correct?

"She put you up to it? How so?" I asked in my normal speaking volume.

"*Shh!*" She held an index finger to her lips. "No one knows—not even Tiffany. I knew Meg from the comedy community, and we'd stayed in touch. We always had each other's backs, even though we had some friendly competition going on. She knew Scott was coming to the show, and she wanted to show she could think quickly on her feet. Have you ever seen one of those comedy competition shows?"

I shook my head, as I rarely watched TV, let alone the shows she referred to.

"Each episode, there's a challenge. For example, in one episode, the contestants are challenged to put together an entire new bit within certain parameters and perform it the same day. In another, they'll plant a heckler in the crowd to see which comedian handles it the best. Meghan thought if she could effectively handle a heckler, it might give her an upper hand with Scott. I'd say it worked."

Even if Tiffany hadn't known their plan, maybe she was aware of Meghan's acquaintance with Kari. But in that case, wouldn't she have assumed it was planned?

Meghan had done a great job of getting the crowd back on her side, even garnering a standing ovation.

While I was still skeptical, the only thing that made me consider she might be telling the truth was how convinced Lainey and Ava had been that her heckling was scripted.

"So, you're saying you and Meghan were...friends?"

She nodded quickly. Although she appeared confident on the surface, her eagerness made me wonder if it was a cover-up. "We were, but for obvious reasons, I had to pretend otherwise."

I sucked in my lips. "Hmm..." Kari had referred to her as *Meg* rather than *Meghan,* a trait that both Tiffany and David exhibited—the two people I knew she'd had personal relationships with.

She crossed her arms. "I can prove it. How else would I know that Meg's ex-boyfriend—the one she obliterated during her set—was in the crowd."

"He was?" I feigned ignorance.

She gave another assured nod with her eyes closed. "Tall guy. Athletic build. Blond hair that's on the darker side. He looked like he just stepped off the golf course and had a baseball cap on."

I wrinkled my forehead. "Maybe..."

"Well, he was always around back in the day when Meg and

I performed open mic nights together. I never cared for him. He avoided me like the plague last night. I'm sure he's painting me in a bad light to the police. That's probably why they're on my case."

"And not because of the heckling?"

She scoffed. "I wouldn't have gone through with the plan if I knew she was going to turn up dead!" She lowered her voice. "Anyway, as I was leaving the comedy show, he was on the phone a couple of doors down from the Italian restaurant above your lounge. I couldn't make out everything he said, but I heard him say something like, 'Everything will be fine once we get her out of the picture.' Of course, at the time I didn't know who he was talking about or what he meant. But once I learned Meg was found dead, his comment haunted me."

I didn't need to fake a shocked reaction. I'm sure my mouth fell open on its own. "Did he see you?"

"Yep. Which is why I'm certain he's doubling down on his smear campaign against me. I have no doubts he's trying to deflect blame."

Everything will be fine once we get her out of the picture. The sentence echoed in my mind.

Who was the *we* David referred to? Was he collaborating with another suspect to kill Meghan? Or was it possible that statement had nothing to do with Meghan at all? *Her* could've been any woman. Had he been talking about getting revenge on Kari?

My mind raced with all the possibilities, though none of them helped me arrive any closer to the truth. She seemed to point fingers in every direction. Was it all a zealous attempt to deflect blame?

I had major doubts about some of the info she'd shared. I struggled to believe Meghan and Kari could've colluded if David was telling the truth about the joke Meghan stole. Unless that was coordinated, too. But what did he have to gain by lying about that?

Plus, what was in the coveted notebook she was willing to dumpster dive for? And why didn't she name David as someone who could've taken her notebook?

Kari had claimed thinking on one's feet was a hallmark of a great comedian. Had everything we'd just discussed in the alley been one long improv act?

EIGHTEEN

I wrapped up my workday at Subplot shortly after my conversation with Kari.

Realizing I hadn't seen Nate since the morning he'd discovered Meghan's body, I sent him a text.

> Hey man, how you holding up?

Though I was wrapped up in solving her murder to help prove Nate couldn't have been involved, I felt horrible that I hadn't been proactively checking in on my friend.

He answered within seconds. Given the unpredictable nature of his job, he almost always kept his notification sounds on so he wouldn't miss a client's urgent message or call.

> Hey, I'm doing alright. Hanging in. You?

Even via text, he didn't seem like his usual playful, vibrant self. He tended to use a lot of emojis and offered random local tidbits. It wasn't uncommon for him to respond with something like, *You'll never guess what I heard at the hardware store.*

Same here, all things considered. Are you free tonight?

I don't have any plans. Want to grab a drink?

Yea, let's do it! How about Bridge Street?

In addition to checking in on Nate, going to Bridge Street Bar might present an opportunity to learn something new about the case, since Garrett had gone there after the comedy show.

Sounds like a plan. Let's aim for 8?

Perfect

~

The bar was a punk-inspired dive a few buildings past the intersection of Bridge and Main Streets. In the opposite direction, a bright green truss bridge with two lanes for cars and a third for pedestrians spanned about a fifth of a mile across the Delaware River. It connected Hope Mills with its equally cool sister town of Lambertdale, New Jersey on the other side, which hosted its own share of attractions and festivals.

When I arrived at the bar by foot, I could hear the pounding drums and slamming guitars of an early-2000s punk rock song pouring outside. After showing the bouncer my ID, I scanned the dimly lit hole-in-the-wall for Nate. Exposed ductwork hung from the rust-tinged tin-tiled ceiling, and most of the red-cushioned barstools along the front of the glossy mahogany bar were taken.

As I squinted, a waving hand at the far end of the bar caught my eye. Then, noticing Nate's bald head, I gave him an acknowledging nod.

"I saved you a seat." Even though he spoke in a lower, softer tone and didn't spring to his feet like he usually would, he still stood up so we could exchange our customary high five, handshake, and one-armed hug combo.

After perching myself on a stool and ordering a crisp tropical IPA, we made brief small talk about Nate's exhausting day building a deck in the excruciating heat before our conversation inevitably drifted to talk about the elephant in the room. Nate was usually a chill guy, especially after a long day of physical labor. But the way he picked at the label of his Mexican beer showed me he was rattled. Understandably so.

"I heard your pocketknife was found at the crime scene."

Nate hung his head. "Who would have done such a thing? I'm sure whoever swiped it at Subplot saw an opportunity to complicate the case and make someone else look suspicious. But then for me to find her body?"

I sipped my beer with bright notes of mango and pineapple, which brought me a small flicker of light as a dark cloud loomed over our conversation. "Are the police giving you a hard time?"

"Dude. I was at the station for *hours* yesterday between waiting around and answering all their questions. They can see pretty clearly that I had no contact with Meghan prior to Sunday. And outside of the show, I didn't really interact with her at all. I know they've got to do their due diligence and explore every possibility, but this sucks." He shook his head and stared straight ahead.

"They can't seriously think you had anything to do with this, right?"

"I don't...think so?" He shrugged. "But enough about me."

"No. Not enough about you. This is important, and I want to make sure you're alright."

He took a swig from his beer bottle. "I'm fine. I promise."

I fought the urge to ask, *Are you sure?*

Nate loved to comfort others, but he struggled to let others do the same for him.

"Seriously, let's talk about something lighter. How are you? I feel like you haven't given me any personal updates in a while. Any coals in the fire, if you know what I mean?" As soon as he'd volleyed the ball of conversation to my court, his tone was suddenly lighter. He nudged my ribcage with a friendly elbow.

"Nah, I'm not seeing anyone." I took a long sip from my glass.

"Are you *interested* in seeing anyone?"

"Well..." Though I hadn't told Nate about my crush on Julian yet, anxiety was slowly building in my chest as I remembered I'd committed to visit Ampersand in less than twenty-four hours to discuss his idea.

He smirked. "Well...?"

"There might be a certain business owner in town."

Nate's face lit up. The whites surrounding his pale blue eyes grew wide. Any hint of his somberness had evaporated. "Who is it? Do I know him?"

"Shh!" I clenched my eyes shut, immediately regretting my shushing. "Sorry. That was rude. I just don't want anyone to hear us."

Nate gestured around us. "Everyone's in conversation, and I doubt anyone can hear us over the loud music playing in here."

I sighed. "You know that new-ish bookstore on Main Street? Ampersand?"

He nodded. "Yeah, I do."

"The owner is a guy named Julian. He came to the lounge with some friends a few months ago, and he left his number for me on the receipt." Being in a bar and unwinding with a drink was doing its business on me.

His mouth hung open. Knowing my friend almost as well as I knew myself, I could feel the joy and excitement radiating from him. "What? Why didn't you tell me about this?"

I shrugged. "I was still dealing with the aftermath of the breakup with Chloe."

"Did you text him?"

"I did, but nothing ever panned out. We've been in touch, though. He has an idea for his store to collaborate with Subplot on something, so I'm going over there tomorrow evening to chat about it."

Nate punched my shoulder teasingly. "Oh, come on. Ask him out. What do you have to lose?"

"Uh...everything." The more I thought about Julian, the more excited I got about spending time with him—and thus the stakes got higher. I wanted him to like me just as much as I liked him. I hoped being previously engaged wouldn't be a deal-breaker. I was just beginning to even *think* about dating again, and it felt safer to avoid it altogether, rather than risk getting hurt—or, even worse, hurt someone else the way I'd hurt Chloe.

"Don't you think that's a *little* bit dramatic?" Nate held out his fingers making a pinching gesture.

"Not at all." I suppressed a smirk, knowing he was right. "I knew I should've kept my mouth shut."

"You're telling me he left his phone number for you and you're still doubting whether or not he might be interested?"

I wished we were sitting at a table so I'd have a place to crawl under and hide from Nate's questions. "You never know. Maybe he wanted to network with me."

"Is that what the kids are calling it these days?" Nate poked his tongue into his cheek.

I waved him off. "Oh, stop it. You know what I mean. He's a

new business owner. I'm a new business owner. He runs a bookstore. I run a literary-themed lounge. I'm sure he wants to do some sort of marketing campaign together."

He gave me another friendly jab on the shoulder. "I think you should ask him out," he said again.

I took the last sip from my beer. *That went down much faster than I wanted it to.* Its juicy tropical flavors balanced out its bitterness—a smooth drink perfect for a summer night. As soon as I set the empty glass on the bar, the bartender asked if I wanted another, and I accepted.

"I need to approach this professionally," I told Nate. "If something develops between us eventually, great. But if not, I'll have a new friend in town. Plus, it makes sense that our businesses could cross-promote each other, and I don't want to lose that."

"Just don't close yourself off to the possibility. You never know what might develop, and if you're so resistant to the idea of getting to know him on a deeper level, you could be missing out on something beautiful."

Though Nate had a tendency to go a step too far sometimes when it came to pushing me out of my comfort zone, I knew it always came from a caring place. Plus, he was right. Although I didn't plan to meet up with Julian purely for romantic reasons, I realized I shouldn't be closed off to the opportunity if it arose.

Our discussion naturally steered away from my crush and back to the murder. I filled Nate in on the clues I'd gathered and the conversations I'd had with multiple suspects since we'd last connected.

As soon as I began to recall my run-in with Kari in the alley this afternoon, he chimed in, sounding very sure of himself. "I know for a fact Meghan didn't put the heckler up to it. It had to have been sabotage."

I crossed one arm across my chest, cupping a palm over my

shoulder. "Really? Because I've heard conflicting stories. How can you be so sure?"

Nate lowered his voice. "After the show, I was floating around, mingling with different people while you were making drinks. Kari was chatting with Tiffany at the merch table by the stage. I couldn't hear what they were talking about, but it seemed like Kari showed Tiffany a video of herself on her phone."

"How do you know that's what she was showing her?"

He stroked his red beard. "Well, her phone was turned to the side, first of all. Usually people do that when they're playing a video. And second, I heard Kari say, 'See, that joke was mine. I'm going to spread it far and wide the second I see her on *In Stitches.*'"

I stared down at the bar's glossy dark wood. "Whoa. So it sounds like Kari had proof her joke was stolen. It sounds like reason to sabotage Meghan, but Kari told me they'd planned for her to give her a hard time during the set. She said Meghan wanted to prove her ability to think on her feet to the Cine-Stream executive who was in attendance."

Nate shrugged. "Kari was probably lying. I'm sure she's trying to cover her tracks." He shook his head and let out a *tsk.* "You should've seen the look on Tiffany's face."

"Shocked?"

"Yes, but also angry."

"Kari claimed Tiffany wasn't in on it. The plan was strictly between her and Meghan."

"Of course she'd say that. How convenient that the only other person who was aware of this supposed plan is now dead."

I nodded with my lips pressed firmly together. "You're not wrong."

Kari had been super sketchy lurking around Subplot, after

all. If Meghan had stolen a joke from her, I could see her jealousy getting the best of her, especially since the stolen joke was the one Scott praised the most.

At the opposite end of the bar, raucous laughter cut through the loud alternative music blaring through the speakers. A group of guys stepped through the front door, either already intoxicated or ready to have a wild night.

"Wait... Is that...?" I squinted through the bar's dim light at the group. "I think that's Garrett, the barber."

Nate, never discreet, craned his neck around me. "Dude. It totally is."

"I was hoping we could learn more from the staff here, but I never imagined he'd actually show up."

As we glanced at one another, our bartender shook her head as she leaned on the counter behind her. "Not again." Her voice cut through the music, unapologetic in her distaste.

The young barback, who was crouched beside her as he swapped out a keg under the counter, popped his head up to catch a glimpse at who'd entered the bar. "These guys suck."

She rolled her eyes at Nate and me, making her disapproval clear. "What a bunch of losers."

Nate leaned toward me and whispered from the corner of his mouth. "You'd think a local business owner would be more careful about his reputation in town. He doesn't sound like a very popular guy in this bar."

I locked eyes with the barback as he stood up directly in front of us. "They're regulars, I take it?"

His lips rumbled with an annoyed, forced laugh. "Not if they keep up this obnoxious behavior. I'm keeping an eye on them."

Our bartender took a step forward and leaned on the bar. "The guy with the mullet made me nearly lose my mind the other night." She had to have been talking about Garrett.

"Was it Sunday, by chance?" I asked.

She exhaled exhaustedly, blowing a tuft of her straight blonde hair from her forehead as she did. "Yeah, a couple of nights ago. Why? You know him?"

Nate chuckled casually. "Know *of* him."

"Lucky you." The bartender smirked as if she was pleased by her wit.

I planted an elbow on the bar. "What'd he do to get under your skin?"

"Just being belligerent."

"Did he have a lot to drink?" I asked.

She shrugged. "Eh. Not really. He had maybe three beers before I cut him off. He was getting progressively angrier."

I chuckled admonishingly. "Really? I wonder why."

She flicked her wrist. "Beats me. He was being all vague saying stuff like, 'I'll show her,' and 'She doesn't know what she's talking about,' and 'I'll show her what a real man looks like.' It made me super uncomfortable."

"Hopefully he didn't stick around here for too long," I said.

"He was here for almost two hours. Two *long* hours." The bartender moved on from our conversation, taking orders from other patrons, serving beers, seltzers, and making quick cocktails.

Her recollection lined up with Garrett's claim that he'd left around ten-thirty. Did he actually go home after leaving Bridge Street Bar, or did he continue to drink somewhere else? Was it possible he bumped into Meghan on his way home? Based on the bartender's recollection, it sounded like Garrett got angry when he was drunk. If he'd crossed paths with Meghan after the bar, could he have taken drastic action to get revenge?

Nate glanced at his watch. "I hate to cut this short, but I have another early day tomorrow."

I swallowed the final few sips of beer left in my glass, never as tasty as a fresh pour, and we requested to close out our tabs.

Though I didn't have an early morning the next day, I never liked to have more than a drink or two when I went out.

Garrett stood behind the row of stools in front of the bar toward the entrance. As we strolled toward the exit, he pointed at a man with slicked-back brown hair. It was Scott, who was dressed in a powder-blue sports coat, which he wore over a checkered shirt with a pair of sunglasses dangling over his chest.

"You were at the show, too. I remember. And I saw you in passing at the police station." Garrett's gruff, slightly slurred speech carried over the Blink-182 song playing over the speakers.

Nate gestured toward Garrett with a turn of his head. "I do *not* want to have to talk to this guy. Let's get the heck out of here," he urged me under his breath.

I shifted my eyes toward the bar's exit, but just as I was about to push the glass front door open, Garrett's deep, gravelly voice called out. "Hey, you guys were there the other night, too."

We both froze. In equal measures, I both wanted to get away from Garrett but also see if I could gather any intel from Scott.

I glanced over at Nate. His face had grown red in embarrassment.

Garrett, not knowing when to stop, continued hollering in our direction. "You own that cocktail lounge. And you were just in for a haircut," he said to me. "And you!" he bellowed at Nate. "You think you're so much better than everyone. At least I still have hair on my head."

My heart sped up in my chest.

I didn't let anyone talk to my friends that way.

NINETEEN

"Your insecurity is showing," I said.

Garrett puffed out his chest and took a few steps closer to me along Bridge Street Bar's varnished concrete floors. "Oh, yeah?"

The friends Garrett walked in with were all having a separate conversation around a high-top table which lined the wall opposite of the bar. Were they embarrassed by their friend's behavior? They certainly weren't involving themselves enough to have his back.

Nate tugged the sleeve of my T-shirt. "We're getting out of here. Come on. Let's go." He usually didn't shy away from uncomfortable situations, but knowing how much he hated being at the center of attention, I wasn't surprised by his urgency.

Scott swiveled around on his barstool. "Why don't you just get outta here, man?" At first, I couldn't tell if his comment was aimed at Garrett or me.

I wiped my clammy hands on my shorts, unsure of how to respond.

Garrett pivoted toward him, once again leading with his brawny chest. "You talkin' to me?"

Scott leaned toward him. "Yeah. You." He didn't seem intimidated in the least. "I know you're committed to your part, but the act's up. You can go home now."

Garrett paused and deflated. Was he disappointed that he didn't get the rise out of Scott he'd hoped for?

A second later, he lurched forward, pushing Scott. "You wanna take this outside?" His voice boomed. "Huh? You wanna go outside?"

The bartender charged toward the end of the bar and yelled. "Enough! You're out."

The bouncer from outside must've heard her shout. He raced inside and looked to the bartender for next steps.

Although the loud music continued to play, the rest of the bar grew silent as patrons gawked in our direction to see what would happen next.

She pointed at Garrett. "Him."

The bouncer approached us, towering over us all. He looked down at Garrett. "Are you going to leave on your own, or do you need me to escort you?"

Garrett grunted. Though he'd been acting erratic ever since I'd seen him enter the bar, he must've had some sense left in him, because without a word, he stormed out on his own. The bouncer followed him out, and a couple of his friends took notice. They ambled slowly outside with flat, annoyed expressions on their faces.

The chatter among bar patrons returned to its original volume.

Scott pinched the bridge of his nose. "Unbelievable." Facing away from the bar, he leaned back, taking a more relaxed posture.

I took a step toward him, probably to Nate's chagrin. "Sorry he was pestering you."

"It's not your fault." He pointed at us with his index and middle fingers on one hand. "You guys work at that cocktail lounge, right?"

Nate and I glanced at one another. Though it was unspoken, I think we both agreed that I better do the talking.

"I do." I placed a hand on my chest and then gestured toward Nate. "This is my friend who helps out there sometimes."

Scott wagged a finger at me. "And I bumped into you on the sidewalk this morning."

I sure hoped he didn't think I was on to him. *Stay cool.* I opened my hand for him to shake. "I'm Reece. Nice to meet you for real."

"Scott." He returned the gesture and offered a handshake to Nate.

Nate inched forward, extended his hand for a shake, and introduced himself.

"I was at the comedy show the other night, and you both looked familiar. What a great space you have down there."

I grinned. "Thanks so much. Are you local?" I played dumb intentionally, hoping I might uncover anything he shared that differed from what I'd already learned.

"Oh, I'm visiting. I'm in from New York City."

I allowed my face to light up. "Oh, wow! I hope you're enjoying Hope Mills, and I'm glad you could catch the comedy show while you were in town."

"Actually, the comedy show was the purpose for my visit. I lead the casting department for Fledgling Studios. It's a film and TV production company." His forehead glistened with sweat, and he pulled open his coat to grab his handkerchief from an interior pocket. As he did, I caught a quick glimpse of a small black notebook tucked inside.

I felt my eyes bulge in their sockets, and I forced myself to blink repeatedly so it didn't look like I was staring. Was it the notebook Kari had been searching high and low for? If so, how had Scott gotten ahold of it? Was it just another black notebook, unrelated to the one she'd claimed was missing? Only the top of the pocket journal had peeked out, so I couldn't tell if it contained a sticker of a pink rose which would identify it without a doubt.

I cleared my throat as I tried to keep my mind on the current conversation while filing my observation away for later. "Fledgling Studios? Weren't they recently acquired by CineStream? I saw it in the news fairly recently."

Scott took a sharp inhale and smoothed his hair. "Yep, that's us."

"It sounds like big news. Congratulations."

He swatted at the air dismissively. "Ah, it's all right. Not a huge deal. It's been a lot of change."

A lump formed in my throat, and I swallowed hard. I hadn't considered until he played the news off as low-key that his career might have been negatively impacted by the acquisition, insider trading suspicions aside. *Way to make it awkward, Reece.*

He sighed. "But I guess it's all good stuff. I'm a casting director, and I was doing some scouting for a comedy competition show—ever heard of *In Stitches*? I was here to watch Meghan Spencer perform. Even though it's TV, comedy is a live experience, so I always make sure I evaluate talent in-person." His eyes drifted toward our feet. "Sadly, we saw how her story ended."

I shook my head. "I still can't believe what happened. It's tragic, and I feel horrible for Meghan and her family and anyone who worked with her."

"Did you end up extending your trip to Hope Mills after her show?" Nate asked.

I'd been wondering the same thing. If Scott was some fancy casting director from New York, I figured he probably had more important things to do in the city than hang around Hope Mills—unless he was trying to cover his tracks, plant evidence, or clear his name from any allegations of wrongdoing.

He picked at a loose thread which protruded from the sleeve of his sports coat. "Yeah. I'm going to watch a play at the Washington Playhouse tomorrow night. They're doing a production of *The Curious Savage*. I have some other TV projects in the pipeline, so I'm planning to scope out some talent there."

His reason for staying in Hope Mills made sense. Washington Playhouse was a local theater which frequently workshopped plays and musicals before they made it to Broadway stages in New York City, so it wasn't out of the realm of possibility that Scott was continuing to work while in town.

"One of my clients saw that show last weekend, and they raved about it," Nate added. "I've seen many shows there, and I'm always blown away by the talent living right here in Hope Mills."

"It's charming, and I love it here—don't get me wrong. But I'd much rather be back in New York. I have tons of office work on my plate, especially after the acquisition."

"I'm sure I couldn't even imagine." I tried to empathize with him. He didn't seem like he wanted to stay in town. I needed to figure out the real reason he'd extended his trip. "Speaking of acting—and I hate to pry—but what did you mean earlier when you told that guy, 'The act's up?'" I asked Scott, hoping my segue didn't feel out of place.

He grasped each hand around the lapels of his sports coat. "I was talking about that terrible acting we saw at the comedy show the other night."

I furrowed my brow. "Acting?"

"Yes. It was absolutely awful."

"Who was acting?" I looked briefly at Nate, who gave me a shrug.

"You couldn't tell? Both the woman who heckled Meghan, and the idiot who just stormed out of the bar."

"I didn't realize they were acting."

"I had a chance to speak with the woman after the show. I was trying to sniff out if Meghan or her manager put her up to it. Of course she denied it, but I know acting—especially bad acting—when I see it. It's my livelihood." He confirmed my earlier suspicion that he might've been evaluating Kari's intentions.

Kari had told me she'd been put up to the task by Meghan, but I wasn't surprised she'd denied it when speaking to Scott. I also wasn't positive she told me the truth. In my opinion, I thought her heckling seemed pretty off the cuff, despite Scott's insistence it was fake.

"Why would any comedian volunteer to be heckled?" Nate asked. "Isn't that setting your own show up for disaster?"

Scott chortled. "I think they were trying to put on a show for me. Comedians need to be lightning quick when it comes to engaging the audience, so I think both scenarios were planned by Meghan to make her appear more adept."

I shrugged. "I'll admit she seemed to win the audience over when dealing with the heckler, but the audience seemed uncomfortable while she was teasing that guy." I pointed toward the door that Garrett had recently exited.

Scott turned his attention to Nate. "No one in that crowd looked as uncomfortable as you."

Nate puffed out a breath. "The whole thing was extremely awkward. I really don't like to be the center of attention or singled out." He raised his right hand beside him. "I promise I was not looped in about any of that. I was horrified."

Scott laughed. "No kidding. Like I said, I know acting when I see it. Your reaction was genuine."

If Scott knew acting so well, was it possible Meghan had secretly enlisted Garrett in the same way Kari had claimed she was? Even with the theory in my mind, I didn't think there was any way he could've been acting based on my trip to the barber shop yesterday. His response seemed too genuine, and his toxically masculine bravado outside of the comedy show supported my suspicion he'd taken her jabs personally. If he'd been acting, I'd think he'd be behaving better amidst a pending murder investigation.

"Excuse me for asking, but did you extend your trip because of what happened to Meghan?" I asked.

He scrunched up his face as if he was in pain while he considered his next words. "I guess you could say that."

"Did you see something important? It's not like you have any ties to the investigation," I said, knowing full well about the insider trading allegations at his company and Meghan's blackmail over the topic. I didn't want Scott to think I was on to him, especially if there was a chance he was dangerous.

"Think again."

"Wait, you do?" Why was he admitting it so openly?

He shrugged. "The police have some ridiculous theory that she approached me and threatened me, causing me to retaliate and kill her. Isn't that the biggest load of baloney you've ever heard?"

I nodded. I tried my best to relate, hoping he might share more. "Yeah. If you're the casting director, you have the power, right? If you didn't want to move forward with Meghan, there wouldn't have been reason for you to retaliate. And besides, even if she'd made a threat, what motivation would you have to cause her any harm?"

Scott snapped. "Exactly my point."

Once again, I recalled Scott's phone call from outside of Subplot before Comedy and Cocktails. *If this doesn't work out the way it's supposed to, I can kiss my career goodbye,* he'd said.

He continued, "I'm not leaving until I get this all cleared up. I have nothing to hide, so I'm here to share whatever I know and cooperate as best as I can."

While I wouldn't have expected Scott to admit his insider trading allegations to essential strangers, his attitude toward the investigation seemed nonchalant. It didn't align at all with the fear Tiffany displayed when she'd visited Subplot this afternoon. He didn't appear like someone who would kill to keep a secret from getting out.

His confidence seemed like reason enough to clear him as a suspect, but I had a bad feeling considering all I'd uncovered—headlines of alleged insider trading at CineStream in the news, his tense phone call in the alley before the show, and Tiffany's insistence that he'd retaliated against Meghan for blackmail. Deep down, I knew there was a chance he could be bluffing. As a casting director in the entertainment industry, he was an expert schmoozer. Of course he'd said all the right things to win me over and make me believe him.

In that moment, I felt shaky. My shallow breath felt like it was stuck inside my chest as I realized Scott was a legitimate person of interest in Meghan's murder and faced my gut feeling that he might've committed the fatal act.

TWENTY

"Well, I guess this is where we part." Nate, his hands buried deep in his pockets, stifled a laugh.

We'd walked separately to Bridge Street Bar earlier in the evening. Though we both lived somewhat nearby, we were equally strict about not drinking and driving. While part of our journeys home overlapped, we had to split off in different directions once we reached the intersections of Main and Mechanic Streets.

After the support he'd shown me as I opened up about my crush, I felt extra grateful to have him in my life. Even before I'd come out to Nate nearly a year ago, I never once doubted our friendship. I could only hope he felt the same from me. Considering the stress he was under, given his discovery of Meghan's body, his pocketknife found at the scene, and the spotlight on him as the investigation progressed, I wished I could snap the puzzle pieces together which would expose the killer once and for all. Unfortunately, the more I learned, the more questions I had, and the more uncertain I felt.

I opened my arms. "Bring it in." We each clapped a hand

together for a handshake and reached our free arms around one another for a hug. "Get home safe."

We released from our embrace.

"You too." He turned right onto the sidewalk along Mechanic Street, then spun around toward me. "Good luck tomorrow night. Let me know how it goes."

I waved him off. "Thanks for reminding me. I'm a wreck over here."

"You'll be fine."

"Night," I called out to him.

Nate echoed the salutation as we each headed our separate directions.

I couldn't wait to get home and sip a steaming mug of chamomile tea with a book in my hand and Jameson curled up on my lap, belly exposed for scratches.

I loved walking home at the end of a good night. I found great comfort in being in solitude with my thoughts when the streets were silent and the rest of the world seemed to be asleep. There was nothing like hearing my own footsteps on Hope Mills's red brick sidewalks as I reflected on my day, pondered my gratitude for my loved ones, and dreamed of the future.

Tonight, however, I couldn't stop the theories floating through my mind as I considered all I'd learned in relation to Meghan's murder.

Although Garrett was clearly offended by her crowd work and showed signs of anger and insecurity, would he have really killed her over a joke? On the other hand, if he had a crush on Meghan and had planned to ask her out, perhaps his insecurity had taken hold. Without uncovering any new information about him, though, and considering other suspects' stronger motives and past histories with the victim, he'd fallen off my radar as a legitimate suspect. Obnoxious? For sure. A murderer?

I wasn't sold.

Garrett had claimed seeing David walking toward the Promenade on the night of Meghan's death, and they clearly had a deep history as a former couple. Why did he bother going to his ex-girlfriend's show in another town? I couldn't rule an ex-partner out so easily. Who knew what deep motivations he might have had to kill her, not to mention the awful claims she'd made about him in her comedy?

I still debated whether Kari's heckling had been staged or off the cuff. Was she Meghan's friend or foe? I couldn't quite read her, but considering her own aspirations for stand-up comedy and Meghan's shot at a big break, I couldn't shake the thought that jealousy might have taken hold.

I also wondered about Tiffany. In addition to the tension I'd witnessed between Meghan and her manager, Kari claimed Tiffany had considered dropping her client. Was their working relationship fatally flawed? Though I'd seen Tiffany's devastation, she'd also admitted her frustrations with the way Meghan often took matters into her own hands—including how she'd potentially blackmailed Scott.

Not only had the talent executive made it clear the police had theories about him, but Tiffany and Kari both had suspicions about him as well. Plus, I'd seen him acting sketchy first-hand on multiple occasions—his phone call outside of Subplot before the comedy show, his newspaper purchase to avoid incriminatory search history. His relaxed demeanor at the bar seemed performative in comparison to my prior interactions, which appeared paranoid. He'd shown concern for his career, and the news confirmed a pending investigation amid the Cine-Stream acquisition of Fledgling Studios. Though I wasn't exactly sure how—or if—she'd done it, I wouldn't have been surprised if Scott had taken extreme measures to keep his name away from the insider trading allegations if they were legitimate.

I'd been so far down my rabbit hole of contemplation that I almost missed the woman sitting on a wooden bench along Main Street near darkened storefronts. I heard sniffles in the still, humid evening air as I approached her. Her wavy hair fell in front of her face as she bowed her head.

I stepped tentatively toward her. "Hey, is everything okay?" I spoke in a soft, friendly tone, just above a whisper.

She startled.

I was surprised she hadn't heard me approaching. "Sorry, I didn't mean to scare you."

The woman glanced up at me. "Yeah, I'm fine." She sat at the far end of the bench, almost as if to take up as little space as possible.

Catching a glimpse of her face under the dim streetlight, I recognized her as the unknown woman I'd been seeing everywhere lately. She'd been at the comedy show, and I'd seen her browsing the used book cart outside of Ampersand yesterday, not far at all from where she was sitting now.

Why did she look so familiar? And why did our paths keep crossing? It had to be chance. However, considering she was at the lounge on the night of Meghan's murder, my curiosity took hold. As much as I hated to suspect ill intent with no concrete evidence, I couldn't help but wonder if she might've had something to do with the murder. Was she crying tears of remorse? Or had she been connected to Meghan somehow? If so, she could be crying tears of sadness.

I pointed at the wide, empty space on the bench beside her. "Mind if I join you?"

She sniffled. "Go for it."

I took a seat and left plenty of space between us. "Can I get you anything?"

She didn't look at me. Her gaze stayed fixed on the sidewalk at her feet. "No," she whispered.

"I apologize if this sounds weird, but I feel like I know you somehow."

She turned toward me briefly, then shifted her attention back to the sidewalk. "You work at that book-themed lounge. I was at the comedy show the other night."

I nodded. "Yeah, I remember that. But I'm talking about before that. Did we go to high school together or something?"

"Where did you go?"

"Here in Hope Mills. You?"

"Lambertdale." She was from across the river. Although our high schools were rivals when it came to sports, a lot of social circles overlapped, due to the schools' proximities to one another.

"Ah, so you're from the dark side—New Jersey," I teased. "Who knows? Maybe we knew each other way back when."

"Yeah," she whispered. "Maybe."

I reached a hand toward her. "I'm Reece. What's your name?"

She didn't shake my hand or answer my question. She only forced a half-smile and gave a small wave.

"Well, pretend I'm a stranger. I guess I already am. Do you need anyone to listen?"

She sighed, the stuffiness in her nose from crying muffling her breath. "I made a mistake. A big mistake."

She wasn't referring to Meghan, was she?

Trying to stay positive and not assume the worst—while also seeing if I could get her to reveal anything else—I said, "I don't know what happened, and it's up to you if you want to share more, but mistakes happen. We're all human. I'm sure you did the best you could."

She let out a small whimper. "I hurt someone who meant

the world to me. And now there's no turning back from it." She shook her head back and forth as if to expel the thought. "I've already said too much. Have a nice night." She stood up from the bench and scurried down the street in the direction from which I'd come. Before I knew it she was gone. Her departure happened so fast, I didn't even consider calling after her.

I hurt someone. No turning back. Her cryptic words echoed through my head. What could she possibly have been referring to?

I allowed more theories to permeate my thoughts as I continued down Main Street in the direction of my apartment.

Had Meghan been a friend to the woman from Lambertdale? Or was I reading too deeply into her words? The mistake she mentioned could've been referring to anything, but I wanted so badly to connect the dots in Meghan's case.

Though I was on the opposite side of the street from The Colonial Inn, my thoughts began to quiet as I approached the hotel. Was there a chance I might bump into David again? The odds felt low. *Ya never know.*

To my surprise, though, a figure did appear to be approaching the inn from the opposite direction. I squinted through the soft orange glow of the streetlights.

The figure appeared feminine. And tall. She had bouncy, curly hair.

Is that who I think it is?

Though many of her defining features were silhouetted by the night, backlit from the lamppost behind her, I had a sneaking suspicion it had to be Tiffany.

I took a small detour into the pocket park where I'd staked out to catch David that morning. It was obscured from the streetlight, so I hoped she hadn't seen me.

As she got closer to the hotel's exterior lighting, her features began to reveal themselves. The woman across the street was definitely Tiffany.

She turned off the sidewalk and hustled up the steps to the Colonial Inn.

Tiffany and David were staying at the same hotel. She had to know David was Meghan's ex, right? Had they had any conversations or conflicts? Was she keeping an eye on him? Were they working together to piece together clues?

Suddenly, I had more questions for her, and I hoped I could find an opportunity to get some answers.

TWENTY-ONE

I tossed and turned all night long. Maybe it was the random bits of information related to the case swirling through my head which interfered with my sleep. Maybe it was the torrential rains pouring down overnight.

Regardless, I slept in a series of short, fitful stretches throughout the night, waking up with my heart slamming in my chest every forty-five minutes or so. After seven, I managed to relax and sleep for a bit longer, but a loud crack of thunder jarred me awake for good.

Rain rapped on my window as gusts of wind whistled through my neighborhood. Though it was long past sunrise, only a dim light glowed behind my bedroom curtains.

Jameson rested on my chest, purring—my favorite sound in the entire world. Once he noticed my eyes were open, he stood on all fours, arched his back to stretch, and yawned.

"*Biiig* stretch." My morning voice was deep with vocal fry. "*Biiig* yawn."

I rolled my head on the pillow to face my alarm clock. Three minutes after eight.

Though Wednesdays were still technically part of my weekend, they tended to be busier than Mondays and Tuesdays as I prepared to open the lounge for another weekend of service. Though it wasn't happening today, once a month on Wednesdays, we hosted the Lifted Spirits Whiskey Club which congregated for whiskey tasting, food pairings, socialization, and camaraderie.

Jameson relocated from my chest to my pillow. He made biscuits before nuzzling into the side of my neck and snuggling up over my shoulder. His rhythmic purring filled my left ear. I reached for my phone on the nightstand. Not wanting to leave the bed quite yet, I figured I could at least do some digital reconnaissance.

I strung a series of related words into the search bar: *Kari Philadelphia comedy don't know how to swim*

And there it was: a video titled, "Kari Kim – I Don't Swim – Stand-Up Comedy." It had been uploaded by Kari herself, eight years before, and it only had a few hundred views.

Though her delivery wasn't anywhere nearly as smooth or as polished as Meghan's, the bit's core was shockingly similar. Meghan had made the joke feel like her own, and her performance had been convincing, but I could absolutely see why Kari would've felt burned. It was her material, after all. On the other hand, I couldn't imagine Kari playing nice and coordinating her heckling with Meghan with a video like this circulating.

I also considered what a risky move it'd been on Meghan's part to steal the segment. Kari's video wasn't hard to find. If Tiffany had been aware of this, I could've imagined she would've been frustrated—if not more—by the move, especially since her career success was directly tied to her client's.

And if Scott had somehow found out about it, perhaps he felt like his time had been wasted, especially since he was in the midst of a major corporate acquisition.

I started a new search on my phone: *CineStream Fledgling Studios acquisition*

The top result was a headline which read TOP EXECUTIVES; FIFTY PERCENT OF FLEDGLING STUDIOS WORKFORCE LAID OFF AMIDST CINESTREAM ACQUISITION.

He hadn't seemed too excited about the acquisition last night, so I wondered if it was causing him more stress than celebration.

I added his name to my search query, but I couldn't find any articles about insider trading which mentioned him. Even if Meghan truly had knowledge of it, Scott was flying under the radar. Had he been associated with the white-collar crime at all?

With a deep breath, I rolled over. If I planned to have a productive day, it was time to get out of bed.

After showering, getting dressed, and making an omelet for breakfast, I refreshed Jameson's water bowl and made sure his automatic feeder was loaded with more than enough food to get him through the day. I crouched down to my knees on the floor and reached for his favorite toy—a long, thin plastic stick with a bundle of feathers at the end, which dangled from an elastic string. Though I could've watched him pounce at it all morning, I knew I'd better head to Subplot to continue working on our fall menu and prepare to open the following evening.

To avoid the pouring rain, I drove to Subplot and parked on the street front of D'Amico's. Once I stepped inside Subplot's windowless walls, the weather became irrelevant, except when an occasional roll of thunder rumbled. Otherwise, I was happy to get lost in my carefully curated literary spirit cave.

Shortly after I arrived, my phone vibrated in my pocket. The incoming call was from Logan Nelson, Ava's boyfriend and the owner of DCDC distillery, one of our main suppliers.

"Hello, this is Reece." I always answered professionally, even when I knew who was at the other end of the line.

"Hey, Reece. Good news. We just bottled an extremely limited, very small batch of a new Limoncello liqueur, and I was wondering if you might want a few bottles. I'm giving you first dibs."

I didn't even have to consider the offer. "Absolutely. Bring some of those by. I'd love to buy some."

Not only was I personally excited to give his new creation a try, but I was always excited to uplift a fellow local business in the town I was proud to call home.

As soon as he mentioned Limoncello, an idea to create a citrusy bourbon cocktail with burnt honey popped in my mind. While lemon made me think of summer, bourbon was my go-to fall spirit. The burnt honey would combine the sweetness of summer with the caramel flavors of fall. The blend of all those flavors seemed like the perfect August drink—especially as yellow buses returned to the streets to take our town's children back to school, Halloween decorations started to pop up in the stores, and pumpkin spice season was about to begin too early.

Logan said, "If you're around, I'll swing by in about fifteen minutes."

When he arrived, his wavy, golden hair was tucked under a soaked bucket hat. He held two bottles between his fingers in one hand, and he had his other hand fully gripped around a third. "I'm not going to let a thunderstorm keep you from my Limoncello," he proudly announced as he stepped into the lounge, his clothes dotted with rain.

He made himself comfortable on a barstool, and we chatted for several minutes about almost everything—the rain, the excruciating heat, how business was going, and of course, Meghan's murder.

"Ava mentioned you two had a sushi date planned last

night." I tried my best to play it cool as a wide smile grew on my face.

Logan nodded.

"So..." I spun my hands in circles, encouraging him to tell me more. "How did it go?"

A huge smirk grew on Logan's face. He removed the bucket hat from his head and ran his fingers through his damp blond locks. "It went really, really well." Although I wouldn't have thought Logan was the giggling type, he let out a full-on giggle.

I'd never seen him act so giddy, but I took it as a positive sign that he was falling in love with Ava. After working so closely with her nearly every day—even in previous roles prior to opening Subplot—it warmed my heart to know such a wonderful person had found a way into her life.

As soon as he left the lounge, I couldn't wait to get started on crafting a cocktail with his Limoncello. Typically, I allowed myself to be much freer when it came to designing a new drink. However, knowing how limited Logan's batch was, I wanted to save as much of the liqueur as possible for customers.

I first got to work on creating a burnt honey sauce. I fetched a hotplate and a saucepan from our small kitchen. As I arranged them on the bar, my phone lit up with a notification.

My heart nearly skipped a beat when I saw the name Julian Garcia on my lock screen.

My giddiness was similar to Logan's as I unlocked my phone and tapped straight to my messaging app. Thank goodness none of my team was around to witness it.

> Hey man, just making sure tonight still works for you

He was surely being proactive in confirming our plans.

I felt like I was buzzing from the inside out as I typed a response.

Yep, looking forward to it! See you at 7?

I turned my phone face down on the bar, too nervous to anticipate a response. Instead, I added honey to the pan, along with a dash of distilled white vinegar, which would keep the final product smooth. I brought the mixture to a boil and added a splash of water and a pinch of salt to further enrich the flavor. Once it reached the ideal temperature, I removed the pan from the hotplate and submerged it in an ice bath to stop the cooking process. From there, I transferred my finished burnt honey to a mason jar.

I couldn't help but turn my phone over again. Another message from Julian awaited me.

Sounds like a plan. We shouldn't be interrupted this time. See you later!

I felt breathless after reading his messages. Was he flirting? Or was he simply referencing how we'd been interrupted by customers the last time we chatted?

My anticipation for our meeting was a bright spot in my week, which was otherwise marred by Meghan's murder. The frustration I felt all night begin to niggle at me as I loaded a scoop of ice into a cocktail shaker. I hoped crafting my new drink might distract me.

I measured out an ounce of Limoncello and poured it into a cocktail shaker, along with two ounces of DCDC double-barrel bourbon, a heaping teaspoon of the burnt honey, and a sprig of rosemary. I jotted down the ingredients I used and their measurements in my notebook as I went.

I pressed the metal lid onto the shaker and shook vigorously for close to a minute to fully dissolve the burnt honey. I swapped the shaker's lid for a strainer attachment to catch any of the rosemary's needle-like leaves and poured the drink into a rocks glass over a single, large ice cube. I dipped a short sprig of rosemary in the glass, just long enough to peek over the rim.

I snapped a picture of the cocktail, which I planned to to post on social media to drum up interest. Customers loved new or limited-edition drinks.

I was finally ready to test it. While the bourbon was strong, the burnt honey gave it a subtle sweetness, made richer by the caramelization process. The Limoncello's brightness further balanced the flavor, while the rosemary added an earthy flair. It tasted like August in a glass. I decided to title the cocktail after William Shakespeare's *A Midsummer Night's Dream* because, well, it was.

After cleaning up the bar and while hand-washing some dishes in our small kitchen, multiple chimes from our doorbell —which was located on the wall beside our secret bookcase entrance—rang throughout the lounge.

I dried my hands and jogged upstairs to answer the door.

Kari stood on the other side, with bags under her eyes as if she'd barely slept. Her hair, which had always been pin-straight with no strand out of place, was frizzy and unkempt.

"Is everything all right?"

She didn't blink. "The police are searching for Scott. They can't find him anywhere. I think he left town."

"The police are looking for him?" Propping the secret bookcase open with my foot, I leaned against the doorframe, not allowing Kari to step inside. Why was she coming to me, of all people? Her frazzled demeanor made me wary to trust her.

With arms folded across her crocheted sleeveless crop top, she nodded adamantly. "Yeah. Have you seen him lately?"

The conversations I'd had since Nate told me he'd found Meghan's body were starting to blend together. "Last night, actually. I was at Bridge Street Bar with a friend, and he was there. Why?" As I said it, the image of a small notebook peeking out of his sports coat pocket flashed through my mind.

Her deep sigh echoed through the vestibule Subplot shared with D'Amico's. "We need to find him. The notebook I told you about yesterday—I'm sure it's long gone now, too." She didn't answer my question.

Did I dare tell her what I'd seen? Anyone could carry a pocket notebook around. Heck, Detective Sharp constantly jotted notes in hers. Plus, how was I to know the notebook belonged to Kari in the first place? Maybe she sought the journal for the wrong reasons. I erred on the side of caution and decided to keep the information to myself. "Why would the police be searching for him? And why do you think he left town?"

She glanced quickly over each shoulder, but in the middle of the afternoon, barely anyone would pass through the vestibule to go to or from D'Amico's. "You haven't heard the latest news?"

I shook my head. "No. I've been in my own little world downstairs. What's going on?"

"Apparently Scott's production company was acquired by CineStream, and news is breaking that he might have been involved in an insider trading scandal. The FBI is in town to investigate, and they're coordinating with the local police." She blew out a deep breath. "A murder *and* insider trading accusations? Those are two serious crimes. And happening within days of each other? I think they're connected. I'll bet Scott got out of Dodge before the media could get ahold of him."

When Tiffany had visited the lounge, she'd implied she alerted the police of her suspicions about his insider trading and that they were coordinating with another jurisdiction. I guessed that meant the Feds were involved.

If what Kari shared was true, it was a game changer for the entire case. Though I had no clue how Meghan would've learned of Scott's business dealings, having confirmation of a federal investigation of his insider trading allegations meant Tiffany's theory held merit. And if he was already caught up in a downward spiral as he tried to cover his tracks, I believed it was more likely he could've killed Meghan in the process.

I folded my arms and shifted my tone to be more inquisitive. "Not to be rude, but why did you come to talk to me about this? And how did you know I was here?"

"Because you're one of the only people I've talked to about this since you saw me out back yesterday. I figured you'd probably be back again around the same time today. And the notebook I told you about—I really think he has it, and I need it back."

"But when we last spoke, you thought a couple of people might have taken it. How can you be so sure Scott has it now?"

"Because I really think he killed Meg," she said.

"Wait. Let me get this straight. Meg's killer would want *your* notebook? Something's not adding up here, and I don't think you're telling me the whole truth."

She grunted. "Fine. It's not my notebook. It was Meg's. I think it contained information that would expose her killer. Okay?"

"Why did you lie about who it belonged to?"

She pressed her palms into each side of her temples. "Because I didn't think you'd help me if you knew the notebook wasn't mine." She removed her hands from her head and continued speaking with one raised index finger. "But now we're wasting time. Scott isn't only a suspect in Meg's murder, but the FBI is also looking into him now as part of another criminal investigation. The man is dangerous, and no one can find him. Are you going to help or not? Did he say anything about leaving town when you saw him last night?"

"He said he was planning to watch *The Curious Savage* at the Washington Playhouse tonight, but considering no one's finding him in town, that probably doesn't help much." Once again, I debated telling her about the notebook I'd spotted in Scott's pocket. She seemed certain that he had it, though, and I still wasn't sold that she was telling the truth. She'd confirmed that she'd previously lied to me, and I was tentative about her new story.

She shook her head in very rapid, small movements. "No, no. Thank you so much. Any information you have helps."

"What if he just went back home?" I asked. "If the police are already on it, I'd leave it to them. They know what they're doing." The words felt ironic to say. Although I trusted the police, my curious and social nature had compelled me to take matters into my own hands ever since Nate had told me of his tragic discovery.

If the police found Scott, they'd find the notebook, too. Was it possible she was trying to reach him before the authorities did? If so, maybe the notebook contained evidence that tied her to Meghan's death, after all—evidence she wanted to destroy.

Both of Kari's arms slumped at her sides. "Well, thank you for telling me about your Scott sighting last night. I'll add it to my timeline. I've got to run."

As abruptly as she'd appeared in my day, she departed, clearly on a mission.

I pulled out my phone and began typing a text to Chloe as I ambled down the stairs.

> I heard a possible suspect in the murder investigation turned up missing. Are you able to confirm?

It wasn't unheard of for Cam to let some inside information slip every now and then.

I moseyed over to the short stage where Meghan had performed her last show and sat on the edge. While I waited for Chloe to respond, I opened a social media app. Sure enough, at the top of my feed was an article shared in a Hope Mills community group: MURDER INVESTIGATION INTENSIFIES AMIDST TALENT EXEC'S ALLEGED INSIDER TRADING. Things weren't looking good for Scott.

I enabled my phone's ringtone sounds so I'd hear Chloe's message as soon as it came through and returned to our small kitchen space to finish washing dishes.

Within a few minutes, a high-pitched *ding* rang out from my pocket. I dried my hands on the towel still draped over my shoulder and reached for my phone. Sure enough, it was a reply from Chloe.

> Yup... Cam was over at mom and dad's when he got the call. Sounded like they needed all hands on deck to try to find the guy

It turned out Kari was more reliable than I'd given her credit for. Despite all the info she shared checking out, I found myself questioning her potential involvement in the murder as I scrubbed the sticky saucepan I'd used to make burnt honey. Was she a friend of Meghan's as she'd claimed—or an enemy, as it'd appeared during the show? And what was in the notebook she was so desperate to find? Was it proof of Scott's guilt —or critical evidence about her which she sought to destroy?

My gut leaned toward Scott, though. I'd seen his sketchy behavior for myself. I saw a notebook in his jacket which fit the description of the one Kari searched for. Official news breaking of his insider trading supported theories he had a lot at stake. As if all of that weren't enough, his sudden disappearance sealed the deal for me.

Confident as I felt, I had no way of knowing where he'd gone. It was pointless for me to leave town to search for him, especially with Subplot opening for service tomorrow night and an already busy schedule—including my plan to meet up with Julian later in the evening.

I wasn't one to admit defeat so easily, but with no ideas for where he might've gone, I could only hope the police would find him sooner rather than later and bring him to justice.

TWENTY-THREE

As a kid, I read anything I could get my hands on, from cereal boxes to the newspaper. Books like Roald Dahl's *Matilda*, E.B. White's *Stuart Little*, and Kate DiCamillo's *Because of Winn-Dixie* were the foundation of my love of reading. By high school, I'd binge-read the classics and Shakespeare and even debated becoming an English teacher. Despite being a fully capable student, I couldn't fathom spending another four years in a classroom. Instead, I was so eager to work in the *real world* that I barely survived my first semester. I'd taken full-time hours on at the restaurant where I'd been working, and I'd worked in the local food and beverage service industry ever since. My love of reading never faded, though. Rather, it set the stage for eventually opening my literary-themed lounge.

Needless to say, spending time in a bookstore after hours and having the whole place to myself was a dream.

But spending time in a bookstore after hours with a dreamy bookstore owner who invited me to join him there? That was heaven—or it would be, if I weren't so nervous.

With my heart racing and unsure of where to begin, I said, "It's really busy out there." From where I stood beside a table of curated fall fiction near the center of the store, I pointed toward the lively evening scene outside of Ampersand on Main Street. Well-dressed couples walked hand in hand, and groups of friends dined outside at restaurants across the street. We were lucky to live in a town that didn't go completely quiet on weeknights; visitors from near and far kept the streets alive year-round.

Julian locked the front entrance and flipped the Books Open sign on the front door to its opposite side, which read Sorry, We're Closed (But Your Books Don't Have to Be!). Then he dimmed the lights so that the store was mainly illuminated by the natural outside light, which was beginning to fade. *Ooh, romance lighting and everything.*

I daydreamed about running my fingers through Julian's lush, wavy hair before reprimanding myself. If only my palms weren't so clammy. *That's not why you're here.* Because I wanted to maintain professional integrity, I tried my best to keep from admiring him, though it was a constant struggle.

He strolled to the back of the store, and I followed him after he passed me. We each took a seat in the reading nook near the register. I sat on a wooden chair with sage-green upholstery that faced the entrance, and Julian sat across from me in a brown leather armchair. An amoeba-shaped coffee table, stacked with staff-recommended books, and a woven area rug tied the space together. The store's relaxed vibe, with its many plants and soft earth tones, helped to calm my jitters.

I kickstarted the conversation. "I'm excited to hear about this collaboration you mentioned the other day."

"Yeah, I'm very excited about the idea. I hope you'll like it." He bit his lower lip as if to suppress a smile. "I read pretty broadly across genres—I kind of have to as a bookseller—but mysteries have always been my favorite." He raised an index finger to his mouth. "*Shh! Don't tell the others.* After meeting a lot of customers and getting to know some of the frequent flyers, I've found a lot of them are big mystery fans, too. I thought we could start a Mysteries and Mixology book club."

I sat forward on my seat. "Ooh! Mysteries and Mixology. That has a nice ring to it."

"I'm thinking we could meet every month. We'd select one mystery novel for members to read—or maybe we could give them options to vote on. Either way, I'd do a display here in the store to sell the book and recruit new members." The words flew out of Julian's mouth, making his enthusiasm for his idea crystal clear.

Swoon! I scooched back on my chair and leaned back, trying to play it cool. "And if we wanted to host the book club in Subplot, you'd be welcome to sell some copies there to any members who hadn't bought the book yet."

Julian clapped his hands together. Watching his excitement made my heart thump in a way I wasn't sure it ever had. "Yay! That's exactly what I was thinking. I was going to ask if we could host it in your lounge, but I was too nervous to ask."

He was nervous...to talk to *me*? I waved off his concern. "I feel like a cocktail lounge is the perfect setting to enjoy a mystery." I extended my arm toward Julian with a closed fist, encouraging him to bump his with mine. "I'm in!"

My heart fluttered as I considered the extra time I'd get to spend with him each month to prepare for the book club. I also admired how well his idea lent itself to both of our businesses—his bookstore and my literary-themed mixology lounge. *A match made in heaven.*

Julian leaned in, clearly delighted by my eagerness. "I don't mean to create extra work for you, but what if you crafted a cocktail or mocktail each month that goes along with the book? We could all sip on them while we discuss."

"That's a great idea. Why not both? I could do a demonstration for the members to make the cocktail before serving it. Maybe I'll even create a bookmark each month with the drink recipe on it. I love your idea, and I can't wait to get started on bringing it to life."

"I'm so glad you're on board with this. Do you think September is too soon to launch it?"

Considering it was early August, we'd have anywhere from four to seven weeks to prepare. "Not at all. We could get it up and running, no problem. Maybe we aim for the last Wednesday each month? The Lifted Spirits Whiskey Club already meets on the second Wednesday of the month."

I loved the idea of Subplot becoming a space for community building on Wednesday nights, and I was glad to add events to our calendar which might attract new customers who might not otherwise stop by the lounge. Perhaps we'd eventually host a different club on every Wednesday of the month.

He grinned confidently. "I'm game. I'm ready to get to work on this. The idea's been brewing in my mind ever since I visited Subplot for the first time. Between opening the bookstore, seeing your lounge, and starting to build more of a community for myself in Pennsylvania, I've been excited to get something like this started."

"You're not from PA?" Since he was about my age and Hope Mills was a small town, I figured he wasn't from here. However, I'd seen him out and about with friends on multiple occasions, so I thought he might've grown up in the surrounding area.

"Nope. How about you?"

"Born and raised in Hope Mills. Where did you move from?"

He planted a palm on each of his knees, leaning toward me. "Texas."

Until he said it, I hadn't quite noticed the subtle Southern drawl that had been in his voice all along.

"I grew up not too far outside of Austin."

"What brought you here, of all places?"

His eyes darted toward the floor. "I, uh...I moved here with someone."

I pressed my lips together. "Ah. An ex?"

He inhaled deeply through his nose. "Yeah," he said as he exhaled.

I had so many questions, but I refrained from asking any of them. Was his ex still around? If Julian was a store owner, he could've set up shop anywhere. Had his ex gotten a job in the area? And why did Julian decide to stay?

"Well, do you at least like it here, despite...?"

His eyes widened. "Oh, absolutely. I love it here. Even as a native Texan, the heat really wore on me. It makes this week's heat wave seem like stepping into an ice box. When I came up here for the first time a couple of years ago to meet my ex's family, I fell in love with a bunch of the small towns throughout Bucks County. There's so much to do here. From the first time I visited, it felt like a dream. I could immediately envision myself living here."

If his ex's family was local, did I know them? If I didn't, I was sure Nate did.

"It's so inspiring—and honestly a bit humbling—to hear the place I've lived all my life was a place of dreams for you. Sometimes I get a bit insecure that I never moved away, but I love it here and never felt a pull to leave."

"I get that. Even despite the awkward circumstances of me moving and staying here, I already feel rooted in this community."

I felt the corners of my mouth tug into a small smile. "Well, I'm glad you stayed. We'll have Mysteries and Mixology to show for it."

He rubbed his clean-shaven chin. His knee bounced up and

down ever so slightly. Was he nervous? "I wanted to ask you another question, but I'm not sure how to ask…"

I suddenly felt suffocated. Was he about to ask what I hoped he would? "Go for it."

"Did…can we…would you—" As Julian stammered over his words, movement near the bookstore's glass front door caught my eye.

The woman I'd seen lurking around town—at Comedy and Cocktails, browsing the book cart, crying on a park bench— stood in the doorway, wearing a yellow sundress. We made eye contact as she raised her arm, about to knock on the bookstore's locked front door.

My breath constricted in my throat. "Don't turn around," I warned Julian as I tried everything in my power to act calm and avert eye contact with the woman as if I hadn't seen her. It killed me to interrupt before Julian could ask his question. "There's this woman I've been seeing around town a lot lately —especially since the comedy show. I swear she looks super familiar, but I can't place her. She's outside the store right now."

As if by instinct, he spun his head around.

"Don't!" I urged under my breath, prompting him to turn back toward me. "I wonder if she had anything to do with the murder." Especially after my run-in with her the night before, when she'd heightened my suspicions after mentioning she'd hurt someone close to her very badly.

Julian didn't say a word. He pushed down on the arms of his chair to hoist himself up to his feet and strode toward the door.

"Julian, please." The door's thick glass muffled her voice, soaked in pain.

"What are you doing here?" His voice boomed through the otherwise quiet store, perhaps to project it loud enough for her to hear on the other side.

"Can we talk?"

Julian didn't respond.

"Please. Just give me five minutes," she begged.

I skittered toward Julian. "Are you okay?"

He let out a deep breath and turned to face me. "Yeah," he whispered.

"Please," she cried.

"Sammi, I can't." His voice trembled. It sounded as wounded as hers.

"You two know each other?"

Julian pinched the bridge of his nose. After making brief eye contact, he stared down at the shop's sandy wood floors. "She's my ex-girlfriend."

TWENTY-FOUR

Ex-girlfriend. The word almost didn't compute in my mind.

I made a mistake, I remembered her saying. *I hurt someone who meant the world to me.*

I should've known it was a stretch to assume she'd been talking about Meghan's murder. Had Sammi been talking about Julian all along? If that was the case, had she broken up with him? Or had she hurt him so bad that he felt like it was time to end the relationship?

The floor-to-ceiling bookshelves around me appeared to shift in my peripheral vision as the room spun around me. Had I misinterpreted all the signs? The receipt with his phone number written on it in blue ink. The drinks we'd shared over the past few months. The invitation to collaborate. The question he was just about to ask me.

I felt embarrassed. Confused. Angry at myself for making assumptions. But also relieved I hadn't tried to make a move.

Add this to my list of reasons why I shouldn't be looking for love.

"Fine." Julian's defeated voice brought me back to the present moment. The click of the lock as he twisted it brought my dizziness to a halt in an instant.

I cleared my throat. "Well, I'll leave you two to it." I spoke in a low register. As devastated as I felt, the last thing I needed was to get in the middle of Julian's reunion with his ex.

"Reece, you don't need to leave." He turned toward Sammi, still standing in the doorway. "We'll only be five minutes."

I shook my head quickly. "No, it's okay. I really want to give you some privacy. We can always chat tomorrow, if that works for you." I tried my best to speak in a friendly yet professional tone.

"I'll text you," he said just under his breath. He pushed the front door open, and I made my way outside, scooting past Sammi.

Why did she look so familiar? She'd confirmed she was from across the river in Lambertdale. Now that I knew her first name, I'd have to ask Nate if he was able to place her.

Might as well not waste any time. I pulled the phone out of my pocket, figuring it was better to reach out to my friend and try to make the connection rather than sulk. I found a nearby park bench—not the same one she'd been crying on last night—and took a seat as the sun fully set.

It all makes sense now. Any time I'd seen Sammi in recent memory, there was always a tie back to Julian. He'd attended Comedy and Cocktails, and she had, too. She'd also stopped by his store earlier in the week and had been sitting on a bench near Ampersand.

> Do you know a woman named Sammy from Lambertdale?

I wasn't sure how she spelled her name, so I gave it my best guess.

> Maybe her name is actually Samantha

Within seconds, three dots danced at the bottom of our text conversation. I wasn't surprised Nate read my message immediately.

Is she around our age?

Yup

Could it be Sammi Franklin?

Remember her from The Perfect Storm?

Memories flashed through my mind like a rewind reel.

When Nate and I each turned twenty-one, we frequented a bar called The Perfect Storm in Lambertdale. They were the only bar in the area which offered trivia night on a Monday, which was the only weeknight I was reliably off work in those days. The bar even offered an Industry Night discount for those of us who worked in the service industry.

Sammi Franklin. The name sounded familiar, but I still couldn't place it. My memory was somewhat hazy.

Did she run trivia night? Was she on one of the regular teams?

No, she didn't play

Remember the woman who used to sing after?

It immediately clicked in my mind.

OHHH

Sammi Franklin was a singer and guitar player who used to set up her P.A. system toward the end of trivia night. By the time we'd wrapped up our game, she began to play a mix of original songs and covers. She was a dynamic performer, ranging from soft, smooth vocals and delicate finger-picking to rhythmic strumming and a warm rasp in her voice when she belted out a big note. In particular, her sultry version of U2's "With Or Without You" stuck out in my mind. She could quiet the room mid-brawl with the way her impassioned voice wailed the chorus.

I hadn't seen her in ten years, which made sense, considering she'd moved to Austin. Though her appearance had matured, Nate's reminder of who she was cemented in my mind that she was the woman I'd been seeing around lately.

I thought she moved away to try and build her career. Only so many gigs you can get around here

Sounds like she moved to Austin

How do you know?

As the warm summer breeze blew through my short hair, I typed a long message explaining I'd been seeing her around town, how I'd seen her in tears last night, and the fact that she was my crush's ex-girlfriend.

Whattttt?!?! Sounds like we have a lot to unpack

We sure did.

I stood up from the bench and walked toward my apartment. As I approached the River Promenade and Washington Playhouse to my left, I checked my watch. Seven forty. When I remembered weeknight productions usually started at seven, I imagined an empty seat inside the theater—the one Scott would've sat in if he hadn't fled town...if he'd been telling the truth about watching *The Curious Savage* at all.

Along my leisurely stroll home, the red, white, and blue flashes of police lights a couple of blocks to my right caught my attention. *What now?* Like a moth to a flame, I gravitated toward them.

Two police SUVs and an ambulance were pulled off on the side of Mechanic Street, where there was a crossing for the Delaware Canal Towpath trail. The red dirt path extended for dozens of miles both north and south of Hope Mills and cut through the heart of town.

The silhouette of a woman with hands clasped behind her neck stood near the emergency vehicles. She rocked ever so slightly as I approached.

"Kari, is that you?"

Her hair had grown even frizzier than when she'd stopped by Subplot this afternoon.

"What's going on? Do you know?" I asked.

She gulped. "They...found..." She sounded breathless. "Scott. He's..." Once again, I feared she might hyperventilate.

I sucked in the deepest breath I could, trying to silently coach her to regulate her breathing. "He's what?"

She let out a shallow exhale. "Dead."

TWENTY-FIVE

"But how could he be...?" Even I couldn't muster the word which should've ended my question. "I felt certain he..."

Concerned as I was for Kari's well-being in that moment—and as shocked as I was to hear the news about Scott—I couldn't help but also feel a wave of defeat crashing down on me. He'd been my top suspect in Meghan's death. I was back to square one.

Had he been murdered as well, or had he taken his own life? I shivered at the thought of both possibilities. If he'd been murdered, had Meghan's killer also killed him? Or had Scott murdered Meghan after all, with his own death serving as revenge—or possibly self-defense?

Kari's breathing turned erratic again.

Pull it together, Reece. I took another deep breath, hoping I could keep both of us from spiraling.

"Did you talk to the police?"

"Yes. But not for very long," she whispered.

"What do they think happened to him?"

She clenched her eyes shut. "He was stabbed."

The confirmation of his murder made me feel unsteady on

my feet. What on earth was going on in Hope Mills? My cozy town was supposed to be known for the arts and culinary excellence, not killing sprees.

"So he didn't leave town after all?" I asked.

"I guess not. He was between some bushes not too far off the trail."

"Did you mention the notebook when you spoke to the police?"

She let out a slight groan as if she was in physical pain. "Yeah."

"And?"

"They searched him for it, but I'm not surprised he didn't have it on him. Maybe it's with his other belongings. Maybe he destroyed it. Maybe whoever killed him took it."

For the notebook to be of value to anyone else meant it must've contained some pretty critical information. Did it contain a plan to kill Meghan? Did it hold secrets about one of the suspects which would end the case once and for all? Beneath all of my questions about what the notebook's contents were more questions about its ownership. Did it really belong to Kari? Was it somebody else's, and she was trying to intercept it? Did she even know what was written inside? Was the notebook even real?

I was so entranced by my questions that I hadn't noticed Detective Sharp striding toward me. Her arms were crossed. "Reece. What brings you here?"

Although our rapport had grown stronger, I knew she probably didn't like seeing me near the action once again. Cam followed her, though he didn't say a word.

Pointing in the direction of my apartment, I said, "I was walking home from downtown, and I saw the lights. With everything going on lately, I was curious."

"So, you decided to walk *toward* the danger?"

My eyes fell to the pavement at my feet. "I'm sorry. I guess I'll be on my way." I glanced up at her, making eye contact for a split second. I nodded curtly and pivoted on one foot to head home.

"And Ms. Kim, if you'll follow me, I have some more questions for you," she said to Kari as I walked away.

I kicked a stone in front of me as I wondered who'd found Scott's body—and how he ended up along the Towpath. Had Kari found Scott herself? She'd been intent on finding him when she stopped by the lounge this afternoon. If so, had she found the notebook on him and taken it?

I visualized all the possibilities like a tree—with more possibilities shooting off like branches, which contained even more possibilities. My mind took a dark turn as I considered whether Kari could have killed Scott. If Scott had killed Meghan, and if she was a friend of Meghan's—as she'd claimed —had she sought revenge? Or had Kari killed Meghan and Scott threatened to turn her in? Perhaps the notebook contained proof. Had Kari somehow learned of Scott's insider trading and used it as leverage?

Trying to keep my mind from completely spiraling out of control with unfounded theories, I took my phone from my pocket.

When the screen illuminated, a string of message notifications from Julian waited for me. Even despite what I'd witnessed between him and Sammi earlier this evening and the chaos surrounding Scott's death, the butterflies wouldn't stop fluttering in my stomach any time his name appeared on my screen.

I am so sorry about earlier...

That was kind of embarrassing

> I can explain

> But anyhow… I love where our collab is
> headed. Let's meet up again soon. I could even
> come to you this time

I had so many questions about Julian and Sammi's relationship, but the answers were none of my business.

It might've been far-fetched, but I also wondered if her heightened emotional state had anything to do with Meghan's death. She'd been in the lounge for Comedy and Cocktails, after all. But with no hard evidence—and considering there were many people in the audience who I didn't consider suspects due to their mere presence—I had to let my suspicions go.

Ampersand was open during the day, and Subplot opened in the evening before the bookstore closed, so aligning our schedules to meet would be difficult over the next several days.

> Don't worry about it at all—you're totally fine!

> The lounge is open the next few nights, but I'll
> be free during the day

To my surprise, he began typing a response seconds after I sent my first reply.

> We usually have a mid-afternoon lull. My
> coworker can handle the store on her own.
> Maybe we could meet up around 2 tomorrow?

I stepped off the sidewalk and leaned against a telephone pole as we volleyed a few other messages back and forth. We settled on a walk around Main Street, starting at Ampersand. Though he'd offered to stop by the lounge, this morning's thunderstorm finally kicked out the oppressive heat wave, and tomorrow's forecast predicted comfortable mid-seventies weather—perfect for a casual stroll.

A couple of minutes later, I'd reached home. I unlocked my front door and stepped inside, greeted by a trill from Jameson—his happy sound which fell somewhere between the sound of a meow and a single purr. Even before I could take off my shoes or turn on the lights, I felt his furry body threading itself through my legs.

"*Meeooow,*" he exclaimed—feline for, *Welcome home! I missed you.*

"Aww, I missed you, too, buddy."

Once I finally turned on the lights and slunk down onto the couch, Jameson leapt up and sat on my lap. He massaged my stomach with his front legs.

I scratched him behind his ears. "How did you know I was hungry for biscuits?"

As glad as I was to be home for the day, I couldn't shake my concerns about what was going on in town. I hoped the police could figure out what happened, because with my top suspect murdered, I felt better off throwing in the towel.

TWENTY-SIX

The following morning was joyful, spent sleeping in, playing with Jameson, and visiting my parents' house for coffee, quiche, and fresh-baked berry muffins on the patio, yet I still strolled toward Ampersand at the corner of Ferry and Main with knots in my stomach that afternoon.

Maybe we should just stay friends, I lamented as I surveyed the charming brick building, weathered by time. Was it wrong for me to still collaborate on Mysteries and Mixology with him with the unrequited feelings I'd developed? I hated to crave something from him he wouldn't be able to give me.

Though I'd sworn I wasn't ready to date again, my feelings told a different story. Unfortunately, it'd only become clear to me after realizing I'd misread the situation.

Julian had been right about the early afternoon lull at the bookstore. Not one customer browsed the store when I arrived a few minutes before two. He let the bookseller behind the counter know he was headed out for a little while.

"Hopefully it'll be slammed by the time you get back. I'll try not to get into too much trouble while you're gone," she said with a playful smile and a wink.

Julian's chocolate-brown knit polo shirt hugged his strong chest and arms. As he stepped outside, he put on his sunglasses and ran his fingers through his luscious, wavy brunette hair. "I am so, so sorry about how things went down last night. I can't believe she showed up."

We walked toward the center of Hope Mills's downtown, in the direction of the Promenade.

I pushed up my sunglasses, which had slid down the bridge of my nose. "No worries. I hope you two were able to work everything out."

He sighed, clearly still frustrated. "I thought everything *was* worked out. She made her decision and left me to pick up the pieces. Then, just as I'm getting ready to move on with my life, she reappears and tries to pull me back to a place where I don't want to return. Is it bad that I want a clean break? Heck, she's the one who wanted this." He seemed desperate to vent.

Though I wasn't sure I was the right person to respond with advice, maybe he just needed someone to listen. "I don't think you should feel ashamed about doing something that is helping you heal." I'd learned that lesson throughout my breakup with Chloe, although our story had played out in quite the opposite way. Many people in my life—and especially in Chloe's— advised us to limit contact with one another, but for us, keeping in touch and being there for one another was essential for each of us to heal.

He scoffed. "Sorry, I shouldn't be burdening you with all of this."

"No, no. It's all right. I'm here for you."

He tucked his hands sheepishly into the pockets of his tan chinos. "Thanks, man."

"I almost hate to bring it up, but I connected the dots last night about why she looked so familiar. I used to watch her perform live at a bar in Lambertdale."

"Yeah, Sammi doesn't sing anymore. She moved to Austin several years ago to build her music career. That's how we met. She really hustled at the beginning, but she liked to party as hard as she worked. She built a following, but the higher she climbed, the more she drank. She drank to the point where she felt like she had no option but to check herself into rehab."

"Is she all right?" From the time I was a kid, my dad always cautioned me about the ways alcohol could ruin lives, informed by his own experience as a bartender and mixologist. It was because of him that I offered an equal number of cocktails and mocktails at Subplot. I sought to create an inclusive environment for all, not just those who drink alcohol.

"Yeah, she's sober now, and I'm grateful for that. I have nothing but respect for her and the hard work she put in to reclaim her life."

"That's good to hear."

"But she never sang again, and she used to sing so beautifully." His voice cracked as he spoke. "We moved to Lambertdale so she could be near her family. I was excited for our new life together, but she crossed paths with an old flame one night, and things were never the same after that."

That explained what she'd said when she was crying on the bench earlier in the week. Between what she'd told me and the way she'd begged Julian to give her another chance, it seemed like she'd felt the negative consequences of her actions.

"Maybe there's still a chance you two can patch things up."

"No," he insisted right away. "I mean it when I say I wish her all the best and hope she finds happiness, but things are one hundred percent over between us. I've had enough time and space to know I'm ready to move forward with whatever's next, and I feel strong in that decision." After a short pause, he took a deep breath. "Anyway, where did we leave off last night?"

I summarized everything we'd talked about regarding

Mysteries and Mixology, including the next steps we'd agreed upon. "I think we're all set to host our first one next month. But when Sammi showed up, you were about to ask me something."

His eyes widened. "Oh. Yeah... I... It was nothing."

"I'm an open book."

As we turned onto the River Promenade, we veered away from the crime scene. Even more flowers, stuffed animals, and votive candles surrounded its perimeter than before.

Julian pointed toward a cluster of red Adirondack chairs under a tree at the very end of the Promenade, where the Aquetong Creek Dam Falls flowed out to the Delaware River. "Can we take a seat?"

"Sure."

I followed him to the chairs in the shade, away from everyone else, and we slunk down into them.

I didn't push Julian to speak. Instead, we sat in silence. I found it difficult to savor the breeze and the delightfully earthy smell which lingered in the air as tension swelled within me. What was likely one minute felt like ten as an impulse to speak overcame me.

"I know there's something you wanted to ask me, but there's been something I've been meaning to tell you."

He sat up straighter in his chair but didn't reply.

I removed my sunglasses and folded them over the front of my T-shirt. "When you left your number for me on your check back in the spring, I think I might have gotten the wrong idea. I thought you were maybe showing interest in a romantic kind of way."

An awkward silence lingered between us. He removed his sunglasses for a second before putting them back on, almost as if they were armor.

"But the truth is...I can't believe I'm about to say this." I cleared my throat. "This is really unlike me. But I think you're really handsome, and you have this energy that makes me want to be around you. I was going to ask if you maybe wanted to grab a drink." Too afraid of what his response might be, I stared straight ahead at the glistening river.

Out of the corner of my eye, I saw Julian's head turn toward me. "I'd like that."

I met his gaze. "You would?" A lump formed in my throat, which made it difficult to get my next words out. "I guess I should be extra clear that I meant grab a drink...together. You know...for real."

"Like a date?"

An embarrassed snicker escaped my mouth. "Yeah. But if I'm reading things wrong, you can tell me. I promise I'll be respectful. When I learned about Sammi..."

He pinched the bridge of his nose. "I know. That was awkward last night. I'm really sorry."

"What? No, there's no need to apologize. I guess it made me think you were...straight. I wouldn't want my crush to ruin the possibility of friendship...or at least collaborating on business projects."

"I'm bisexual." He let out a deep, shaky exhale.

A wave of heat rose on the back of my neck. Why had I been so close-minded? At first, I'd supposed he was gay and then immediately ruled him out as straight when I'd learned about Sammi. I felt frustrated with myself for making assumptions—and embarrassed that it never even occurred to me he might be bi. It was impossible to understand someone's identity without them sharing.

"I'm honored that you felt comfortable to share that with me." It was true, despite my personal embarrassment. It meant a lot that he'd come out to me and shared more about his recent experiences.

"My answer is yes to the date, by the way," he said.

The butterflies in my stomach flew up to my heart.

He gazed out over the shimmering Delaware River, not looking in my direction. Taking a chance, I leaned forward and reached out for his hand, still death-gripped around the arm of his red Adirondack.

"Hey," I whispered, letting my hand rest gently on top of his. As soon as our skin made contact, I felt a jolt of bliss surge up my arm and radiate through my body. "Is this okay?"

He didn't move his hand. "This is great."

"I'm here for you."

He turned to face me, removing his sunglasses with his free hand to reveal his watery chocolate-brown eyes. "If your question still stands, I'd love to grab a drink...together."

I stroked his hand with mine. "Are you free on Monday night?"

He glanced up at the boughs of the tree hanging above me, as if he might see his calendar up there. "I believe so. Let's plan on it."

"How about we go to Penn's? Is that cool with you?" Penn's Brewery and Biergarten had a lovely rooftop, perfect for watching the sunset over our cozy town on a summer evening. I couldn't wait to see Julian's golden-hour glow.

"Sounds great," he said. "It's a date." His hands were much more relaxed, no longer clenching. He tapped his flat palms on both arms of his chair before pulling himself forward on his slanted seat. "I hate to run off, but I should get back to the shop soon."

We each stood and roamed slowly up the Promenade, closer to the shops which lined it, with our hands tucked nervously in our pockets. I buzzed on the inside, but I tried my best to play it cool. I had a date with Julian Garcia in a few days. It was a glimmer of light in the middle of a dark week.

As we approached the taped-off crime scene, police came

into view. I squinted and made out Cam and Detective Sharp among the authorities near the scene. Thank goodness they hadn't spotted me with another suspect.

"Reece, is that you?" Cam called out.

My chest muscles tightened. Though he and I were on good terms, I felt awkward strolling along the Promenade with Julian in front of him. I'd gotten a glimpse into Julian's past, and I didn't know how or when I'd ever tell him about mine.

Plus, I didn't want Julian to get the wrong impression about my involvement in the investigation.

"Sure is," I hollered back. I turned to Julian and spoke in a hushed tone. "I've been in touch with the police, given the victim performed her show in my lounge hours before she—"

"Why don't you go talk to them, and I'll head back to the store. I'll text you closer to Monday to confirm we're still on."

"Perfect. Enjoy the rest of your day. I can't wait."

He smiled. "Me too." And then he was off.

I headed toward Cam. "Any closer to figuring out who did this?"

He rested his hands on his waist, just above his duty belt. "Yes, and no. The second homicide really threw a wrench into the investigation."

Yeah. It did for mine, too.

"Was Scott Simmons the second victim?"

He scanned the area around us. He didn't say a word, but he gave me the slightest nod to confirm.

"I'd heard a rumor that the FBI came looking for him and it seemed like he'd left town. I figured he went home or somewhere private. How'd he end up dead along the trail?"

"We were assisting some federal agents in relation to another case. We'd located Scott's accommodations, but he was nowhere to be found when we showed up, so we looked at other avenues to get in touch with him. Once we finally found him, though, it unfortunately seemed like he'd been where he ended up for about twelve hours."

I shook my head. "That's awful."

Cam's eyes turned toward the Promenade's concrete walkway at his feet. "I've been in this line of work for over a dozen years now, but I will never understand what could drive someone to take a life."

"How did you...find him?"

He pressed his lips together, clearly hesitant to answer me. "A jogger who was out on the trail this evening did. I really can't share anything more."

After wrapping my brief conversation with Cam, I walked toward Subplot. Knowing the police were also stumped didn't bring me any comfort.

Thinking through everything I knew as I stepped along the brick sidewalk, I asked myself what motives each of my suspects had to kill both Meghan *and* Scott—assuming one person was responsible for both murders.

I felt comfortable eliminating Garrett as a possibility. While he might've killed Meghan over her joke in a drunken fit of rage, I had no reason to believe he would've killed Scott. I'd seen them interact at Bridge Street Bar. Garrett had been an obnoxious jerk, but he gave everyone a hard time.

Meghan and Tiffany had a tense relationship, and I'd learned Tiffany had potentially considered dropping her client. She'd also thought Scott had been out to get her. Could she possibly have killed him in self-defense if he thought she knew something about his insider trading?

Kari claimed to be Meghan's friend, but Meghan had stolen her joke. If Kari was jealous of Meghan's career, she could've killed her. Plus, given her concern about the missing notebook and her eagerness to locate Scott, could he have known she was guilty? He'd seemed pretty confident her heckling wasn't authentic, so maybe he was on to her.

And then there was David, the spurned ex-boyfriend. Had he killed Meghan for reasons related to their relationship? I racked my brain for reasons he might've killed Scott, but my mind kept coming up blank. Though the jogger who discovered Scott's body could've been anybody, I couldn't help but make the association with David, as I'd seen him out for multiple runs. Could he have killed Scott and called in the body on the trail to deflect blame? It was a stretch, but I filed the theory away just in case it'd come in handy later.

TWENTY-SEVEN

With a lengthy to-do list to prep the lounge for what I hoped would be a busy weekend of service, I didn't waste any time heading directly to Subplot after meeting up with Julian and my quick run-in with Cam.

I'd sent Nate a quick text to let him know about what I'd just learned. With his knowledge of almost everything that went on around town, I wondered if he'd heard or seen anything more since we last spoke.

I spent the afternoon cleaning the lounge, experimenting with flavors for our autumn menu, and handling payroll for my team.

"Does anyone mind if I turn these overhead lights off a bit early? They're starting to give me a headache," Ava called out from across the lounge.

"I don't mind," Lainey answered as she removed outdated flyers from our community event bulletin board. She was more than a maître d'. If she saw something that needed to be done, she hopped in feet-first to do it, which I always appreciated.

Dante paused from wiping down a table to give a thumbs-up.

I nodded. "Go for it."

We typically worked under bright, fluorescent lighting when the lounge wasn't open so we weren't spending all of our waking hours in darkness. Especially as we chopped fresh fruit and other garnishes for our drinks in preparation for the evening's service, the overhead lighting helped us stay safe. Luckily, our ingredient prep had been completed for the day.

When Ava flipped off the lights, my eyes slowly adjusted to the lounge's cozy glow. I took it as a signal to turn off my phone's notifications, not wanting a vibration in my pocket to take me out of my presence and focus.

In honor of summer, we'd changed the color of the strip lights which lined the top perimeter of the lounge to a soft pink, which brightened the space and conjured images of summer in my mind—pink lemonade, watermelon, flamingo pool floats, and strawberry ice cream.

I added a teaspoon of burnt honey to my shaker as I taught Ava how to prepare my new A Midsummer Night's Dream cocktail.

"Logan's been so excited about this new liqueur." She beamed as she spoke about her boyfriend. "I texted him about this cocktail, and I'm hoping he can swing by tonight to give it a taste."

I added the bourbon, Limoncello, rosemary, and ice to the shaker. "Oh no. The pressure's on now," I joked.

As I shook the drink vigorously for a minute, I couldn't keep my mind from drifting to everything I knew about the case so far. Random bits of information appeared in my mind like scattered pieces of a jigsaw puzzle.

Tiffany's fear that Scott had been after her. David jogging through town. Kari searching for a pocket journal in the alley. The black notebook in Scott's blue sports coat. Kari's presence at last night's crime scene. How did it all fit together?

"I think it's been a minute." Ava jarred me back to the present moment.

I stopped shaking the cocktail. "Whoa, I guess I got lost in a daydream."

I placed a large ice cube in the center of a rocks glass with a sprig of rosemary and strained my shaken concoction over it. The beverage was a bright, golden hue, just like an orange-yellow leaf from a hickory tree at peak fall foliage. I couldn't wait for autumn to descend upon Hope Mills.

Preparations for the evening continued until our team huddle at ten to six. After putting our hands in the center of our circle and raising them with a cheer, Lainey headed up the staircase to open Subplot for business and began escorting parties of customers down to the lounge. Dante floated around the lounge to greet our guests, fill their water glasses, and take their orders. Ava and I did the same for those seated at the bar.

No surprises tonight, please. As badly as I wanted to figure out exactly what'd happened to Meghan, I hoped nothing haywire would happen at the lounge tonight. Subplot was supposed to be an escape.

As the lounge steadily filled with guests, I found my rhythm chatting with and waiting on them, along with mixing and serving drinks, and keeping my workspace tidy as I went. The first several hours of service flew by as I entered a flow state. I loved when my body and mind were so attuned to the present moment that I felt like I was on autopilot, knowing exactly what to do to work as efficiently as possible.

"Order up," I said with a smile as I spun around on my heels to serve a Giant Peach mocktail to a patron at the bar.

"This drink looks stunning." Her phone was at the ready to snap a photo of the photogenic cocktail, which was sprinkled with our house-made chili-lime seasoning and garnished with a peach slice and a single basil leaf.

A few seats down, I noticed another man getting settled at the bar out of the corner of my eye as Lainey headed back toward the staircase that led upstairs to her host stand.

I sidestepped to greet the man in a white golf polo with dirty blond hair, who appeared deep in thought as he studied the menu bound in a hardcover book.

"Welcome to Subplot," I said. "Is this your first time visiting us?" It was my standard script.

"It's not. We've met before." When he looked up, his eyes—I couldn't tell if they were hazel or green—caught my attention immediately, even in the dim lounge lighting. It was David. I'd never seen him without his beat-up coral baseball cap.

"I'm so sorry—David, right?"

"Yessir."

"I didn't recognize you at first." I reached for an empty glass and poured water from a carafe. "Let me know if you have any questions about the menu."

"All good." He let out a single forced chuckle and peered down at the menu again. "I think I know what I want already. I'd like to try the Fahrenheit S'more Fifty-One, please."

"You got it."

To prepare it, I added bourbon, a hint of chocolate whiskey, and our special house-made syrup, created with actual toasted marshmallows, to a mixing glass with ice and stirred. I strained it over a large ice cube in a rocks glass. Using a blowtorch, I toasted a large marshmallow, which I used as a garnish. I drizzled the marshmallow with a light chocolate ganache and finished it with a sprinkled pinch of graham cracker crumbs. If I weren't on the clock, I would've loved to have sipped on the campfire-inspired drink.

I slid the finished cocktail in front of David. "Enjoy!"

While I wanted to confront him about what Kari had overheard him say—*Everything will be fine once we get her out of the picture*—as well as whether or not he'd gone for a jog yesterday, I knew it wasn't the time or place. I had a business to run, and I couldn't let my sleuthing get in the way, even as badly as I wanted to figure out once and for all who'd killed Meghan and Scott.

In addition to the handful of customers I waited on at the bar, I also served a couple of groups at seating pods throughout the lounge. I made my way out from behind the bar to refill their waters, take orders for another round, and collect empty glasses from the customers I was responsible for waiting on.

Across the lounge, in Ava's section, Kari sat alone at a table for two.

Lainey beelined over to me. She must've realized I was taking note of Kari. "You recognize her, right?"

I nodded. "The heckler from the comedy show."

"I know we try to seat solo guests at the bar, but she saw someone seated there who made her uncomfortable, so I made an exception."

David.

"That's totally fine. I always trust your judgment."

A heaviness sunk from my chest to my stomach. Was it a coincidence that both Kari and David were in the lounge? Had they coordinated it? Had they set out to do reconnaissance in the venue of Meghan's final performance? If Kari had indeed overheard David's comment about getting Meghan out of the picture, was she following him around?

Please, no drama. No action. As hard as I wished, I knew I needed to keep a close eye on the two of them.

"Pssst!" The loud hiss which cut through the rumble of conversation and soft electronica playing over the speakers not only caught my attention but also turned the heads of a few patrons.

Turning toward it, Kari waved me over to her seating pod, and I obliged. I hoped no other customers would listen in.

"Hey, Kari. What's up?"

"I'm going to skip over the funny business. You know that's him, right? At the bar," she half-whispered.

"Who? Meghan's ex-boyfriend?"

She peered around cautiously. "Mm-hmm. I'd keep an eye on him if I were you. I sure am."

"I recognized him from the other night." I tried to keep my cards somewhat close to my chest, not wanting to reveal anything about my prior interactions with him.

She looked to her friend and then back at me. "I have a bad feeling about that guy."

I inhaled through clenched teeth. "I'll keep that in mind." I tried to be diplomatic, not wanting to share anything with her, but also wanting to ask if she'd learned anything new since I'd seen her the night before. I'd be keeping an eye on her, too.

Noticing Lainey had seated a new party in my section, I let Kari know I needed to get back to work.

I stopped by the nearby table to greet the group which had just arrived and took their orders.

When I returned behind the bar to prepare their drinks, I observed David as discreetly as I could. He wasn't even halfway through his drink yet, and he held his phone to his ear with one hand and plugged his open ear with the other. His wrinkled forehead and unblinking eyes told me he was alarmed. I glanced across the lounge to keep an eye on Kari.

Amidst the chatter and music floating through the lounge —which acted as a natural filter to block out specific conversations—I couldn't make out exactly what he was saying. Luckily, he faced me directly, and my station behind the bar was close enough that I could make out bits and pieces.

"I'll be heading back soon," I thought I heard him say. He

stood up from his stool and waved to get my attention, though I'd already been keeping my eye on him. "Sorry, babe—you're breaking up a bit. Let me step aside for a second." He made eye contact with me, gestured at his rocks glass, and mouthed, *Be right back.*

I gave him a thumbs-up. He wouldn't skip out on his tab, would he?

As David left the bar through the rarely used downstairs exit, one word replayed in my mind over and over.

Babe.

By the sounds of it, there was another woman in the picture. If he'd called someone *babe* just a few days after Meghan's death, had he actually begged her for another chance, as Garrett had claimed? It was possible, if David was in a non-exclusive relationship or ready to cheat. Maybe he'd moved on from Meghan more than he'd let on. But if that were the case, it lessened his motive for revenge. I also imagined it lessened his motive to seek justice. Why was he really still here? And why had he made the trip to Hope Mills for Meghan's show in the first place?

Surveying the glasses of the other customers seated at the bar, I noticed a few needed water refills. I reached under the bar for a fresh carafe of chilled water and topped off all their glasses.

Over their shoulders, I stared through the darkness.

A sinking feeling of defeat tugged at my chest as my vision seemed to zoom in on an empty armchair deeper in the lounge. *Where did Kari go?*

I shifted my eyes to David's empty seat.

Babe.

The hair on the back of my neck must've been standing straight up as a what-if formed in my mind.

I eyed Kari's vacant seat again. *There's no way...is there?*

TWENTY-EIGHT

David eventually returned from his phone call several minutes later, but it appeared Kari was long gone. Had they come to Subplot to meet up? Were they co-conspirators?

Wait a second. My kneejerk theory didn't make sense. Kari hadn't been on the phone, which meant David hadn't been calling her *babe*. Unless it was all a ruse. Maybe he wanted me to think he was talking to another woman.

That's enough, Reece. I admitted I was officially spiraling, but I didn't let it stop me from imagining them getting up to no good in the alley behind the lounge.

With David back at the bar, I needed to tread lightly and choose my next words carefully if I decided to say anything at all beyond small talk. Luckily, I was preparing drinks while Dante stood at the opposite end of the bar, waiting to deliver them to guests in his seating section. *Good, I look busy.*

He guzzled down the remainder of his Fahrenheit S'more Fifty-One cocktail, a strange contrast compared to how long he'd nursed the first half. The way he leaned forward on the bar and appeared taller than the guests beside him, it seemed he was only half-sitting on his stool. His posture was rigid—not at all as relaxed as he'd been before he stepped out for his call. He waved me over, and I pretended he'd caught my attention. He asked me to close out his tab.

I hustled toward our point of sale system to print out his check. I grabbed a thick mass-market paperback from the stack beside the register, which sat below a sign that read, TBR PILE. A customer had given the *To-Be-Read* sign as a gift, and it made me smile despite the tension swelling in my chest. As I sandwiched his tab into the worn copy of *The Da Vinci Code*, I spoke quietly into the lapel mic clipped to my shirt. Ava, Dante, Lainey, and I each wore one, along with an earpiece that allowed us to communicate with one another.

"I'm going to need to step out for a few minutes. I'm so sorry. Could you please cover for me?"

"No problem. I'll cover your sections," Dante answered first.

"And I can pop down to help fill waters and clean up empty glasses," Lainey offered.

"I'll stay behind the bar and take care of your guests here until you get back," Ava chimed in through her mic, although she stood beside me, so the others could hear.

I felt so grateful for my agile team, always ready to pivot to help one another out when we needed to be flexible.

"Sounds like a plan."

I spun around and slid the book in front of David. "No rush."

He already held out his credit card between his index and middle fingers.

I nodded and took his card, swiped it, and printed his final receipt.

He scribbled a tip amount and his signature before making a quick exit up the front stairs.

As soon as he was out of view, I hustled around the bar and through our rarely-used—especially in the middle of service—

downstairs exit. The sun had set, and it was already dark outside.

I jogged down the gravel alley behind Subplot and turned up the narrow cement footpath along the side of the building, which led to Main Street. Standing on the sidewalk in front of D'Amico's, I surveyed Main Street in both directions. I spotted David's white polo under the soft orange glow of streetlights. He headed in the direction of the Colonial Inn.

"David!" I hissed, hoping I was loud enough to catch his attention, but not so loud that I'd cause concern if anyone beyond him could hear me.

He froze, then pivoted slowly toward me. Once he realized who was calling his name, he sped up.

"Wait!" I called out.

"Sorry, man. I've got somewhere to be. I can't stick around."

I desperately wanted to chase him down and figure out what he was up to, but seeing how he'd sped out of the lounge and not wanting to unnecessarily escalate the situation, I decided it probably wasn't in my best interest to follow him. I was also likely overthinking the situation as I felt tormented by the theories I'd formed. Plus, I needed to get back to work.

I felt my shoulders droop as I retreated down the pathway toward Subplot's back alley. Looking up to the sky dotted with stars, I found myself asking for a sign that would put the mystery surrounding Meghan's death to rest. I let out a frustrated grunt. *I can't wait to put this all behind me.*

"The door's locked up here, everyone," Lainey called down the steps. "Watch your eyes." She flipped the fluorescent lights on as soon as the last party departed Subplot a few minutes after one-thirty, bringing everything around me into brighter focus once I'd allowed my eyes to adjust. Without our colorful, dim lighting and no sounds of drinks being shaken or blended, the lounge felt like a strange shell of itself.

Throughout the remainder of the evening, I couldn't shake the feeling of defeat I'd felt since learning of Scott's murder. Though I'd grown suspicious of David and felt like I'd gathered some interesting tidbits tonight, I didn't feel any closer to ending this week's chaos.

I slumped onto a barstool, facing the bar as my team surrounded me from behind. "How would you all like to head home a little early tonight?"

"Reece, what's going on?" Dante, who was never afraid to speak up, asked from his position at the end of the bar.

"Nothing." Knowing my staff would want more of an explanation to be sure I was all right, I elaborated. "I'm just feeling really stressed about the murders that happened in town this week. It haunts me to think about how Meghan performed her last show ever in that corner." I pointed backwards over my shoulder with my thumb in the general direction of our small stage.

Ava, who'd been collecting empty glasses in a plastic tub, approached me from behind. She placed a comforting hand on my back. "Reece, we're here for you. You do so much for us. Please, let us support you."

"Thank you. It's just...sometimes getting lost in my work is my way of coping. I don't mind staying here to clean up the lounge on my own." I wanted nothing more than to blast some Liz Phair and tackle a laundry list of chores.

"Well, if you change your mind, I'll be on standby," Lainey offered.

"I'm sure any of us would be happy to come back to help you if you need us," Ava said.

I wiped the moisture from my eyes. "Thank you all. Seriously. I appreciate you more than you'll ever know." I swiveled around on my barstool to look each of my team members in the eye. I was truly the luckiest guy in the world to get to work with each of them.

The team collected their personal belongings and left the lounge together through the secret bookcase upstairs. Soon, my sulking feelings would disappear as I collected dirty glasses and loaded them into our industrial dishwasher, wiped down tables, and straightened all the bottles behind the bar to ensure their labels faced outward.

But before I got to it and turned on some music, I sat still on the barstool, enjoying a few peaceful moments of silent solitude. Though Subplot was a huge investment and responsibility, I found solace in the space I'd created, and I loved to admire it. It was a place I could feel proud to call my own.

A couple of minutes later, with both feet planted on the ground, I spun around on my barstool, ready to check off all the closing tasks for the evening. As I did, though, I felt a flat object dragging beneath one foot. Had a customer dropped something?

Trapped under my white sneaker was a black pocket-sized notebook.

I leapt off the barstool and crouched down to pick it up. I turned it over, revealing a glossy sticker with a pale-pink illustration of a rose. I began to shake as I felt the emotional weight of what I held in my hands. Was this the key piece of evidence which would help me solve Meghan's and Scott's murders?

I counted the barstools on either side of me.

I'd been sitting in the exact spot David had been before he rushed out.

TWENTY-NINE

I leafed through the journal. Most of the notes jotted inside appeared to be random observations.

> Take Your Kids to Work Day? More like Forced Brainwashing to Humanize Your Co-workers Day.

Another line read:

> I'm not the only one who thinks it's icky when realtors print their faces on park benches, right? Yeah, that's a no for me.

One page contained what looked to be a free-verse poem:

> Soothed by the glow of the
> Golden refrigerator light,
> I cradle my emotional-support

Bag of shredded cheese.

Though I wasn't in a headspace to laugh, there was no doubt the scribbles inside had a humorous bend to them. My best guess was that the journal was a collection of inspiration for comedy.

Was I holding Kari's lost notebook? It was exactly how she'd described it. How had David gotten ahold of it? And what would it have meant to Scott? Was it proof of jokes Meghan had stolen? Did it implicate Scott in Meghan's murder somehow?

If it'd been in David's possession, was it possible he'd killed Scott and taken it from him? How would he have known to look there? Had Kari handed the notebook off to Scott after the comedy show? Had Scott stolen it somehow? All my questions assumed it was the same notebook I'd seen in Scott's pocket, but it was also possible he had one of his own, completely unrelated to the one now in my possession.

Regardless of how he'd gotten his hands on the notebook, I found it highly unlikely he would've accidentally dropped it here. Wouldn't he have been more careful with such an important piece of evidence? Unless he'd left it behind intentionally. But why?

I flipped through the pages and then checked the front cover. Were my eyes deceiving me? I blinked hard, as if it might change what I saw. Of course, it hadn't.

Meghan Spencer's name was inscribed in blue ink on the inside cover.

Why had Kari been searching for a notebook that wasn't hers? Was it a further act of sabotage? Or was she aware that the notebook contained useful information which could help her find justice? Though I'd had my doubts, she'd claimed to be friends with Meghan, and her knowledge of this journal might've been proof of it.

My heart pounded, and my vision blurred and refocused over and over. Finding the notebook at the stool where David sat felt like confirmation he at least knew something about the murders—or possibly had something to do with one or both of them.

I continued leafing through the small journal, skimming its pages of Meghan's seeds of inspiration. *Is there incriminating information about David in here?* Even if there was, how could any of it be proven to be true? David confronted Meghan herself after the show Sunday, claiming she'd falsified details of their relationship in her set. Just because something was written in her journal didn't make it fact. However, I trusted its authenticity, figuring it probably wasn't meant to be read by anyone but Meghan.

And then, as I reached the end of her entries—about two-thirds of the way through the book—objective observations were interspersed between her stream-of-consciousness comedic musings.

> *She claimed there weren't enough rooms at The Flora House.*

> *I wish David would quit hanging around. Move on already!*

> *I think he's using me to get to her.*

My fingers trembled as I flipped through the pages. I closed the notebook and placed it on the bar.

"How did I miss this?" I mumbled to myself.

I paced frenetically in the open area between the barstools and a couple of the lounge's seating pods.

David's words echoed in my mind as the pieces began to fall into place.

Everything will be fine once we get her out of the picture.

I'll be heading back soon.

Babe.

An image of Tiffany hustling up the front steps of the Colonial Inn popped into my mind.

"They've been seeing each other." I whispered, feeling vindicated as I made sense of the situation in my mind.

I couldn't imagine Meghan would've been pleased if she'd realized David and Tiffany—her loathed ex-boyfriend and manager—were seeing one another. Had she confronted her manager about it? If Tiffany was aware that multiple people in the area had plausible motives to want Meghan dead, had she taken advantage of the opportunity to knock her client off?

I'd never seen Tiffany and David interact, but it made sense they'd try not to be seen together. They each pointed blame in multiple directions, but never at one another.

Though it could've all been in my head, I didn't want to risk Tiffany getting away. Especially since she knew I had suspicions about David, I feared she might flee.

I called Detective Sharp's direct cell phone. I'd added her to my contacts when I'd received previous instructions to call her immediately if I saw or heard anything related to the investigation.

She skipped a greeting when she answered and got straight down to business. "Reece... Is everything all right?"

"Meghan's killer—and possibly Scott's, too. I think it was Meghan's manager, Tiffany. She's staying at the Colonial Inn."

I explained my rationale for why I suspected David and Tiffany might have been acting together. I told her I'd found a notebook that looked like it belonged to Meghan in the lounge as I was cleaning.

Detective Sharp let me know that she, along with another officer, would head over to the inn. She asked me for a few additional details and told me to keep the notebook in a secure place in Subplot.

"Will you be there for a while?"

"I was just finishing up around here, so I was about to head home. But I can stay here as long as you need," I offered before we ended our call.

I rested my phone on the bar. Following her instruction, I took Meghan's notebook to my office and locked it inside. I clipped my carabiner of keys to a belt loop on my jeans.

As I collected the trash to take out back, there was a lightness in my step. I hoped that if the police could prove my theory was right and potentially get a confession from Tiffany, I could finally move forward.

I stepped outside into the cool evening air—much cooler than it had been over the last week—with two large trash bags at my side. The shadowy alley was silent and void of any police activity, which was a relief. The forensics team must've collected their evidence.

I turned toward the dumpster in the faint light, ready to finish my final task.

But then, just before I took my first step into the gentle breeze, I heard a woman's calm voice, just above a whisper, behind me.

"Don't move."

THIRTY

My breath caught in my chest.

Following the voice's order, I kept my focus straight ahead. As bad as I wanted to turn my head to confirm who was standing behind me, I didn't dare disobey. I couldn't let what'd happened to Meghan and Scott happen to me.

Was it Tiffany? Or maybe Kari? It was difficult to make out the hushed voice.

A quick click echoed through the alley. A second later, I saw a gloved hand raising the blade of a pocketknife toward my neck.

"If you move, you die," she whispered. "Got it? It won't take much pressure for this thing to make a cut."

I could sense that the person hovering behind me was taller than me, partially from the way the woman's voice seemed to descend into my ear and from the upward angle from which she held the knife against my throat.

It has to be Tiffany. Kari wasn't nearly as tall as she was.

"I've got you exactly where I want you," she hissed. "You thought you were so smart, pinning this on David. But he told me you were sticking your nose where it didn't belong. Bet you didn't expect to see me here."

She must have been waiting to confront me. Had I given David the impression that I was onto him? Or maybe since he'd misplaced Meghan's journal in the lounge, Tiffany had come looking for it.

"*You* killed Meghan, didn't you?"

Tiffany let out an evil cackle. "So what if I did? Where's the proof?"

"Tiffany, would you please put the knife down? Can't we talk about this?" I begged through shaky breaths.

"I'd say we're talking just fine the way things are. Although I think I'd prefer to have this conversation indoors." She didn't deny her identity.

"No. I'd say we're able to talk just fine out here."

"Awww," she moaned coldly. "Don't go back on your word, Reece. You said I was welcome here any time. We're going to pivot toward the door, and we'll have a little chat in private. Okay?"

I gulped carefully, afraid my Adam's apple might graze the blade as I swallowed. "Fine, then."

As we spun toward the door, she kept talking. "You love to act like you're so interested in helping. You weasel around, asking people questions and searching for clues, as if you really care, when really, you're just trying to keep your own nose clean."

I pulled the door's unlocked handle down and stepped inside with the knife's blade at my throat and Tiffany just inches behind me.

"I believed you wanted justice for Meghan, but now I know it's not the case. *You're* the one trying to keep your nose clean. It was *you*," I said as we crossed the threshold into the air-conditioned lounge.

Tiffany pressed the flat side of the blade into my neck, careful not to cut me, but enough to make me freeze in my tracks. "I'd choose my words a bit more wisely if I were in your vulnerable position."

The door slammed shut behind us, causing me to jolt.

"Let's go over there," Tiffany instructed.

I rotated my head to the left. With her free hand, she pointed at the bar. I shuffled my feet in that direction, and she followed closely behind.

"Your phone," she barked. "It's mine now. I'm not going to let you get out of this so easy."

I could only hope the police had shown up to the Colonial Inn, were unable to locate Tiffany, and thought to come check on me.

"Tiffany, can we please sit down and talk about this?"

She tapped the knife's blade on my neck ever so lightly. "I'm not letting you out of my reach. Now keep moving. Hands in your pocket. Now."

I obeyed, scuffling closer toward the bar. As soon as we were within arm's reach of my phone, Tiffany reached for it with her free hand. She tucked it away, presumably into her back pocket.

"There. That wasn't so bad, was it? See how well things work when you listen to what I say? No one needs to get hurt here."

As angry as her condescending tone made me, I knew anything I rebutted would only aggravate her, and I didn't want her to draw any blood.

"Now, where is the notebook?" she demanded.

"Notebook?"

"Oh, don't play dumb. You know exactly what I'm talking about. Meg's notebook. David *accidentally dropped it*," she said in a mocking tone. She gently pressed the flat, dull side of the knife into my throat to remind me it was there. "I know it's somewhere in here."

"It's in the office," I admitted. I wished my keys weren't clipped to my jeans. If only they'd been in my pocket. I could have curled my knuckles around them and had a fighting chance to escape Tiffany's threat.

"Let's not waste time. To the office we go."

I let out a deep sigh and paced toward the office. My keys jangled with each step.

"The keys stay around your waist. Got it?"

I grunted in response and angled my right hip toward the doorknob, allowing me to unlock the door without unclipping the carabiner.

"I knew it." She chuckled as soon as we stepped into my workspace. The weighted door fell shut on its own behind us. The journal lay on my desk, rose sticker side up. "It's mine now. Keep it moving."

Once we reached the desk, she confiscated the notebook. "Very good." I figured she tucked it into her pocket, along with my phone.

"Okay. You can go now," I said.

She snickered diabolically. "Oh, we're not done." In my lower peripheral vision, I could see the movement of her wrist as she waved the knife in front of my neck. "I'm not so heartless that I'd leave without giving you all the juicy details you've been looking for all week."

My heart threatened to beat out of my chest. My breathing accelerated. If she promised to tell me everything, she probably intended to kill me.

THIRTY-ONE

"Wouldn't you rather get a head start? You can get far away before I have a chance to get ahold of the police. You have my phone." I didn't dare clue her in that I'd already called the police. I could only hope they might be on their way to me once they realized Tiffany wasn't at her hotel. The detective knew I had a key piece of evidence in my possession.

She drew in a sharp breath. "See, I don't intend for you to get in touch with them at all. So, spill. How are you so certain it was me? Humor me."

"Tiffany, can you please put the knife down?" I urged. I felt hopeless standing in the center of my small, windowless office. At such a late hour, it was unlikely anyone else was in the building. Heidi and her team had likely gone home already. Even if I screamed, no one would hear me.

She pressed the flat side of the blade into my neck again, making me afraid I was one deep breath away from a fatal slice in my skin.

"Tiffany. Tiffany. Please," I begged through shallow, shaky breaths. "If you kill me right now, you're going to have more blood on your hands. It's going to be even harder to hide your guilt from the police. Are you prepared for that? You've already murdered two people."

It had become abundantly clear Tiffany operated on emotion more than logic, so I needed to tread carefully.

I felt her lighten the pressure on my neck ever so slightly. *Hopefully I'm getting through to her.*

"How can you be so sure?" She really wanted to know. Perhaps she was trying to assess how likely it was that she could get away with her crimes.

"Did Meghan know you and David were together?" I didn't answer her question directly. The more I could keep her talking, the longer I could stretch out the time, hopefully increasing chances I might be found alive.

"Together?" She spat the word out like she'd taken a shot of something stiff with no chaser.

"You've been staying at the same hotel as David. And you've been staying there together, haven't you?"

"So, what if we were?"

The knife's dull edge pressed harder into my neck again, causing my already-shallow breathing to quicken. "I'm sure Meghan didn't like that her ex-boyfriend, who she clearly despised, was sleeping with her manager—who she was supposed to be able to trust to grow her career."

"Don't even start with me about trust. Don't think for a second that I would've jeopardized Meg's career. I did *every-thing* for her career. My entire world revolved around her. Shouldn't I be able to do *anything* for myself?" Luckily, as her emotions escalated, she relented the pressure she applied to my neck.

Though Tiffany seemed to have been Meghan's biggest supporter, willing to do anything to help build her client's career, cracks had formed in her apparent loyalty. And understandably so. Not only was Meghan's blackmail illegal, it was a huge breach of trust.

"Tiffany, don't do anything else you'd regret," I pleaded.

"I'm too far along for that now." She pressed the flat edge of the blade against my neck. The ever-changing levels of pressure she applied were torturous. How much longer would it be before I felt blood trickling down my neck? It was a miracle the blade hadn't yet torn my skin, and it felt like time was running out to negotiate my way out of my vulnerable position.

I took shallow, tentative breaths, not sure how much longer I could endure her pushing and pulling. This time, I feared her fuse would be much shorter. *One wrong move, and I'm done for.*

She stroked my neck ever so slightly with the knife, grazing my stubble as if she were shaving me.

"Tiffany, I know deep down, this isn't who you are. I see the real you." Considering her erratic behavior and seemingly unstable emotions, I hoped I could talk the knife away from my neck. I'd felt for myself how her fluctuating emotions had made her press harder or let up.

I sensed the slightest trembling in her voice. "It wasn't supposed to go this way. It all spiraled out of control."

Keep her talking. "She pushed you to the edge, didn't she?" I played into the tension that I'd witnessed between them before the show, although I wondered if Meghan's attitude toward Tiffany was because she was aware of her secret relationship with David.

Her shoulders slouched, and the knife lost contact with my skin, though she didn't retreat entirely. *It's working.*

"After her show, we were going to celebrate Scott's interest in casting her for *In Stitches*. But she'd put the pieces together that I'd been seeing David, and she was pissed. We bickered back and forth, and I tried to show her how her entire career was thanks to *me*. Everything I did was for *her*. David was the one thing in my life that was for *me*, but she didn't want me to have it. When she charged at me with clenched fists, I knew it was going to get ugly for at least one of us. Luckily, I had my height and strength going for me. I wasn't going to let her get between me and David."

Though I couldn't fathom it for myself, it seemed Tiffany felt killing Meghan was her only option to be with David in that moment.

"When I pushed her, she lost her balance and hit her head on the arm of an Adirondack chair when she fell. It knocked her out."

The Adirondack chairs along the Promenade were all bright red. Had there been any blood splatter on the chair that Meghan hit when she fell? Had there been any blood at all? Either way, I wondered if Meghan might have left a trace of DNA behind that could validate Tiffany's story.

As I stared at the blank office wall in front of me, time stood still. I feared my time—and Tiffany's patience—would run out soon if I didn't find a way out of the room.

"Why didn't you call for help? Were you afraid?" I asked.

"Once she was on the ground, it was clear she wasn't going to make it. She fell hard. And I was sick of devoting my life to helping her."

It wasn't impossible, but I had a hard time believing that hitting her head on a composite wood Adirondack chair was enough to kill her. Her head would've had to hit the chair's arm at the perfect angle and location to be fatal. Considering her fall was the result of a push, maybe she had a brain bleed that ultimately led to her death.

"So, you checked her pulse, and...?"

"No. I could just tell she was gone."

"She hit her head on a chair from being pushed and died instantly? With no blood?"

Her eyes filled with tears. It seemed she was beginning to crumple under my scrutiny. Was she finally admitting the weight of what she'd done? "Fine—After she fell, I couldn't face what I'd done. I didn't know what to do. I had to cover my tracks, so I dumped her in the river."

I fought every urge to cover my mouth with my hands, not wanting to risk being slashed with the pocketknife less than an inch away from me. "I can't believe you left her to die. You could have called for help and saved her."

"There was no saving her. I didn't want to save her. She couldn't have cared less about what was best for me. She never took my advice, even though I always had her best interest in mind. And then when she tried to get between me and David? *Psh.* I was done worrying about what was best for her."

How could she have been so invested in her client's career and care so little about her as a person? I found it difficult to understand Tiffany's motivations, but I also would never understand what could drive a person to take a life—let alone possibly two.

I still wasn't convinced Meghan's death was accidental. "You meant to kill her, didn't you? I can't think of any other reason why you would've swiped my friend's pocketknife. I think you knew you'd need to plant fake evidence."

"I found it lying around on the floor after the show. I meant to hand it over for your lost and found."

I highly doubted it. Luckily, she couldn't see the angry glare on my face. "And you killed Scott, too. I don't know how, but you did."

"How dare you!" she growled.

"Was he after you for knowing about his insider trading? Are you going to try to claim you killed him in self-defense?"

She laughed deviously under her breath. "You're so gullible.

I saw the news about insider trading at his company, so I used that knowledge to pin Meghan's murder on him."

"So he wasn't actually involved?"

"Not until I decided to involve him. It sure fooled everybody. It fooled you, huh?"

I could barely comprehend how she'd fabricated a story about Scott to steer suspicion away from herself. She'd turned an innocent man into my—and likely the police's—top suspect.

Suddenly, a click echoed through the office.

Time seemed to accelerate as so much happened in a matter of seconds.

My breath caught in my throat.

The knife in Tiffany's hand still hovered too close for comfort in front of me, though she'd grown shaky.

The office door whooshed open.

"Drop it!" a familiar man's voice ordered. Without looking, I knew it was Cam, even though I rarely ever heard him speak with such a forceful tone.

Fearful as I still was, I still managed to take my first full, deep breath in quite some time.

I remained frozen as Tiffany lowered the knife.

Daring to glance over my shoulder, I saw Cam standing in the hallway. He propped the office door open with his foot. He must have been extra stealthy when entering the lounge, likely through the unlocked basement door. I hadn't heard a peep outside of the office, though the air conditioning's white noise and my tense conversation with Tiffany likely drowned out any sound.

"Hands up," he commanded.

Tiffany raised both hands beside her head and folded the pocketknife shut in one hand. I followed suit, even though I figured the instruction was directed only at her.

Tiffany's head dipped. There was no doubt in my mind that she knew she'd been caught for good.

Cam lowered his gun and stepped into the office. "I'll take that," he said as he confiscated the pocketknife. "Hands behind your back." He reached for handcuffs on his waist.

"She took my phone," I said just above a whisper.

He allowed her to remove my phone from her back pocket before fastening the cuffs around her wrists and escorting her out of the lounge.

As they turned the corner, Detective Sharp stepped into view. I felt relieved I'd called in my concerns about Tiffany as soon as I'd put the pieces together.

Detective Sharp didn't blink as she approached me. "Are you all right?" I'd never heard her speak in such a high-pitched or whispery tone. Though she always maintained profession- alism and had a duty to remain objective, I sensed genuine concern in her voice.

"How did you...?" I started to ask.

"When we couldn't locate Tiffany at the hotel, I tried to call you. When you didn't answer, I had a bad feeling. We headed here right away and heard arguing in the office as soon as we stepped inside."

Though I'd been standing in the same spot since I'd been coerced into my office, I was still somehow out of breath. "Thank you. You saved my life."

Detective Sharp took a step closer and put a comforting hand on my shoulder. She nodded solemnly at me. After removing her hand, she retrieved the palm-sized notebook from her maroon blazer. "How did she find you?"

I let out a shallow, exhausted exhale as I gained more control over my breathing. "She was waiting for me outside when I went to take out the trash. She's been seeing Meghan's ex-boyfriend, David, and I suspect he told her I was onto them.

She told me everything because she was ready to kill me, too. She killed Meghan Spencer."

"And Scott Simmons, too?"

My stomach was in knots. "We didn't get that far, but it was implied."

The detective jotted notes at lightning speed as I summarized everything that happened since I'd stepped foot into the alley. I recounted everything I'd learned about Meghan's final interaction with Tiffany and how she'd falsified accusations related to Scott's business dealings.

As relieved as I was to know Tiffany was in custody, I still had so many questions. Most of them revolved around Scott, whose death I still hadn't fully processed. Why exactly had Tiffany killed him? Had she lured him to the Towpath, or had he confronted her?

I also wondered about David. It had become clear Tiffany hadn't been operating from a stable frame of mind. Was David in on Meghan's murder? Had he realized Tiffany was out of control? If so, I had a hard time wondering why on Earth he would've stayed with her.

Detective Sharp clicked her pen shut and tapped her notebook against her flat palm. "And the notebook she found in here?"

"I couldn't see what she did with it, but I think she put it in her pocket. It's probably still on her."

She placed her notebook back into her blazer. "I better get back to the station. I have a busy night ahead of me. Can I give you a ride home on my way?"

I shook my head. "Nah. But thank you. I'll lock up here and walk back. It'll be a good way for me to decompress. And besides, at least I know it's safe out there now."

THIRTY-TWO

Nate's text had arrived at five forty-seven the following morning. His message was accompanied by a link to an article on the *Hope Mills Local* website. The headline read Viral Comedian Meghan Spencer's Manager Charged with Two Counts of Homicide.

According to my alarm clock, it was a few minutes before nine-thirty. I felt terrible for not texting him last night, but after all I'd been through, I'd headed straight to bed after getting home.

Jameson, who was curled up on my pillow just above my shoulder, purred lovingly in my ear as I typed a response.

Over the summer, my parents and I began having a standing weekly coffee meetup on Friday mornings.

Nate replied immediately with a rapid-fire series of texts.

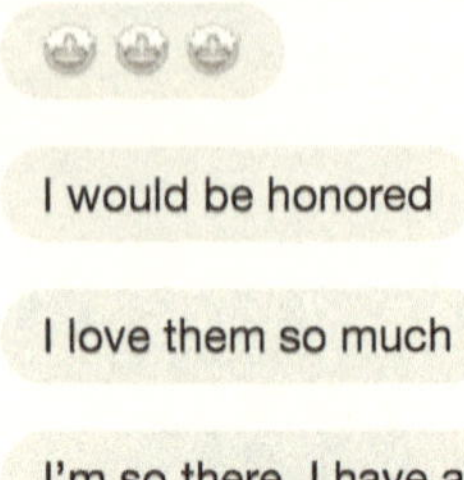

I would be honored

I love them so much

I'm so there. I have an opening in my schedule
til 11

From my comfortable, stretched-out position in my warm bed in my cool, air-conditioned bedroom with Jameson nuzzled against me, there was nothing I wanted to do more than roll over and go back to sleep.

However, I looked forward to seeing my parents, and I knew I owed it to Nate to fill him in on everything that had gone down last night.

Ok awesome! See you there soon

After slipping into some athletic wear, fitting a baseball cap over my disheveled hair, refreshing Jameson's water bowl, and topping off his food, I headed for Riverside Roastery in what was shaping up to be another hot and humid August day.

As I passed the Colonial Inn on my way, there were no signs of anything out of the ordinary. I had no doubts Tiffany remained in police custody, and I wondered what had happened to David. Had he played any role in Meghan's death? How aware was he of everything Tiffany had done over the past week, especially if they'd been staying there together?

As I approached the coffee shop via its rear entrance along the Promenade, Nate accompanied my parents from the opposite direction. While he was dressed in his typical tattered, paint-streaked work wear, my parents were dressed like they'd just finished playing pickleball at the community courts.

Once we were all within earshot of one another, my dad poked a thumb into Nate's chest over his shoulder. "Look who we picked up on the way."

Nate shrugged. "I heard you all were getting coffee. I didn't want to miss out on the fun."

My mom's face glowed. "It's so wonderful to have coffee with *both* sons today."

I opened my arms and first hugged my mom. "The whole crew is back together." I loved how my parents treated Nate like a member of the family. Considering how close we'd been ever since he'd moved to Hope Mills and how much time we spent together throughout high school and beyond, he was the closest thing I'd ever have to a brother.

"Talk about perfect timing," my dad said as we embraced.

Nate and I clapped our hands together and pulled one another in for our customary one-armed hug.

Inside, we each ordered a drink. The iced blueberry pie latte had a chokehold on me, and I couldn't resist ordering it yet again. With fall just weeks away—and the fall menu likely launching toward the end of August—I knew my time with the delicious latte was limited. Nate ordered a plain cold brew, and my parents each ordered a black coffee and added milk and sugar to their mugs at the self-service condiment station.

We sat at a table near the front windows overlooking Main Street with vibrant purple flowers in hanging baskets in view. Understandably, our conversation started with the biggest news Hope Mills had seen in quite some time.

"So, it was Tiffany all along?" Nate asked.

I nodded as I swallowed a gulp of my iced latte.

My dad let out a disappointed sigh. "I saw the article in the

Local this morning. If she was charged with two counts already, then she must've confessed everything."

"And *two* counts of homicide? What's that all about?" Nate asked.

I grimaced. "Sorry, I didn't tell you. But yes. She came clean to me about killing them both."

Nate practically choked on a swig of cold brew. "Came clean to *you*? Why? How?"

I inhaled sharply with a wince. "She...uh...paid me a little visit at the lounge last night, after we'd closed."

My parents and Nate gave me confused stares without saying a word. They all leaned in closer as I summarized our run-in. "Luckily, I'd already called the police to tell them about my suspicions, so they came to my rescue." I tried to downplay the intensity of the situation, not wanting to worry them unnecessarily after the fact.

My mom, who cried any time she so much as saw a cardinal in the backyard, was in tears. "This world. Oh, what you've been through. I hate that I can't protect you."

Though my dad was sensitive and empathetic, he was masterful at maintaining a stoic demeanor to balance her strong emotions.

I feared Nate had turned to stone after hearing what I'd said, based on the way he froze, his eyes wide and unblinking, his glass of cold brew dripping condensation down his arm as he prepared to take a sip. "You weren't lying when you told me you had a bunch to fill me in on," he eventually said.

I summarized details I'd learned about the case since our last meetup at Bridge Street Bar.

I concluded my story by glancing at Nate. "Needless to say, you're finally in the clear." I picked up my iced latte and raised it toward him. "Cheers to that."

Nate's coffee remained on the table. He massaged his

temples and shook his head, probably stunned to take in all the information I'd dumped. "I owe you big time."

"You don't owe me anything. I know you'd do the same for me."

Nate squinted at me, as if something was wrong.

I tucked my chin into my chest, looking down at my shirt. "What? Do I have a stain?"

Nate chuckled. "No, I'm looking over your shoulder. Is that Cam and Chloe?"

In particular, my mom perked up at the sound of Chloe's name. She absolutely adored her would-have-been daughter-in-law.

Sure enough, Chloe and Cam were waiting in line together at the espresso bar. I almost hadn't recognized Cam without his police uniform. Like Chloe, he was dressed in gym attire.

"*Pssst!*" Nate hissed loudly, not only catching their attention, but also nearly everyone else in Riverside Roastery.

As soon as they made eye contact with us, they abandoned the line and made a beeline for our table. We all stood up and exchanged a series of handshakes and hugs.

Chloe clasped my arms as we released from our quick embrace. "How are you holding up? Cam told me about what happened last night."

"Honestly, I'm still a bit shaken. Luckily, a good night's sleep helped." I turned toward her brother. "Did you get any sleep last night?"

With arms crossed, Cam rocked on his heels. He had tired bags under his eyes. "Barely. But I'm used to it. My sleep schedule is forever messed up."

"Why don't you two sit down?" She looked to her brother. "I'll go order our drinks and join you."

Nate dragged two more chairs to our table, and we took a seat while Chloe headed to the coffee bar.

"There's so much about this situation that hasn't completely clicked together yet for me," I said, speaking to Cam. I lowered my voice, mindful that details about the case had to stay under wraps. "I figured out Tiffany and David were together. But why would he have left that notebook behind in the lounge? It was clearly a critical piece of evidence. It had to have been intentional, right?"

Cam scanned the coffee shop. "That aligns with the story she told during our interrogation," he said quietly from his position across from me. "It sounds like there was trouble in paradise."

My parents and Nate didn't chime in, but they appeared deeply engaged in our conversation, with eyes wide open.

As I continued to speak, I stayed mindful of my volume, especially when mentioning any names. "There was no other explanation that made sense to me. It was too much of a linchpin in the case to be left behind so casually. There seemed to be some incriminating stuff written in there. Besides her funny little observations, it seems like Meghan was catching on to her manager's fishy behavior."

He nodded in agreement.

"I still can't figure out Scott's murder, though. Was he actually on the run? Because from what Tiffany told me right before Detective Sharp showed up, he hadn't actually engaged in any insider trading." I hoped we weren't alienating everyone else at the table by carrying on our conversation without offering additional context, but I was too eager to fill in the gaps in my knowledge.

Cam turned his chin down toward his chest and let out a perturbed grunt. "We're still learning more, but he was keeping a low profile as the news started to break. There was some major drama happening at his company with the acquisition, but there was no concrete evidence of any wrongdoing on his part. We believe Tiffany saw news of insider trading at CineStream and called in an anonymous tip to create an apparent motive for Scott."

"Earlier this week, Tiffany told me Meghan had been blackmailing Scott, and she thought he'd killed her to keep his secret from getting out. But it never added up to me how Meghan would've learned of his alleged insider trading in the first place."

He gave me a curt nod. "Of course, the insider trading investigation is with the Feds, but it doesn't seem like her claims were accurate. She used her knowledge of the situation to her advantage to make him look super guilty."

My mouth was agape with amazement as Chloe joined us at the table, a mug in each hand—one for her and one for her brother.

"However," Cam said as he slid the tangerine mug toward him, "Tiffany claimed Scott had been in possession of the notebook."

"Really?" I figured Tiffany took it from Scott after she'd killed him. Clearly, it contained information that didn't paint her in the best light, and she'd gone so far as to come back for it at Subplot. "How would Scott have gotten ahold of it?"

"Tiffany thinks Meghan handed it to him."

"Why would she share a book of unfinished jokes and half-baked ideas with a casting director she'd just met?"

He shrugged. "We may never know for sure, especially now that both of them are sadly no longer with us."

When Kari had gone searching for the notebook, was it because she was aware it held the truth? Maybe she'd been telling the truth all along about her friendship with Meghan, and she knew it'd avenge her death.

Nate tsked. "This is a lot to take in."

Chloe shook her head, probably in disbelief. My parents barely reacted, probably stunned by all the information.

I furrowed my brow. "Wait...let me make sure I've got this all straight. Tiffany had been sleeping around with Meghan's ex-boyfriend. When Meghan found out, she was none too happy and planned to confront Tiffany. When she did, her manager pushed her and knocked her out. Instead of trying to help her client, she dumped her in the river and left her to die. Tiffany, aware of the CineStream scandal, tried to shift suspicion to Scott. Meanwhile, he had clues in the notebook given to him by Meghan. Scott, upset by her false accusations of his insider trading, probably had Tiffany figured out and went after her, but she killed him, too."

Cam, who'd just taken a small gulp from his beverage, bobbed his head. "I'm sure there's much more to be uncovered, but that seems to be the gist of it." I was sure he was privy to more information than he could share with me, especially in a public space.

Everyone around the table exchanged stunned eye contact as the conversation on the topic tapered off to its natural conclusion.

"In brighter news..." Nate spoke up to pivot the discussion to something a bit more lighthearted.

We continued to catch up on the more mundane aspects of everyone's lives, which I was perfectly okay with. My parents asked Chloe and Cam about their parents. Chloe shared more about her recent trip to Florida. Nate shared he'd been contracted to build a custom gazebo at a nearby winery. We all laughed as my parents teased each other about their pickleball abilities.

"Is there anything new going on with you, Reece?" Cam asked. "Besides everything that happened this week, of course."

After all the excitement I'd experienced, I was more than

ready for my life to return to normal. I was anxious to get back to Subplot for the remainder of the weekend and put the finishing touches on our fall cocktail and mocktail menus with Ava.

It wasn't until Cam asked his question that I remembered my upcoming date with Julian. Butterflies swarmed in my stomach at the thought of it. The image of my hand on his began to play on a loop in my mind. I felt a grin forming on my face. "Nope, it's business as usual for me."

THIRTY-THREE

Although I was desperate to play it cool, I bounced nervously on my heels as I stood on the sidewalk outside of Ampersand on Monday evening.

Yesterday, Julian texted me to confirm we were still on for Penn's Brewery and Biergarten tonight. I offered to meet him at the bookstore around seven so we could walk over together, knowing it'd likely take several minutes after the turn of the hour for him to close up shop.

Penn's was a German-inspired bar and restaurant located in the heart of downtown Hope Mills. It featured two bars—one inside with its brew tanks visible behind a glass wall, and one outside as part of its rooftop beer garden.

With the heat wave vanquished, the warm evening air was delightful. Considering how muggy it'd been for most of the week before, I didn't take the ideal weather for granted.

A high-pitched bell tinkled behind me twice as a door opened and closed.

There he was. He wore a short-sleeved floral button-down shirt tucked into a pair of gray slacks with hems at his ankles, just above his fashionable white sneakers.

Is this my reality? I took a deep breath to center myself in the present moment.

The way Julian's wavy brown hair seemed to float when blown by gentle gusts of wind made me inwardly swoon as he pulled the door handle to confirm it was locked.

I strode slowly toward him, planting my heel firmly on the brick sidewalk with each step.

His face lit up as soon as we made eye contact. "Hey, there." He gave me a single wave. "Rumor has it you're a hero."

"Hero?" I stroked my stubbled cheek. "I don't know about that."

He swatted at the air as if to reject my statement. "Don't sell yourself short. Take the compliment."

Though I'd connected the dots and made the phone call to Detective Sharp which led to Tiffany's arrest, it hadn't been without tumult. My near brush with death at Tiffany's hand kept me from feeling like a hero. Mainly, I felt extremely lucky.

I hoped my response to his compliment hadn't seemed rude or dismissive. I'm sure it came off as awkward.

Julian took a step closer to me and opened his arms for a hug. "Good to see you."

I leaned in toward him with a strange blend of excitement and hesitation swirling in my chest. Though I'd admitted I was gay and had come a long way in accepting myself, going on a date with another man for the first time felt like a new mountain to climb.

"Good to see you, too."

Our embrace felt markedly different from when I hugged a friend like Nate. Even as we briefly wrapped our arms around one another for a couple of seconds, I couldn't help but note the sensation of his strong back beneath his soft shirt and his firm chest briefly pressed against mine. Julian was the perfect blend of gentleness and strength.

After releasing from our hug, he gestured down the street in the direction of Penn's. "Shall we?"

I nodded. "We shall." After taking a few slow paces down the sidewalk, I said, "I've been really looking forward to this."

"Me, too."

After arriving to the ivy-covered brick building, which had been converted from an old warehouse, we decided to spend our evening in the beer garden.

Stepping out onto Penn's rooftop, I admired the sky's pink and purple hues with streaks of orange and yellow clouds. Julian's skin radiated in the golden hour light, which magnified all his handsome features.

"Wow!" He took off his sunglasses to admire the vibrant sky. His wide smile glowed brighter than the setting sun. "Look at this. This view is incredible." His delight was palpable. The way he surrendered himself to be swept away by such a simple joy made me wish that moment could last forever. *Just when I thought he couldn't get any more beautiful.*

We took a few seconds to take in the scene around us. The pink, yellow, and white potted flowers scattered throughout the rooftop. The bar with a seemingly endless row of beer taps. Groups seated at long picnic tables. The friendly competition between an older couple playing corn hole in an open area at the opposite end of the space.

Julian tucked one hand in his pocket and gestured at the bar with the other. "Can I buy you a drink?"

"Are you sure?"

He furrowed his brow. Was he annoyed? Was he surprised?

Why did you say that, Reece? I was terrified I'd screw everything up somehow.

"Of course," he said. "That's why I asked."

Well, this is new. Though I hadn't been on a first date since I first started seeing Chloe about seven years ago, I was used to paying. My instinct was to insist on offering to cover it, but not wanting to deny his kind gesture, I accepted.

"Sure. Thank you so much. Let's see what they have on tap."

Julian ordered a watermelon sour beer while I opted for a citrusy IPA, each served in a pint-sized glass mug.

I pointed toward a small round table along the beer garden's far side, which was parallel to the Promenade. "I think I found a spot for us."

"Talk about a prime location."

He trailed slightly behind me as I seemingly floated toward the high-top. It was a wonder my mug, filled to the brim, didn't spill.

We stepped to the rooftop's edge on one side of the table and leaned against the metal railing which rose just below our chests. The sunset was behind us as we faced east, but the vibrant sky it created reflected on the wide Delaware River as it flowed as far as the eye could see in either direction.

I raised my mug toward him. He mirrored the gesture, and we clinked our glasses together.

"Cheers!" I said.

"Cheers." His deep tone was breathy and relaxed.

We both took a sip and placed our glasses on the table beside us.

Still leaning against the railing, we stared south at the river, which seemed to melt into the lush mountains along the horizon. The sky seemed to be darkening by the minute, causing the slight ripples in the placid water to start to fade from view.

Julian inched closer toward me.

Chills surged down my spine as I felt his arm brush against mine.

He gently nudged me with his elbow. "It doesn't get any more perfect than this, does it?"

I smirked and leaned into him. "It really doesn't."

Dear reader,

Thank you for taking the time to read Reece's second adventure, *Pour Choices!* I hope you enjoyed being back in Hope Mills with the Subplot crew again.

If you could please leave an honest review wherever you buy books or track your reading, I would be very grateful. Reviews from readers like you help others find my story.

I'd also encourage you to sign up for my newsletter. About once a month, I send out an update with exclusive content for subscribers, including giveaways, recipes, glimpses into my writing process, deleted scenes, and updates about future books.

www.adrianandover.com/newsletter

Also, please find me on social media using the links on the next page. I'd love to stay connected!

Thanks again for spending time with me in this story. I wish you peace, joy, and light. Take care of yourself.

Sincerely,
Adrian 🤍

STAY IN TOUCH WITH ME

Visit my website:

www.adrianandover.com

Let's connect on social media:

instagram.com/adrianandover

facebook.com/adrianandover

threads.com/@adrianandover

bsky.app/profile/adrianandover.com

youtube.com/@adrianandover

ACKNOWLEDGMENTS

First and foremost, I must thank my wonderful family and friends for supporting me in all I do. I am a lucky man to have so much love in my life in all directions.

Thank you to my beta readers, Anna Champagne, Kat Webb, Jennifer Moriarity, and Patrick Ardinger. It's always a bit nerve-racking to share a manuscript for the first time, but I know my work is in good hands when I send it off to all of you. I'm so grateful for all the ways your feedback helped me shape this story.

Special thanks to Kelly Eleneski, my 5 A.M. writing buddy. Editing this book was so much fun, thanks to our early morning sprints.

I am grateful for the team that helped bring this book to life: my cover designer Dawn Adams, my editor Bryn Donovan, and my proofreader Ericka Turnbull. Thank you for lending your talents to this book. I am proud to present it to the world because of the care you've shown with my story.

Even though writing is a solitary craft, I never feel like I'm writing or publishing alone. So many authors have offered me support, and in turn, I feel like I have the greatest colleagues in the world! In alphabetical order: Ellie Alexander, Nicole Asselin, Sarah E. Burr, Paula Charles, Leah Dobrinska, M.S. Greene, J.C. Kenney, Kara Lacey, Annie McEwen, Korina Moss, Christina Romeril, Eryn Scott. I'm sure I'm leaving out some folks (unintentionally), so please forgive me if I haven't listed you here, and allow this thanks to extend to *everyone* in the mystery writing community who showed me such kindness during my debut year.

To the mystery community—thank you for welcoming me in. Before publishing *Whiskey Business* last year, I never would have imagined the beautiful connections I'd form with so many people, from readers to fellow writers to content creators. I've been fortunate to be a part of several communities over the years, but this one is extra special.

And to you, dear reader. Thank you for spending time with me in the pages of this book. Your support means the world to me, and I can't wait to share more stories with you. Sending you lots of love!

ABOUT THE AUTHOR

Adrian Andover is the Lefty Award and Agatha Award-winning author of the Mixology Lounge Mystery series. When he's not reading, writing, revising, or publishing a story, he enjoys long walks, attending live music events, and spending quality time with friends in his chosen hometown of Asbury Park, NJ.